The Involuntary
CONCUBINE

L.M. CHAMPION

ISBN 978-1-956001-85-3 (paperback)
ISBN 978-1-956001-86-0 (digital)

Printed in the United States of America

PART 1

ONE

The balmy Wednesday morning of the first week of May was unceremoniously interrupted by a cacophonous screeching of many collective brakes and bleating horns, immediately followed by a horrendous and frightening explosion of sound that resonated angrily, echoing throughout the busy intersection and into the nearby shops and commercial environs. The T-bone impact of the collision flipped the shiny white sedan and drove it sideways, sending it rolling awkwardly for twenty yards. The driver's door and the center column of the door frame collapsed and were driven into the driver's compartment as though struck with the full force of Thor's mighty hammer. The hips of the young woman driving were pinned in her seat and her torso was driven sharply down into the passenger seat by the impact. She lay motionless, her listless head and neck canted awkwardly toward the rear of the car.

Morning rush hour traffic came to a dead still stop. The scene was eerily silent as onlookers assessed what had just happened. The collective consensus was that the driver of a large gray delivery truck had been texting or doing something with his phone, was oblivious of the intersection, and had breached the red light, failing completely to apply his brakes until after impact. The truck was fully loaded and weighed considerably more than the light sedan of the victim. The truck driver was unscathed.

A bystander immediately rushed to the injured woman's car. He tried to open her door, but it was impossibly bent and twisted. Groups of drivers and bystanders gathered here and there along the roadway as sirens could be heard, the Doppler effect of their cries growing louder and closer. The fire department arrived first, followed by an ambulance. A paramedic rushed immediately to the passenger side of the victim's car where he was able to assess her condition, as two burly firemen quickly took action and began cutting the door and doorframe away on the driver's side. The paramedic called for an oxygen bottle and mask, telling his partner that the young woman was unconscious and having difficulty breathing.

Although traffic noise in the distance could be heard, the eerie silence prevailed in the immediate area as though out of respect for the fate of the injured woman. As three Sheriff's cruisers arrived, onlookers and drivers silently migrated toward the cruisers, forming a ragtag line and waiting their turn to absolve the young blond driver of any liability for the collision. A collection of observations were heard up and down the queue: "He was texting; he wasn't watching; bless her heart, she never saw it coming; she isn't moving;" and "Thank goodness, the hospital is close-by."

After considerable effort, the seemingly lifeless victim was freed and carefully lifted from the mangled wreckage. She was placed on a gurney, which was efficiently lifted into the ambulance as the crowd watched.

"Oh, dear God," a woman moaned, "she still hasn't moved."

TWO

I answered my ringing phone as I walked into my office. I heard the voice of the Surgery Coordinator tell me perfunctorily, "We're going to need you in Surgery Two. Auto accident, possible pneumothorax and a punctured lung, broken pelvis, and various bones. Should be here in twenty minutes."

"I'm in the building and on my way," I announced. So much for a quiet morning.

I reached surgery, scrubbed, dressed and gloved. A nurse assistant had my equipment waiting for me in the surgery theater as I walked in, followed by the surgeon.

"Good morning, Dub. I'm glad it's you who will be working with us."

"Thanks, Dr. Gillespie. What do you have?" I asked, despite what I had been told.

"Primary is a punctured lung and traumatic pneumothorax. Get her stable and I'll take a look."

I am Dub Wade. I am a perfusionist. I'm a specialist, not a doctor. I operate the cardio-pulmonary bypass machine–CPB or heart-lung machine–during surgery to ensure proper and continuous blood and airflow for the patient. I work closely with anesthesiologists and surgeons.

Bob Gillespie, the surgeon, and Rhia Khiladi, the anesthesiologist, are both excellent doctors and I like working with them. The patient was already intubated. The nurse anesthetist and I got her hooked up and Dr. Khiladi anesthetized her. We then stepped out of the way to observe and maintain the patient.

She looked to be in her mid-twenties and appeared to be tall, slender and blonde. Her face had been cleaned of blood, but some remained in her hair. Despite the multiple bruises and abrasions that had quickly become apparent, it was obvious that she was a very pretty woman.

Dr. Gillespie opened, quickly assessed her condition, and systematically, but quickly began clamping bleeding arteries and prioritizing damage. She had a great deal of ancillary bleeding in the abdominal area, probably from the seat belt, which was a significant concern to Dr. Gillespie. He had the young woman's bleeding stopped and her lung repaired and functioning in less than three hours. He addressed the internal bleeding and injuries. He scrutinized the operating cavity but found no further damage. He closed and the orthopedists took over. In cases like this, there may be a pair, as there was today, to deal with multiple bone and joint injuries in order to lessen the time in surgery and under anesthesia.

I generally deal with complicated cardio-pulmonary cases. I seldom have ancillary procedures in my cases. I didn't know the two orthopedic surgeons, but I liked their manner and was impressed with their skill and efficiency. I gathered that they either had a shared practice or had worked together before.

We finally closed a little before two o'clock. I went to the cafeteria for a light lunch and then closed my eyes for a few minutes in my chair in my office. I was back in surgery at three o'clock for an uncomplicated surgery on a geriatric patient.

THREE

I showered and changed from scrubs to jeans and a loose polo before I left the hospital. It had been a long day and I didn't feel like going home to an empty house again this evening. I either need a dog or a girlfriend. I'm getting tired of eating alone and going home to an empty house.

I decided to stop at Keenan's Bar and Grill on my way home to watch the game and have supper. Keenan's is a popular after-work watering hole. On one side are a very comfortable and spacious bar and a working dining area. On the other side is a complete and separate restaurant with ample seating in an environment rich with thick fabrics and carpet, polished woods and sound absorption material in the ceiling so that one doesn't have to shout to be heard. It provides an ideal environment for every occasion, is reasonably priced, and it draws a crowd of all ages, but is especially popular with attractive and successful businesspersons and up-and-coming young professionals.

I settled onto a barstool and ordered a glass of wine as I fixed my gaze on the television above the bar. It was the second inning, Astros versus Angels at home. Jose Altuve had just crossed home plate after a two-run homer that put us ahead two to zero. Man, we have a real chance this year. They're looking good.

I was caught up in the game when a woman's pleasant, but dull voice next to me asked if the stool on my left was taken. Without looking up, I replied, "No. It's all yours."

"What's the score?" she asked listlessly.

"Two, zip, us," I answered as I turned to look at her. Wow. Beautiful girl. She has to be meeting someone. She looked at me, smiled half-heartedly, and looked for the bartender. She looked exhausted.

"How many outs?" she asked.

"None."

"Well, at least the Astros are having a good day," she said bleakly, without looking up.

"Bad day?" I asked.

She nodded. "Yes," she intoned morosely, "very."

She stared straight ahead into the polished mirror behind the bar. In the reflection, I saw tears appear in the corners of her eyes. She dabbed at her eyes and sniffled; then the tears came stronger. She clasped her hands together on the bar and shook her head, then shook with emotion that brought more tears.

I handed her a bar napkin and she wiped at her tears.

"Thank you," she said softly. She sniffled and looked at me.

Touching my hand, she said with sincerity, "I'm sorry. It's been a rotten day."

"I'm sorry that it has been so rotten. Can I buy you a drink?"

"Thank you. But I would be terrible company."

"It's okay. If you want to be left alone, I understand. If you want to talk, I'm a good listener. Your call. The offer still goes for the drink. No strings attached."

The bartender came to us and asked if I wanted another. I looked at her and asked, "Is Ferrari Carano cab okay with you?"

She wiped away the last tears, attempted a smile, and said softly, "Yes. Thank you."

The bartender nodded, turned to the counter behind him, found the open bottle, and poured two large glasses of wine.

She took a sip of her wine and looked at me. Her expression was moribund.

"My best friend was seriously injured in an auto accident this morning. She was hit by a careless guy driving a big delivery truck. He was texting and ran a red light. He hit her so hard it drove the door into her and pinned her inside the car. I've been at the hospital all day. She is in intensive care right now, but it was touch and go for a while this morning. They called me because I'm listed as the person to notify in case of emergency, but they made me go home because I'm not family, even though she is like a sister to me. She has no family here. She's unconscious and there is nothing I can do there. The nurse said she would call me if I am needed.

"I'm sorry. I can only imagine how upset you must be," I offered sympathetically. "Where is your friend?"

"At Methodist Hospital here in The Woodlands."

I nodded. Her friend has to be the same person who came in this morning.

I decided not to mention to her that I had been in surgery with her friend that morning. She seemed to be getting her mind off the sadness a little and I didn't want to bring the unpleasant back up.

She extended her hand and gave me a wan smile.

"I'm Elizabeth Barton. Liz to my friends. My friend who was hurt is Jill Hancock.

"Dub Wade," I said, taking her hand. "I'm pleased to meet you… and very sorry for your friend's injuries."

I knew Liz was a Texas girl when she didn't ask about my nickname.

"How long have the two of you been friends?"

"Since grammar school."

"Where did you grow up?"

"Here. We went to high school right here in The Woodlands, then to Texas A&M together. We graduated three years ago and now we work together and live together."

"What do you do?"

"We're financial analysts for ExxonMobil."

"How did you manage to swing that?"

"We're legacies. Our fathers are Aggies and Petroleum Engineers for ExxonMobil. They were best friends in college and were hired together. She and I graduated tied for fifth place in our class and, like our fathers, were hired as a package deal." She laughed. "We've been very fortunate."

"Sounds like it. How did you manage to stay so close together all those years?"

"We lived on the same street as kids. Our daddies seemed to always be on the same project. Now, our parents are in South America. Our daddies are on the Guyana Project. So, she and I are the only family either of us has here right now. We're more like sisters than best friends. I talked to her mother today and she will fly in tomorrow. Her fiancé is in Alaska, and he will be here tomorrow as well.

"I just feel so helpless right now. There isn't anything I can do for her.

"We sometimes come here after work, so I came here because it's familiar… and I don't want to go home without her." She paused, mournfully looking into space.

"Is there anything I can do to help you?"

"No. But, thank you." She said without looking at me. "I just need to work through this." She sighed, as if in effort to dispel her mood, and turned to me. "Do you come here often?"

"I've been in here three or four times. My company expanded and took office space in The Woodlands. I was transferred up here. I like this place and will probably come frequently. I imagine we'll see each other here occasionally."

She gave me a wan smile and nodded. "What do you do?"

"I'm a Perfusionist."

"Is that a kind of musician?"

I laughed.

"No; although it does sound like that, doesn't it? A Perfusionist operates extracorporeal circulation and auto-transfusion equipment during any medical procedure where it is necessary to support or temporarily replace the patient's circulatory or respiratory function. Extracorporeal means any procedure or related activity outside the body. In simple terms, we keep the blood and breath flowing during operations. We work in the operating room with the surgeons and operating room staff."

"Well, I've learned something new." She smiled at me. "How did you become a Perfusionist?"

"I have a degree in Life Sciences from A&M. I work for a group of Perfusionists who have a lot of business in the medical center and other major surgery centers in Texas, Louisiana, Oklahoma, and New Mexico. I graduated six years ago. My company interviewed me on campus and we hit it off, so I just kind of fell into the job.

"So, you're an Aggie also?"

"You bet."

I looked up at the television.

"Three to two, their way now."

She smiled. "Thank you. Just talking has helped me. It doesn't relieve my concern, but it's been nice talking with you."

I presumed her comment was a prelude to leaving. I was enjoying her company and was impressed with her. She was intelligent and well-spoken. She was nicely dressed in well-tailored slacks and a fitted silk blouse. I'm an inch over six feet tall and she must have been at least five-ten in her flats. She was slender, trim and nicely built, with beautiful hands and delicate fingers. Her auburn hair hung in soft waves to her shoulders, was thick and full, and nicely cut. And she had the whitest, perfect teeth and sparkling hazel eyes.

I didn't want her to leave, and I was getting hungry, so I asked if she would join me for dinner.

She hesitated.

"Have you eaten today?"

"I had some crackers and a diet Coke at the hospital. That's all since breakfast, which was a protein bar."

"I hate to sound like my mother, but you probably need to eat. You aren't going to do Jill any good if you make yourself sick in the process."

She smiled and accepted. There was a waitlist in the dining room, so we ordered dinner at the bar and another glass of wine. We talked about ourselves and she seemed to relax some. Jill's fiancé and Jill's mother called during dinner to advise her of their arrival times.

The ball game ended in our favor. The news came on and there was an account of a missing college coed. The reporter went into a short editorial on the growing problem of human trafficking, forced prostitution, and child slavery. She stated that in the United States in 2019 there were 212,723 male and 235,367 female missing persons under age twenty-one; and 98,285 male and 62,823 female missing persons over twenty-one, according to NCIC, the National Crime Information Center.

She went on to say that, in 2018 in the US, there were 10,949 reported cases of human trafficking. Of those cases, sex trafficking comprised 7,859. Texas reported 1,000 cases that year. And we learned that twenty-five percent of all human trafficking is said to travel through Houston, that fifty percent of human trafficking victims are sixteen under, and that eighty percent are women and girls

In 2015, Houston had the highest number of trafficking victims in the US comprised of 274 women and 45 men. She finished with the fact that, according to a recently released report by the State Department, the top three nations of origin for victims of human trafficking in 2018 were the United States, Mexico, and the Philippines.

Liz shook her head. "There are a lot of sick people in this world. That's so sad. I hope they find her soon. I can't imagine how frightening an experience like that must be and how hopeless she must feel. It has to be one of every woman's most frightening nightmares."

I agreed.

FOUR

I asked Liz if she wanted to stay and talk a little while longer. I didn't want the evening to end. And despite her protests that she was okay, I had the feeling she didn't want to go home to an empty house. She morosely said that she should probably go home. I waved off her offer to split the bill and paid the check, then walked her to her car.

"Thank you for dinner. That was sweet of you."

She paused thoughtfully, then stood on her toes and gently gave me a quick kiss on my cheek.

I smiled and nodded. You're welcome."

As I turned to go, she took my arm and quietly repeated herself, "Thank you. This would have been a terrible evening by myself." Her voice was despondent. "Thank you for being such good company."

She gently leaned her cheek against my chest and I wrapped one arm around her shoulders. She was warm against me and felt good. She made no move to disengage for a moment, then said softly, stoically, "Good night."

"Good night," I replied as I stepped away, then turned back. "May I call you?"

Her smile, though wan, was reassuring as she gave me her number and I tapped it into my phone. Then, she asked for my number. She looked into my eyes and her expression was so sad. The anguish in her eyes looked two steps from thoroughly frightened, and she looked a little tipsy.

"Liz, will you be okay tonight?"

She paused for a long moment, looking down.

"Yes," she replied with no conviction. She paused. "No… I don't know. I'm so worried about Jill. And I know what it will be like going home and knowing why she isn't there."

I saw small tears glisten in the corners of her eyes. I gently touched her arm. I knew I was okay, but I was pretty sure she felt the wine more than I.

"I'm not sure you should be driving. Would you like me to drive you home? I can come for you tomorrow morning and bring you back to your car?"

She was thoughtful for a moment, then nodded. "That would be nice. I'm not sure I could pass a breathalyzer. And I don't need any more grief today."

We walked to my car and I settled her in. She gave directions. It was only a seven-minute drive. Her home was in a nice development of attractive patio homes. I parked on the driveway and walked her to her door, where I took her hands.

"I hope you can get some sleep tonight. What time would you like me to come for you tomorrow?"

She started to speak but hesitated. I saw tears glisten in her eyes. She looked down, sniffled, and looked up at me, apprehension in her face.

"I know how this must sound, but would you like to come in for a minute. I'm not quite ready to be here alone."

"Yes; if you're sure."

"I know I should just bite the bullet, but I don't want to be alone right now. I know I'm taking advantage of you, but you've been so nice and you've made me feel… better."

Her words sounded genuine and I didn't try to read anything into them. The effect this was having on her was obvious.

"Of course. I want you to be okay."

I followed her inside. A night light illuminated a very neat and tidy kitchen on one side, and I could see the subdued glow of a lamp coming from her living room ahead of us. She dropped her purse and briefcase on a side table.

"Would you mind if I changed out of my work clothes?"

"Not at all."

"I'll make some coffee when I come back."

"I'll be glad to do that if you'll point me in the right direction," I offered. "It will probably do us both some good."

She pointed me to the coffee pot and showed me where coffee and filters were. I put a pot on to brew and went into the living room.

I sat, feeling a little awkward and looking around. It was a warm, inviting room, resplendent in subtle colors, polished hardwoods, and good fabrics. There was a nice coffee table bordered on one side by a handsome couch with two complementary wing chairs on either end of the table. The rest of the room was occupied by two attractive club chairs with a drink table, a pair of tall bookcases filled with books, and a white baby grand piano. Her home was beautifully decorated and very comfortable.

She entered from across the room, barefoot and fetching in short shorts and a Texas A&M T-shirt.

"Music?" she asked.

I nodded.

"Alexa, play the relaxation station," she instructed and Alexa complied.

She smiled as she walked into the kitchen. "Thank you for making coffee." She took two cups from the cabinet and filled them. "Cream or sugar?"

"Just black, thanks," I replied.

She seemed to be functioning all right, but I knew the adrenaline from the day would wear off and the alcohol would hit her pretty soon.

We sat at each end of the sofa, facing each other.

"Your home is very nice." I nodded at the piano. "Do you play?"

"Yes. We both play–piano lessons together since we were eight. We enjoy many of the same things and have similar tastes. As I said, we're more like sisters."

"Have you lived here long?"

"We bought this home two years ago with a little help from our parents. We flipped for the master bedroom and I won, which has been nice since Jill spends many nights and most weekends at Richard's house– at least, she did until he went to Alaska on a temporary assignment. Jill and Richard are getting married in September and the plan is for me to buy them out and live here."

Tears started and she looked so unhappy. "That is if she recovers from this."

She stepped out of the room and returned with a handful of tissue, dabbing at her eyes.

"I'm sorry, Dub. This is so upsetting." She stepped to me, took my forearms, and laid her head against my chest. "You've helped so much this evening." She sighed as she laid her palms flat against my chest. "You were right. You are a good listener."

I put an arm around her and stroked her head. After a moment, she looked up at me. "I'm sorry. Would you like to drink your coffee before it gets cold? I think I got us off track."

She looked at me.

"Dub? For W?"

It was a rhetorical question. I nodded.

"William Ellis Wade. Ellis was my mother's maiden name."

We talked. She more than I, but she needed to talk, to keep her mind occupied. She refilled our cups. We talked and it got later. At one point, I offered to leave so that she could go to bed. She said she knew she would only lie awake thinking of Jill. She set her empty cup on the table and scooted down the couch to lean against me.

She laid her head against my shoulder and whispered, "Do you mind if I just sit here with you for a little while?"

I put my arm around her shoulder and shook my head. "Not at all."

She snuggled against me and whispered, "Thank you."

She took my hand as she said, almost to herself, "Isn't it coincidental that you came into my life at a time when… when I needed someone comforting?"

It hit her. The adrenaline was gone and the alcohol kicked in. Her breathing became slow and even. She was asleep. The long, emotional day had caught up with her.

Now, what do I do?

I slowly extricated myself, took the cups to the kitchen, and rinsed them. I looked back at her. She hadn't moved. I walked down the hall and found her bedroom by the faint light that came from the living room and a night light in the room.

On her dresser, I saw a picture of a nice-looking young man dressed in the uniform of an Army First Lieutenant wearing a tan Ranger's beret sitting on her dresser. I was pretty sure that meant she was taken.

I turned her bedcovers down and went back to the couch.

I got one arm under her legs and the other around her, lifting her into my arms. She moaned and snuggled against me. I carefully walked back to her bedroom and gently laid her on the bed. As I reached for the sheet and blanket to cover her, she grasped my forearm and sleepily said, very softly, "Don't go. I don't want to be alone."

She tugged on my arm, pulling me down next to her. She cuddled into me, nuzzling her head into the hollow of my neck, and whispered, "Thank you."

We lay quietly like that. I assumed she would go to sleep and I would again extract myself and go home. When I thought she was asleep, I began to move slowly. She moaned softly, put her arm over my chest, and pulled my head to her, nestling into the crook of my neck.

Oookay, now what do I do?

"Hold me," she whispered. I did.

She had one arm on my chest and was pressed close to me. She gently kissed my cheek. "Go to sleep," she whispered. "It's too late for you to go home." She was asleep again in seconds.

I was perplexed. But, she was right. It was late and I was tired, but I was wide awake. I looked down at the girl sleeping next to me and wanted to laugh out loud. I like being in bed with a beautiful woman, but this was a first. But she needed a friend and, hopefully, I had helped—and it just seemed to happen naturally.

It will be interesting to see where this goes next. I'm sure she will be embarrassed tomorrow. I dropped my shoes by the bed, pulled the covers over us, closed my eyes, and went to sleep with her warm against me. She smelled good.

FIVE

I woke at six-thirty to the smell of coffee and a gentle touch on my hand. I opened my eyes and saw her standing next to me, a cup of black coffee in her hand, and an embarrassed smile on her face. She was still dressed in her shorts and the A&M shirt from last night.

"Good morning," I said, looking into her eyes as I scooted upward and leaned against the headboard.

"Good morning," she said uncertainly as she handed me the cup.

She straightened her shoulders and looked back at me.

"My behavior was totally out of bounds last night. I think it would be best if we didn't see each other again. I'm so embarrassed. I could never be comfortable around you.

"Last night, you listened. You made me feel at ease. Being with you was very comfortable.

"You could have taken advantage of me, but you didn't. Thank you… for being a gentleman. I don't know what you think of me right now, but it matters to me whatever that is. I know that I took advantage of your kindness. We hardly know each other—and I took advantage of your kindness."

I patted the bed next to me and motioned for her to sit. She did

I put my index finger against her lips.

"Sh. I think you are one of the most delightful and attractive women I have ever met. Despite the unhappy circumstances that led to our meeting, I am happy that we have met. I know you have a lot to deal with right now. I'm happy if my company was helpful."

I thought for a moment, then went out on a limb.

"I noticed the picture last night." I nodded toward the Army Officer. "I assume he isn't your brother. I won't cause you any problems."

She took a deep breath, was silent for a long moment, then said softly, "He is gone. You can't cause me any problems."

"I'm sincerely sorry to hear that; I won't ask questions. But knowing that, within the bounds of decorum, I would be devastated if you don't want to see me again when life is less stressful for you. Besides, if you think about it, last night was our fourth date. How can you say we hardly know each other? I think it's okay to accept comfort from a fella after four dates, don't you?"

She looked at me quizzically.

"We met, had drinks, and talked."

I held up one finger.

"Then, we had dinner and talked–that was our second date."

I held up two fingers, then flipped up three fingers.

"On our third date, you invited me to your home for coffee, and we talked more. By that time, I was pretty well taken with you."

I smiled gently and looked her in the eyes.

"On our fourth date," I held up four fingers, "we slept together… even if it was only in the platonic sense."

I held both hands up, palms out and fingers expanded, as I cocked my head to the side with a wry smile.

"And I think we've gotten to know each other pretty well in a short time, don't you?"

She blushed and laughed.

"I know you have a lot more to deal with in the coming days. I'll repeat what I said to you last night. 'How can I help?' I'm here for you.

And I certainly want to get to know you better when time permits. Does that help you?"

She nodded silently, smiled embarrassedly, and tentatively touched my hand.

"Yes. I'm sorry. I didn't mean to be so abrupt. I owe you more than that. I'll get over my embarrassment."

"There is no need for you to be embarrassed."

She stood and smiled a crooked, awkward smile.

"Thank you. I'll get Jill's mother at nine o'clock at Intercontinental Airport. Her fiancé arrives at Hobby Airport at ten. He'll be fine. He'll get a cab or limo to his townhouse and drive to the hospital. I don't know what to expect for a few days, but I would like to get to know each other better when that is possible. We may be on hold for a while. That isn't what I want, but it's all I can offer right now. Jill is the priority at the moment."

She looked into my eyes and touched my arm.

"Dub, thank you. I still feel awkward, but the idea that it was our fourth date helps. You're a clever man. I'll think of us like that."

SIX

At that moment, my cell phone rang. It was a number from the hospital. I answered and heard the voice of Dr. Melbourne, Chief of Surgery at the hospital.

"Dub, I'm glad I caught you. A young lady who was admitted yesterday has been rushed back into surgery with a collapsed lung. She has been intubated and is steady at the moment. We need a Perfusionist and the on-call is thirty minutes away. Are you close enough to help?"

"I'll be there in ten minutes. I'll need a set of scrubs. Would you have someone assemble the necessary equipment?" He agreed.

"Dr. Melbourne, is her name Jill Hancock?"

"Why… yes. How did you know?"

"I know her best friend. And I worked her surgery yesterday with Dr. Gillespie. I'm on my way now."

I turned to Liz. She looked both alarmed and puzzled.

"I was in surgery with her yesterday. She had great care from an excellent surgeon.

"Don't be alarmed. Her lung collapsed. It happens sometimes. She has been taken to surgery. They need a Perfusionist. I'm sure she will be all right. They are on top of things."

"Why didn't you tell me last night?"

"I wanted to keep your mind off Jill, last night. I didn't want to remind you of what happened."

She smiled and said, very softly, "Thank you. Thank you for being there last night."

As I was reaching for my shoes, I remembered that her car was at Keenan's

"Oh–I can drop you at your car if we hurry."

"I can get one of my neighbors to do that. You get to the hospital."

I hugged her and kissed her cheek.

"See you after surgery."

When I arrived, a nurse I know well met me with scrubs and helped me prep. Jill and the surgeon were ready to go as soon as I checked my machines. I connected Jill and gave the thumbs up. I had worked with Dr. French, the surgeon many times and we got on well together. She was one of my favorites and one of the best. In the worst of emergencies, she was always gracious and composed and instilled a sense of quiet optimism in everyone around her. Today was no exception.

The problem had been identified before I reached the hospital, so the only thing that was necessary once I took over Jill's vital functions was for Dr. French to do her thing.

"What do we have?" I asked as she began.

"I understand you were in surgery with her yesterday."

I nodded.

"Then you know her initial condition. She was on a monitor last night and she was being watched for any signs of infection or pneumonia. She had a great deal of internal bleeding caused both by the impact and by the seat belt. That may be the problem. The lung collapsed this morning, but that sometimes happens, as you know. We'll get her fixed."

In three hours, I was taking Jill off my machine and she was quietly rolled to the recovery room in the intensive care unit. Everything had gone well.

As we were removing our gowns, gloves, hats, and booties, Dr. French said, "Dr. Melbourne mentioned that you know this young lady."

"I know her best friend. I haven't yet had the pleasure of meeting Jill other than in an operating room. Thanks for taking such good care of her today."

"That's my job," she said with a smile. She took my arm and offered, "Why don't you come with me to see the family."

When we walked into the waiting lounge, Liz looked up in surprise at me in my scrubs walking in with Dr. French, still in her scrubs. She could tell from our smiles that the surgery had gone well. Liz's eyes were as big a silver dollars and she had an ear-to-ear smile. Dr. French introduced herself and Liz quickly introduced Vivian, Jill's mother, to Dr. French and me.

Dr. French explained what had happened to Jill, how she had repaired the problem, and she very kindly described my involvement in the surgery–both this morning and yesterday. Vivian and Liz asked questions. Liz stepped next to me and–surprise–quietly smiled at me and took my hand. Dr. French noticed and smiled at me.

When she had done all she could for them, she told them that she would be checking on Jill each day for the next week and would instruct the nurses to keep them and me informed. She said Jill should be awake in about an hour and suggested we get some lunch while we waited.

As she passed me, she patted my arm and said quietly, "I like your friend, Dub. And it appears she likes you more than a little."

She smiled broadly when she spoke, then told me she would see me next week.

Vivian asked me to join them and I agreed. We opted for the cafeteria so that we could be close to Jill. Just as we were seated, Richard came into the cafeteria, spotted Liz, and came to us, giving Vivian and Liz a hug. Liz introduced me. We shook hands and he joined us.

Vivian asked Liz how long we had been seeing each other. Liz was quick.

"We met at Keenan's, the pub near our home. My day had been long and I wasn't ready to go home. Jill couldn't join me, so I stopped in for a glass of wine. Dub was sitting at the bar and we struck up a conversation about the Astros. Their game was on the television. After that, he asked me to dinner. Then we had drinks again. Last night I was very upset; I didn't want to be alone. I asked Dub to keep me company. He did. He's a good listener and he helped me get through the evening. We've had four dates."

Richard smiled at Liz. "I'm glad you weren't alone, Liz."

"Thank you. Dub was there when I needed a sympathetic ear. He made everything better at a terrible time. He was my anchor yesterday. Dub was there yesterday for Jill, he was there last night when I needed someone to listen, and now he has again helped Jill. Who would have thought my anchor yesterday would be involved in Jill's surgery yesterday and today."

Vivian smiled and said, "It is quite a coincidence, isn't it."

Richard offered his thanks and shook my hand again.

After lunch, we arranged for HIPPA forms for Liz, Richard, and me. Liz kissed my cheek and told me she would call me later.

SEVEN

Liz called at five o'clock. She told me that Jill's condition and status were unchanged. She said that Vivian would stay at her home tonight and that she would have dinner with Vivian and Richard and his parents at the hospital that evening. I listened and asked a couple of questions about Jill. I wanted to see Liz but didn't want to push at a time like this.

As if she had read my mind, she said, "I would love to see you, but there just won't be time or the opportunity this evening."

"I understand. Call me when you can."   She called at ten o'clock.

"How are you doing?" I asked.

"I'm tired. The whole day was stressful. It was good to see her awake, but she was incredibly groggy. We talked to her doctors and feel optimistic about her recovery, but it is going to be slow and she will need physical therapy. We're going to meet back at the hospital tomorrow at nine o'clock."

"How are you doing, really?"

"I'm okay, I guess. I'm worried, concerned that she has a long road to recovery ahead of her. I'm angry at the person who caused this. I'm afraid this is going to upset their wedding plans. And that will upset her."

"One thing at a time," I said.

"You're right. I understand that."

"Is there anything I can do for you?"

"I wish I could put my head on your shoulder right now. I'd like that very much."

"I wish you could, too. That would be very nice."

I heard her take a deep breath. "Dub… I still don't know what to say about last night. I'm… uncomfortable about what you think of me."

"I think you are an attractive, intelligent woman. I admire your loyalty and love for your friend… and I'd like very much to see you again when Jill's situation is less exigent and you have some time. Four dates just weren't enough."

She laughed. It was good to hear her laugh.

"I'd like that. Isn't it ironic that a terrible incident brought you into my life? I want to think that was a good sign—the silver lining in an otherwise dark cloud."

"I like the way you think."

"Dub?"

"Yes."

"Vivian is going to stay with me tonight and tomorrow night. I may not be able to see you other than at the hospital for a few days. I'm sorry. That isn't what I want, but she is my second mother. I need to be here for her and Jill."

"I understand. We can talk by phone when you have time.

We talked and laughed and teased for another few minutes. I told her to get a good night's sleep.

"Dub?"

"Yes."

"I'm glad I met you. Thank you for being there for me last night."

"You're welcome. It was my pleasure. Sleep well, pretty lady."

She giggled and said good night.

You kind of like her, don't you, Wade? There must be a good explanation for the picture.

EIGHT

She called at four o'clock, Thursday afternoon. Jill was awake and reasonably alert. Richard's parents were at the hospital. Former neighbors with whom Vivian would stay the next week were coming at six o'clock. She said Vivian would go to dinner with her friends, who would bring her to Liz's place after dinner, and Richard would have dinner with his parents.

I saw my chance. "If you aren't too tired, would you like to have dinner tonight?"

"Very much," she replied. "Actually, that was Vivian's suggestion. She said that you and I probably needed a little time together."

"I knew there was a good reason that I liked Vivian," I said with a laugh.

She said she wanted to go home, shower, and change clothes before this evening. She asked if I could pick her up at six-thirty.

"Sure. Where would you like to go for dinner?"

"Someplace casual and quiet."

"Coco's?"

"That would be perfect."

Coco's was a small, family-owned and run Italian restaurant that had tried too hard when it first opened. The food had been good, but not great. The menu had been too abundant and the live music on Fridays and Saturdays was too loud. From somewhere, they got some good advice early enough to avoid failing.

Soon, the menu was manageable and the food improved greatly. They did away with the live music and added carpet and padding here and there to absorb sound. The dress norm became business casual, and absolutely no cutoff jeans. It had quickly become a favorite of couples and small groups of baby boomers and young professionals. That attracted the media and they received a nice article in Houston magazine, which also helped their popularity. Now, it was reservations only on weekends. I had planned ahead this morning and made a late reservation in hopes of time with Liz.

I stopped at the florist and bought a dozen yellow roses. I knocked at six-thirty. She opened the door wearing a happy smile, a pretty white sundress that hugged her curves, and simple flat sandals. Her hair was in a ponytail and she looked young and vibrant.

"Wow. You look beautiful. I like your dress."

"Thank you," she said softly, taking my hand, and inviting me in.

"Oh, what beautiful roses. Thank you. I love roses."

She closed the door, stood on tiptoe, and kissed my cheek.

"I've been looking forward to seeing you."

"Good, because I've certainly been looking forward to seeing you."

She hugged me and I slipped my arms around her. Without a second thought, I kissed her. She immediately went taut and stepped away.

"I'm sorry. I shouldn't have done that, but I've wanted to do that since the first evening, sitting on your couch."

She looked into my eyes and smiled.

"We've had four dates now. I think a kiss might be in order."

She stretched up to me and she returned my kiss. I ran my tongue across her lips and she invited it in as she did likewise.

She sighed and said softly, "Oh, I'm glad you're here."

"I can't believe it has only been one day. I feel as though we've been together since the beginning of time," I replied.

She looked into my eyes and nodded with a warm smile.

"What a romantic thing to say." She kissed me again. "I understand exactly what you mean."

She went for a vase and set about arranging the roses, smiling at me a dozen times as she did.

As she was arranging, her phone rang. She excused herself without looking at the phone and answered it. The caller spoke and she immediately tensed and looked unhappy.

"No," she said firmly.

"No," she repeated.

"Please. Don't call me again." She hung up and shook her head, a solemn look on her face.

"Are you okay?"

She sighed deeply, turned to me, and smiled.

"Yes. I'm sorry. I should have checked the caller ID before I answered."

"Anything I need to worry about?"

She took my hand and smiled gently.

"No, Dub. I assure you that you have nothing to worry about. I'll explain another time. There is a lot I should tell you, but let's enjoy ourselves tonight."

I took her at her word, but I was curious. Maybe this had been the guy in the picture.

NINE

We drove to the restaurant and held hands in the car. She took my arm as we walked to the restaurant and held my hand as we checked in with the hostess. It was nice—surprising, but nice. I realized that I was ready to have a woman in my life again. And, at that moment, I was certain she was that woman.

We were told it would be a ten to fifteen-minute wait. We went into the bar and found one empty bar stool. She sat. I stood and couldn't keep my eyes off her. She was as pretty as any woman I had ever met—absolutely eye-catching, but appearing completely comfortable in her own skin. I had once heard Grace Kelly described that way and I was sure the description fit Liz, as well. We ordered wine, were served, and sipped. She told me about Jill and her day.

Our table was ready and our drinks were taken to the table as we followed, comfortably holding hands again. Our waitress, a cute young woman who appeared to be a college student, arrived and introduced herself as Sofie. She smiled. "You two certainly seem happy. Is this a special occasion?"

We smiled and Liz surprised me. "Yes; it's our first formal date. What do you think the chances are that there will be a second?"

The girl laughed heartily. "If the look on your faces is any indication, I say yes. You look well-suited to each other, and happy. I take it from what you said that you've known each other for a short while."

"Circumstance brought us together unexpectedly and we learned that we liked being together. And, here we are," Liz said with a happy laugh.

We thanked her. We ordered dinner and a bottle of wine. We held hands and talked until the owner of the restaurant appeared at our table, accompanied by Sofie, who carried a champagne flute in each hand.

He introduced himself as Samuel Linz.

"Sofie told us about your question to her. The staff took a vote. We all think there will be a second date."

A young man appeared behind him with an ice bucket containing a bottle of champagne. "And we've brought you some champagne to celebrate your first date

Linz opened the bottle and poured as he said, "We hope to see you with us often."

Another reason this restaurant was so popular—they knew how to treat their guests. He had just made this our favorite restaurant for many meals to come.

We beamed and thanked him. He shook my hand and kissed Liz's hand. We toasted each other and noticed the glances of those around us. Several clapped. The couple at the next table had heard his words and they offered us good wishes.

Liz smiled brightly at me, and I said quietly to her, "Well, pretty lady, it appears that you're going to have to do this with me at least one more time."

"Oh, please! Don't throw me in that briar patch."

I laughed.

I love her sense of humor and her smile.

"Did I mention that I like your dress?"

"Thank you. I believe you did mention that. I was hoping you would like it."

She kissed my cheek.

"It's nice of you to notice."

We talked easily throughout dinner and a shared dessert. Despite the seriousness sitting out there in the background, we made each other laugh and smile. As we left, we saw the owner and waved.

"See you soon," I mouthed.

He nodded and gave us a thumbs up.

We got to the car and, as I moved to open her door, Liz spun into me and wrapped her arms around my neck. She pressed against me and kissed me gently.

"Thank you. I don't know when I've enjoyed a dinner out so much. I like being with you."

I returned her kiss.

"And I like being with you."

We held hands all the way to her house. I pulled into her drive and shut the engine down.

"It looks like Vivian is already here," she said. "I'm sorry. I was hoping we could have a few minutes to ourselves before she arrived. She will stay with her friends beginning Monday night. I'm sorry, but I should be with her until then."

"I understand"

She leaned into me and gave me one helluva goodnight kiss.

PART 2

TEN

I was in surgery Friday morning, and it went into overtime. When we finally finished and I had all of my equipment back in order, I started upstairs to see if Liz was with Jill. It's my habit to use the stairs in the hospital rather than the elevator. Jill's floor was only two above where I was. I entered the stairwell and immediately heard the voices of two persons arguing above me.

The voices were subdued, but strong enough to easily be heard in the confines of the stairwell. As I started to back out gracefully, I heard what sounded like Liz's voice telling the other person to leave her alone.

I heard her say, "It was nice of you to visit Jill, but don't think that puts you back in my good graces. And I'm not sorry if I ruined things for you with Melissa. You've proven that you are neither trustworthy nor faithful. Why in the world would you think I would want to get back into a relationship with someone who can't be trusted? I don't have feelings for you."

A man's voice said, "The last I heard, you haven't had a date since you walked out. Or, are you seeing someone now?"

"Please go."

"Why? Are you seeing someone now?"

There was a pause. Then, Liz spoke matter of factly and evenly.

"Yes. I've met someone and I care for him very much. I believe he cares for me. He's a good person, and he's honest and trustworthy."

"Well, he'd better watch his back."

"Don't threaten me… or him. Please leave."

I heard the door open and he hissed, "Don't walk away from me."

There was a long pause and he swore crudely and abundantly. The door closed. I assumed he had left the stairwell and gone after Liz.

I didn't like what I had heard and I was concerned for Liz. I took the steps two at a time. I reached the door, collected myself, and calmly entered the hallway. I didn't see Liz.

I started toward Jill's room. As I passed the visitor's lounge, I saw Liz, Vivian, and Richard. They each wore a strained look and stared at a man standing in front of them. He was about my height, heavier, and a little older than I. He was nicely dressed and had a good haircut.

I entered the room. Vivian saw me first and gave me a helpless look. I walked to the group and asked, "Is everything all right?"

The stranger turned to me and barked, "Who are you?"

Diplomatically, Vivian said, "Damon, this is Dub Wade. Dub was in surgery with Jill. He has been very helpful to us."

When she said that, Richard greeted me by name, and Liz stepped close to me.

"Dub, this is Damon Clark," Liz said. "He came to pay his respect to Jill."

He looked at me. Seeing me in scrubs, he made an errant assumption.

"What are you? Are you a doctor?"

He didn't offer his hand, nor did I.

"I'm a friend, Damon,"

Liz stepped closer to me and took my hand. As she did, she said, "Thank you for coming by, Damon. We'll tell Jill you asked about her?"

We all stood silently, looking at Damon, and he at me.

Without looking at Liz, he asked, "Is this the guy?"

I squeezed her hand and answered for her, "Actually, Damon, I think I am."

He glared at me and hissed, "You better watch your back," as he turned on his heel and walked out of the room and down the hall.

"Excuse me for a sec," I said.

I walked to the head nurse and gave her Clark's name and the instruction that he wasn't to be allowed on the floor as long as Jill was a patient. She knew me well enough to agree without any further approval. I returned to the waiting room.

"Well, he won't be back up here. I'm sorry if he upset you all. Hopefully, he didn't upset Jill."

I left for my office, saying goodbye and telling Liz to call me if Clark showed up at the hospital. She nodded and gave me a quick kiss. Damon Clark is definitely not the guy in the picture, so maybe my first guess was correct and he was her brother.

On my way out, I stopped in to see Robert Munoz, the Director of Security for the hospital. I didn't know him well, but I liked him. I explained what had happened and he said he would give notice to all of his personnel to watch for Clark. He asked what I knew about the guy and I told him I knew nothing about Clark. He said he would see what he could find out. I thanked him and went on my way.

At four o'clock, Liz called.

"Hi. Do you have dinner plans this evening?"

"No, I said, inwardly hopeful that Vivian's plans had changed in our favor.

"Would you like to join the three of us for a late dinner? We have a meeting with Jill's doctors at the end of the day, so I may have some news And Richard and Vivian would like to get to know you better."

"Sure," I replied. "What time and where?"

It wasn't what I had hoped for, but I took it as a good sign.

As Liz hung up, my phone signaled an incoming call from Robert Munoz.

"Dub, I'm glad I caught you before you left. Do you have a minute?"

"Sure. What's up?"

"I heard from my contact at the Houston Police department. He couldn't tell me much but said Clark has a flag from Narcotics. He said someone in Narcotics would give me a call Monday and give me more information. He did say that Clark also has a flag indicating he could be dangerous.

"I have a supervisor who is retired from the Houston Police Department. He worked Narcotics for a time. His name is Tim Carrell. He says the flag is pretty broad, meaning the guy could be a user, a dealer, or just suspected of some kind of drug activity. And the dangerous note could be anything from a hot temper to homicidal. I know that isn't much, but we're watching for him if he comes back here. Tell your girlfriend to call the police or sheriff if he comes around.

I thanked him for his help.

Great. This guy could be a real problem, especially if he does drugs.

ELEVEN

Damon Clark was in a foul mood. He wanted a drink but didn't have time. He drove to his office and strode angrily through the entrance. His secretary took one look at him and asked, "Bad day?"

"Yeah," he replied. "Shitty day.

"Tell Bobby I want to see him," he instructed her as he went into his office

Bobby Duvall was his second in command. Duvall knew the business and could run it as well as Clark. They had been friends for more than fifteen years. They had met in juvenile detention when they were both sixteen. Both were born ne're-do-wells and con men. Both were reasonably good-looking and were personable when they wanted to be.

Duvall entered, took one look at Clark, and asked, "Bad day?"

"That seems to be the question of the day," Clark replied. "Yeah, shitty day," he repeated.

"Do you want to talk about it?"

"Yeah. I had this all worked out. That bitch Liz was going to be my ticket to respectability. I'm gonna buy this business from my uncle and get away from the drugs. Having a wife who is a college graduate with parents who have respectable educations and jobs is what I need to move up in this state.

"Uncle John had a good idea when we started the deli chain and then began moving weed through these shops, and it has worked well for several years now. But now, I think he wants to move a lot of weed in, and I'm getting a bad feeling. We've kept it quiet so far, but I think we could be asking for trouble if we escalate.

"I think it's a big mistake. It will influence the deli clientele and kill the deli business. The delis are my ticket out of here. I want to get them clean, and I think Uncle John is moving in the other direction. And it will probably get us back in jail. I'm not going back to jail and I'm not going to prison. And I don't think you want to, either."

"You got that right, brother," Duvall affirmed. "So, what's the problem?"

"She gave me the brush off and now she's seeing some doctor."

"How do you know that?"

"Her best friend was in a bad car accident. I was gonna be a nice guy and pay respects to her friend. You know, get back in her good graces. I went to the hospital this morning. I thought going up there to see her friend would get me on her good side again. When I suggested we should get back together, she told me to leave."

"Yeah, well. You said she found out about that girl in San Antonio–Melissa. I'm sure that pissed her off."

"Melissa was just company when I was over there, just like the girl in Austin. I still don't know how she found out about Melissa.

"Anyway, the guy was at the hospital when I was there. She introduced me to him. He got wise with me. I got hot and told him to watch his back. Now, I have to find a way to get rid of him, to scare him off."

"Why? Is she that important to you? There are plenty of women out there."

"For guys like us, there aren't many women out there who have a college education, a good job, and a good family. I want to get ahead, maybe get into politics. I don't want to be just another ex-juvenile delinquent with a GED. I'll never get into college, but she would be nice window dressing if I'm going to get anywhere."

"What makes you think you can compete with a doctor?"

"He's a young guy. Probably up to his ass in school loans and not making much at this stage. I can give her anything she wants. I'm already making good money."

"So, you think that scaring him off will get her back?"

"Maybe not, but if I can't have her, no one else is going to have her."

"Man, you're not thinking straight."

"Maybe not, but I want to have some fun with him. The whole time I was there, he was just looking down his nose at me and gloating."

"So, what are you going to do?"

Damon was silent for a moment. Then he smiled.

"I'm going to send Hector out to give him a little message."

Within his world, he handled the delicatessens and the take-out business. Bobby backed up Damon, especially when Damon went out of town. Hector Gomez handled the procurement of stolen vehicles and parts for Damon's uncle, John Candelero, and provided muscle when needed. John Candelero ran everything in compartmentalized operations.

Bobby shook his head.

"Hector's not too bright. Give him good instructions. He knows how to keep his mouth shut, but he gets confused sometimes. Do you want me to do it?"

"No. You aren't scary enough. Hector will be okay. I only want to scare the guy enough to get him out of the picture."

TWELVE

I finished some paperwork. I went home, showered, shaved, and dressed casually for dinner. I was waiting at our table when they arrived. They all looked tired.

We ordered. As we ate, Vivian, Richard and I told each other about ourselves. I had liked each of them from the moment we met. Both were very complimentary of Liz and encouraged a relationship between Liz and me. I casually asked Liz about Damon. Both she and Vivian quickly assured me that he was in the past.

"I believe that, but humor me. Tell me about him."

I saw recognition in Richard's expression and he nodded his head.

Liz responded.

"A few months ago, last fall before Richard left for Alaska, he and Jill invited me to a concert. Before the concert, we went to dinner. We had a drink at the bar while we were waiting for our table. Damon was at the bar and he struck up a conversation. He asked for my phone number and called a few days later. He seemed nice, and he acted nice. We dated. Two months ago, I learned that I wasn't the only one. I broke it off."

"Well, I can certainly understand that. And I'm happy for you–and me–that you did. What does he do for a living?'

Liz answered. "His uncle owns several delicatessens in Houston, Austin, and San Antonio. Damon operates them for his uncle. As I learned, he has a girl in each city.

"Does he have business partners?"

"I think so," Liz said.

"He does, in the legal sense," Richard added. "He told me his uncle owns three corporations. I don't know the names of those corporations, but one of them is a partner in the deli business, which is incorporated as Deli Texas, Inc. He must make a nice income from the businesses because he drives a Land Rover with all the bells and whistles."

"How long did you date?"

"Three or four months. Actually four, I guess."

"How did you find out about the other women?"

"We were out one night. I went to the ladies room. When I returned, his back was to me. He was talking to some man I had never seen before. I heard the man ask him if that girl in San Antonio was new, and he called her by name–Melissa Rice. I heard the name clearly.

"Damon said yes. The guy asked him what happened to the one he had been dating and Damon mumbled something I didn't hear. I just stood off to the side, fumbled in my purse, and listened without watching them closely. I don't think the man noticed me. They shook hands and the man left.

"Damon turned one way and I stepped to his other side and touched his arm as if I had just walked up. We went to the bar for a drink. As the bartender was setting our drinks on the bar and Damon was reaching for his wallet, I asked when he was going to see Melissa again. He dropped his wallet and knocked over his drink trying to turn toward me. The bartender got the mess cleaned up and brought him a new drink. He turned to me and his eyes were cold. Very tersely, he asked who told me about Melissa.

"He never asked, 'Melissa who?' He never denied her. He just wanted to know who told me about her. When he turned to look at me, the expression on his face and the coldness in his eyes told me all I needed to know. Mr. Nice Guy was just an act.

"'Does it really matter?' I replied.

"I removed the expensive watch he had given me and a ring that he had given me and laid them on the bar in front of him. I picked up my purse and left. He never came after me, never tried to explain, and never apologized.

"He called once shortly after that and left a message demanding that I tell him who told me about Melissa. I ignored his call. But I did go online and I found Melissa Rice in San Antonio. I sent her a message and she called me. We had a very nice talk and she thanked me for outing him.

"He has left phone messages saying that he wants to fix things, to get back together, but he has never apologized. It was he who called the night we went to Coco's.

"Since that experience, I've had no desire to have another man in my life."

She paused, blushing a little. "Until now."

She gave me a smile that would melt butter.

"What else can you tell me about him?"

"He's in the past, Dub. Why do you want to know about him?"

"Because I'm not sure he will stay in the past and I want to be prepared. I think this morning was a good indication of what you can expect. Give me until Tuesday and I will tell you more if there is any more to tell. Until Tuesday, just trust me… and stay alert."

"You're scaring me a little, Dub."

"How hard was the look in his eyes when he turned on you that night at the bar?"

She paused, looking directly at me. Then, her gaze shifted inward and she said, after a moment, "Scary hard."

I didn't pursue the subject anymore that night. We paid for our check. Richard and I walked Liz and Vivian to Liz's car. Liz gave me a good night kiss and whispered, "I'll miss you.

"I'll miss you, too. Sleep well tonight. Call me when you can."

"I need to tell you something. I'll call in a little while," she said quietly.

She smiled as she got into the driver's seat and they drove away.

You really do like her; don't you Wade?

THIRTEEN

Richard was waiting as I turned. I arched my brows questioningly and he asked, "Are you up for another glass of wine? I may have something of interest to you."

I nodded. "My treat."

When we were seated with a glass of wine for each of us, he spoke.

"Jill and I never liked that guy. He tried too hard. He tried to buy Liz's affection and our friendship. That first night, he paid for our bar bill. It was a nice gesture, but it was a prelude. Every time we went out, he wanted to pick up the tab. Jill and Liz and I go to local places; he wanted to go to the expensive, glitzy places. He talked a lot about local politics and how he could run things better–as if he had the skills to do so.

"He gave her an expensive ring. She didn't want to take it, but he convinced her. For Christmas, he gave her a Rolex. She didn't want to accept it either, but he finally convinced her. For her birthday, he tried to give her a BMW convertible. She thanked him and flatly refused to accept it. We think she was ready to break it off about the time she learned of the woman in San Antonio.

"That has no bearing on anything, but I thought you should know. And I think you need to understand who Liz is. You know that Jill and Liz have known each other since God's dog was a pup. Jill and I met when we were all juniors at A&M. At about the same time, Liz started dating a junior who was in the Corp of Cadets. You're an Aggie so you know about the Corp."

I nodded.

"His name was Phillip Taylor." He laughed. "We used to kid Liz that, if they married, her married name would be Elizabeth Taylor."

"Anyway, Phil was right up at the top of the chain of command of The Corp. He was a great Aggie, a great student, and a great person. He was a very caring guy and would do anything for his friends. The four of us were together constantly. Phil became one of my best friends.

"We graduated and you know Jill's and Liz's story. Phil accepted a commission in the Army. He spent one year as an Intelligence Officer, then applied to Ranger School. He was at the top of his class. We were all on the right path to success. I won't say Phil was breezing through Ranger training–that would be an insult to Rangers because it's certainly no breeze–but he was again at the top of his class. He completed jump school and was to make his final jump.

"Something happened. He made a perfect exit from the aircraft. Before he pulled his cord, a bird hit him full in the face. The film of the exercise showed he was dazed and just fell for a few seconds.

"My understanding is that twelve hundred fifty feet is the base safe level. He was seen struggling to pull the cord and they think he finally did at nine hundred feet. He was still dazed. He landed hard and all wrong. The bottom line is that he broke his back and both legs. A broken rib punctured one lung. He was paralyzed from the waist down. Liz was a basket case; she was devastated. The three of us were.

"Phil was in Walter Reed in Bethesda, Maryland. Liz was here. Because they were not married, she was not eligible for travel at military expense to Maryland. Her parents and her coworkers started a fund for airfare and she spent as much time as she could with Phil. ExxonMobil was very considerate and worked with her schedule for a year. At the end of her second year on the job, Phil contracted pneumonia and died shortly thereafter.

"That is part of Liz's fear now. Phil essentially died of a lung puncture from a broken rib. And Jill is suffering from the same injury.

"Phil was the love of her life."

Curiosity resolved. The picture must be Phillip.

"They were going to be married. When Phil died, the three of us were devastated. Liz was a zombie and became a recluse for a while. She worked and slept. She kept it all bottled inside her. Occasionally she would go to dinner with us. Her mother and father were out of the country, so we were all she had. Like Vivian is doing now, her mother came here for a while to be with her, but there wasn't much any of us could do or say that helped her. She suffered for nearly a year, but she is strong, realistic, and practical. She began to come out of her shell.

"The night she met Clark was the first attention she had received–or at least accepted–from a man since Phil died. He seemed nice enough that first night and at first, but Jill and I agreed that he was almost too nice. And then the weekends that he said he had to be out of town began. We wanted to warn her off, but his attention seemed to make her happy at first and helped her shed the cocoon in which she had wrapped herself. But, as I said, he tried too hard. He gave her things, but never himself.

"According to Jill, he constantly pressed Liz to sleep with him, but she refused. She said she felt it would be an insult to the memory of Phil and what they had together. Jill said Liz never slept with him. Until that night she met Clark, she had refused dates and would go nowhere other than work with Jill and me. She fell back into that pattern after Clark.

"Honestly, I was truly scared for Liz when Jill was injured. She had lost the love of her life to an accident. And now she was once again faced with a similar situation. When I learned of Jill's injuries and finally got my head wrapped around the fact that Jill wasn't going to die, my next thought was of Liz. Without Jill, she had no one here to be there for her. She's a strong girl, but even the strongest of us can only handle so much. I tried to call her Wednesday night, the night of the accident, but I couldn't get a call through to her phone.

"From what I've seen and heard, it was you who got her through that first night and who is keeping her afloat now. From what I've seen of you, I think you are very much like Phil. And it seems obvious that she is very taken with you.

"That's history, but I think you should know who she is. She's the genuine article and the man who wins her heart will be a very lucky man, indeed. In my humble and biased opinion. Jill and Liz are two of the finest women I have ever met.

"Now, as for Mr. Personality. Everything I'm going to say is just opinion, hearsay, and supposition. I don't have one fact of proof.

"One of my two remaining best friends is here in Houston. The son of one of his neighbors died of a drug overdose several months ago. He told me that it was judged an accidental suicide and taken no further. The father has taken it upon himself to find out who was selling drugs to his son. My friend says the father has had little success. He tried talking to all his son's friends, but they are either afraid to say from whom these kids get their drugs or they just don't know. However, one of the kids told him it was as easy as takeout from the deli. I found the metaphor to be a little too close to home.

"I don't know to whom the father told that bit of information, but I just got a funny feeling about that statement, and about Clark when we found out how much money old Damon makes selling deli sandwiches.

"And, like Liz, I've heard the guy when he is angry. And I've seen his face. One evening, the four of us went to dinner and he drove, as he always did. As we were walking back to the car after dinner, a young guy–I guess between eighteen and twenty-one–backed into Clark's Land Rover. Clark told us to get in the Land Rover and that he was going to talk to the driver. The girls got in, but I watched… and listened. The other driver had no insurance. Clark took the guy's license and said the guy could have it back when he brought Clark ten thousand in cash. Then, he threatened to kill the guy if he didn't bring the cash within a week. He held up the license and waved it in the guy's face like he was saying I know where you live. He didn't sound like he was kidding.

"When he turned and saw me, he gave me a hard look and told me I should be in the car. Then he asked if I heard what he said. I played dumb. I told him I didn't hear anything and just watched because I thought he might need a witness. We were never buddy-buddy, and we sure haven't been since that night.

"I hope Clark really is out of our lives, but I don't think he is. His display at the hospital was just like his behavior the night of the car incident. I don't know if he ever followed through or if the guy brought him cash, but Clark is scary."

We talked a little longer about Liz and Jill, then went home.

So Clark is a bully. But he isn't the kind that gets in the other person's face. Clark is one of the behind-your-back bullies to watch out for. They are more likely to follow through on a threat.

Liz called as I was driving.

"Dub, I'm sorry, but I was told this afternoon that I have to be in a meeting in Dallas Monday morning. I'm booked on a flight out Sunday afternoon. I want so much to see you, but it will be Monday night or Tuesday before that can happen."

Her voice broke a little as she said softly, "Please don't give up on me."

I chuckled softly.

"How could I do that? We have a date to return to Coco's."

She giggled.

"That's right. We do."

We said good night and she told me she would call in the morning.

FOURTEEN

Liz called Saturday morning. I offered to take them to dinner. She said Richard would probably have dinner with his parents since he was flying back on Sunday, and she thought she and Vivian would be tired after a long day. She asked if I would come to her home and offered to prepare dinner. I suggested that I cook at her house and have it ready when they arrived.

She protested, but not too hard. I told her I make a mean Irish stew and she accepted for her and Vivian.

I went to the hospital to see Jill and to ensure that I saw Richard before he left. Liz gave me a spare key to her place. When Liz and Vivian arrived, they looked less tired and stressed than they had Friday night. They said Jill had a good day. They complimented my stew and we had a pleasant evening together. I learned a lot about Vivian. It was easy to see why Liz considered her to be a second mother.

I offered Liz a late lunch on Sunday and a ride to the airport.

"Thank you, Dub. That would be very nice."

Her smile lit the room.

Sunday, I met Liz at the hospital where she left her car in the parking garage. We had a quiet, wistful lunch. For me, and I think for both of us, the inability to have some time alone was wearing thin. I drove her to the airport and we were both quiet.

On the way into the airport complex, I pulled into the telephone lot where one waits for arriving passengers to call. Liz looked at me curiously. I parked in the back, under a large live oak tree.

"Airport security won't let us park in front of the terminal long enough for a decent kiss before we unload your bag."

She laughed out loud, unbuckled her seatbelt, and pulled me to her. She gave me a great, warm kiss and took my face in her hands.

"Promise you won't give up on us," she murmured with a grin on her face, but concern in her eyes.

I tipped her chin up and kissed her slowly. I kissed her a second time. We slowly explored with our tongues and teased with our lips.

"I'm not giving up. I kind of like the new girl in my life."

She nodded her head and smiled warmly.

"I like the way you think."

"And we are definitely going to find some quiet time together this week," I said as I looked into her eyes. "That's a promise."

"I promise, too," she said softly as we kissed again.

FIFTEEN

I had two surgeries on Monday. There wasn't time between the two to check my phone. When I finally got my equipment shut down, cleaned, and stored properly, it was two o'clock and I was hungry. I went to the cafeteria, got a sandwich and some soup, and checked my phone. There was a message from a Detective Asimov.

I returned the call and he arranged to meet me at hospital security at three o'clock in Robert Munoz's office. I explained to Asimov what had happened with Clark at the hospital and his comment about watching my back. I also told him of the incident involving Clark that Richard had described to me, but did not mention what Richard told me about drugs. Asimov took notes and asked some perfunctory questions. He asked for my home address and my office address and phone numbers. He asked if there had been any further contact or threats. I said no and he closed his notebook, giving me his card and telling me to call if there were any more incidents with Clark.

When he rose to leave, I said, "I understood that Clark's name was flagged in the system for narcotics.

"He had a misdemeanor possession charge when he was nineteen. Nothing since then," he said dismissively. "Call me if there is anything clsc."

I said I would.

When he was gone, I asked Robert if they had a security film from the day Clark made the statements to me. He played with his computer and pulled up footage from the entrances to the hospital and at the elevator on Jill's floor. I confirmed the time of the incident and he scrolled through the footage at the elevator at that time. It didn't take long to find Clark, both coming and going. He isolated Clark in still shots and printed two clear pictures of him.

"I'll keep these, just in case," he said as he put the photos in his desk drawer. "Let me know if you see him around the hospital.

I nodded, thanked him, shook hands, and left.

PART 3

SIXTEEN

Liz was scheduled to arrive at five-forty Tuesday evening. I stopped by my office, then drove home. I checked her flight and it was on time. Just as I cleared the screen, she called.

"My flight is on time and I can't wait to see you."

Yes! I did a little fist pump.

"Call me when you are in baggage claim. I'll be waiting in the phone lot and will meet you outside of the baggage claim area. Would you like dinner?"

"I'd like a glass of wine and a light dinner."

She called from the baggage area and was waiting at the curb when I pulled up. I popped the tail door of my SUV. She deposited her bag, jumped inside, and gave me a huge kiss. An insensitive security woman blew her whistle and motioned me out of the area. Liz quietly took my hand and kissed my palm. It was nice.

"I don't want to go to a restaurant. I just want to be alone with you."

"Your place or mine?"

She was quiet a moment. "I don't want to go home to an empty house just yet. And I haven't seen your home. Is that too presumptuous?"

"No. I'd like that." I gave her a big grin. "I'd like that very, very much."

"Good. I've called Jill and told her I would see her tomorrow. She said she's doing well."

We arrived at my home. She asked me to bring her bag in with us. I thought that was a good sign.

Inside, she squeezed my hand and told me my home was very warm and inviting. I told her she was invited anytime, and we laughed and grinned conspiratorially.

My home is very open and spacious. I set the sound system to play pleasant light jazz throughout the house. I took her bag to the guest room, then led her to the kitchen. She looked around. "This is very nice. And very spacious. How many bedrooms do you have?"

"Three and a dedicated study," I replied as I poured wine for us. I hand her a glass and invited, "Bring your wine and I'll give you the butler's tour." As we wandered into and out of rooms, she was very complimentary. "This is very comfortable and very handsome. And what I could see of your landscaping also looks wonderful. It fits you perfectly. You must be very happy here."

"I am. When I learned that I would be reassigned to the Woodlands, I contacted a realtor and told her exactly what I wanted. Two days later, she brought me here. I didn't need to look any farther. It was designed and built by a bachelor who added a lot of guy-friendly options. He came into a large inheritance and built a larger, similar home not far from here. He had added a rain shower head in the bath, double pane windows, a small wine closet, a cedar closet, and some other things."

"What kind of other things?

"I'll show you one of my favorite additions." I took her to the garage where I showed her a six by eight-foot independently air-conditioned alcove that held a speed bag and a heavy punching bag. I pointed to the speed bag. "Do you know what that is?"

"It's a boxing bag."

"Close enough. It's called a speed bag. The purpose is to give a boxer quick hands. And I love working out on it."

"Show me."

I gave her a quick demonstration. She set her drink down and tried to imitate me, but failed. She only hit the bag twice.

"How do you do it?"

I explained the mechanics and showed her the rhythm in slow motion. She tried again and, after three or four tries, began to feel the rhythm.

"Good job!"

She smiled her thanks. "That could be quite a workout."

"It is, but it's a great workout."

"Do you box?"

"I know how, but I don't box anymore."

"How did you learn?"

"Our neighbor when I was growing up, Mr. McCain, had boxed in the Navy and had been a self-defense instructor. His son, Carter, and I were the same age and were good friends. Mr. McCain taught us to box and to use the speed bag and the big bag. He bought gloves and helmets—with good nose guards—and taught us how to fight with our fists. Carter and I tried it a few times without the helmets and both got our noses smashed. Hurt like the dickens!! That ended any desire to get in the ring again without protection.

"He also taught us some tactics for self-defense and introduced us to martial arts. And, I've also had some other self-defense training that helped."

"Have you ever been in a real fight?"

I paused. "Yes. A few as a kid. Once as an adult."

"Did boxing help you?"

"Yes."

"You're an interesting man. You'll have to tell me some stories sometime."

I shrugged. "There isn't much to tell. For right now, how about another glass of wine and some dinner?"

We fixed a simple salad. We ate and talked. After a few minutes, she looked at me as a mischievous smile appeared at the corners of her mouth.

"All this happened pretty fast, didn't it?" she asked

I nodded. "Indeed, it did."

"Does that bother you? Does my behavior the first night bother you?"

"No. I generally know my mind… and what interests me. It didn't take me long that first night to know that I was interested in you."

"Because you thought I would sleep with you?"

"No. I knew you were upset. I knew it was wrong to take advantage of you that night. I liked you and wanted to help you get through the night. I do have some scruples."

"Are you dating anyone now? Am I just the new girl?"

"No. To both. There hasn't been anyone for almost three months."

She took a drink. "This has all been incredibly unexpected… and nice. Are you okay with us?

"Surprised and very okay."

We sat quietly for a while. A lot of random thoughts marched through my head, but each time, she popped into the picture and stood front and center. I liked her. And it wasn't just the sex that I hoped would come.

"What would you like?" I asked.

"I know we should get some sleep. It's getting late and I want to be at the hospital by nine tomorrow morning." She set her glass on the table. "But I'm not ready to end the evening. Are you?"

I grinned and shook my head. I stood and she came into my arms. And it all seemed so natural and comfortable. We kissed and touched and explored until need overwhelmed us. We walked hand in hand to my bedroom where we eagerly undressed each other.

"Are you," I began, and she nodded.

"I'm on birth control."

She took my hand and we tumbled into bed. It was wonderful.

Afterward, we quietly lay together, she on her side with one arm over my chest and one leg over my thigh. We sighed and murmured and teased each other until need took over. We again made love and peaked compatibly. We soon found ourselves back in the same position with her arm and leg over me.

She sighed and yawned, cuddling closer to me. We again lay quietly together, occasionally kissing or touching.

"Would you like me to take you home?'

She shook her head. "No. I'd like to sleep next to you all night, right here." She kissed me coquettishly. "If that's okay with you," she murmured as she reached for me and I grinned from ear to ear.

SEVENTEEN

I woke early Wednesday morning. Liz was sound asleep, purring softly as she lay next to me. I knew she must have been very tired and we had plenty of time before we needed to leave for the hospital, so I let her sleep.

I made coffee and showered quietly. As I was rinsing the soap and shampoo off, the shower door opened behind me and two delicate hands slipped around my waist. I felt Liz's cheek nuzzle against my back and felt her naked body press against me.

How can this day possibly go wrong?

"Good morning," she murmured, as I turned and pulled her to me. She kissed me wonderfully.

"Good morning," I replied, returning her kiss.

She giggled delightfully. Without a word, we made love as easily under the warm shower as if we had been together for months.

"You get dry and let me shower," she said, as she gently pushed me out the door. Her naked body was a sight to behold. "Then I need a cup of coffee."

"Coffee coming up, ma'am," I said with a laugh.

We dressed and ate a quick breakfast. I had two surgeries that day beginning at ten o'clock. I suggested that she could take my car from the hospital to her office after she looked in on Jill this morning, and then pick me up at the end of the day when she came back to see Jill.

I drove us to the hospital and parked in the doctors' parking lot. Dr. Melbourne had been kind enough to get me a pass into the lot, which requires a windshield device to trigger the gates. As we passed through the gate and it lowered behind me, I heard car horns sounding. I looked in my rearview mirror and saw a nondescript white van caught between the closed gate and a short line of cars behind it. We parked and I gave Liz my keys.

As we walked toward the hospital, we both looked at the immobile van. The window was down and someone, apparently the driver of the car with an open door behind the van, was gesturing to the van driver, a large Hispanic man with a ponytail. They were shouting at each other. A security car arrived as we crossed the drive and walked into the hospital. We went to see Jill, then Liz left for her office and I walked downstairs to prepare for surgery. I didn't give the van another thought.

My day went well. Between surgeries, I relaxed and replayed our morning in my mind. I smiled a lot. She was smart and pretty and personable. I liked her a lot.

After the second surgery, I gathered my paperwork to go upstairs to my office. Surgery is on the second floor. My office is on the third floor. As I neared the door into the stairwell on the second floor, something caught my eye that registered, but not distinctively. I heard footsteps coming toward the stairwell door as I started up the stairs. As I stepped onto the mid-level landing, the door behind me opened and an accented voice called, "Hey, you. Wait a minute?"

I realized what I had seen as I was going to the stairwell. It was the ponytail of the guy who was in the white van.

Mrs. Wade did not raise a fool for a son. And I was not going to get caught on a small, tight landing between floors by a guy much bigger than I. It was a pretty safe bet that he wasn't there to tell me I had won the Publisher's Clearing House Award.

I continued up the stairs. His footfalls were quick behind me as he yelled, "Wait. I just wanna talk to you."

I stepped onto the third floor and moved to the center of the hallway. At my end, there were four offices. At the other end was a break room, a nurse's station, and then a T-hallway that held recovery rooms and post-surgery intensive care. I stepped away from the nurse's station toward my office and laid my papers on the floor away from me. In the worst case, I knew there was a fire alarm five feet from where I stood.

The guy burst into the hallway and never looked toward the nurse's station. His eyes were fixed on me.

"You wanted to talk to me. Go ahead. Talk," I said loudly enough to be heard down the hall. I looked behind the rogue and saw the desk nurse watching us.

Ponytail stepped toward me and growled, "I got a message for you,"

He wore a Mexican wedding shirt outside his trousers. As he spoke, he lifted the hem of his shirt and grasped the hilt of what looked to be a large knife.

As I stepped into a defensive position, I saw over his shoulder the nurse lift the phone to her mouth with one hand and reach for the security button on her desk with the other.

He was oblivious to what was happening behind him and there was no other sound in the hallway. He pulled the knife with his right hand and extended it toward me.

"You didn't watch your back," he advised as he stepped toward me and made a little threatening jab at me.

Okay, Wade. Remember what Mr. McCain taught you.

I have not had anyone come at me with a knife except the play knife Mr. McCain used when he gave us lessons, but I did have a guy once come at me with a short club. I stepped back a half step and Ponytail did just what I knew he would do. He stepped toward me with the knife extended.

As Mr. McCain had taught us, instead of retreating I quickly stepped toward Ponytail and to his right. I grabbed his wrist with my right hand as I had been taught and spun my left shoulder and side into his right side, pulling his right arm around me. Ponytail's free hand was away from me and the knife was now pointed away from me.

Mr. McCain's next instruction to us had been to either head butt his nose for a person of our height or stomp on his right instep for a bigger assailant. I stomped with everything I had in me.

He yelled in pain and his right knee reflexively contracted from the pain in his foot causing his weight to drop onto his right side and his left leg to tense. *Don't mess up now, Wade.* With all my strength, I drove the cupped heel of my left hand into the center point of his straightened right arm, his elbow, and then did it a second time with all my strength. He was beefy and strong. My blow didn't break his elbow, but it hurt enough that he cried out in pain and dropped the knife.

Now, it was a piece of cake. I spun away from him on my right foot, still holding his wrist. I shifted my weight and balanced on my left foot as I drove my right heel into the side of his knee. The knee gave way and he went down. Still holding his right wrist, I kicked him hard on the point of his chin. His head bounced against the floor. He moaned and slumped, dazed, but not unconscious. Still holding his wrist, I kicked his chin again and his head thumped against the floor. If he wasn't unconscious now, he was very dazed and not moving.

I heard feet pounding from down the hall as a security officer ran toward us, his weapon in his hand.

I stepped back and raised my hands to chest level. "I work here. He followed me into the stairwell and attacked me here. The desk nurse saw everything."

He told me to stand where I was. He handcuffed ponytail as the nurse walked quickly toward us.

"That man attacked Mr. Wade with a knife. I saw him do it," she called to the security officer.

In quick succession, another security officer arrived followed closely by Robert Munoz, Head of Security. Robert looked at me and then at Ponytail.

"Big son-of-a-bitch, isn't he!"

The nurse quickly told Robert what she had seen. Robert looked at me with a big smile, and asked quietly, "Jesus, Dub. You took this guy down by yourself?"

I nodded. "A lot of luck and a good instructor when I was younger. If that hadn't worked, I was going to pull the fire alarm."

Robert laughed heartily. "Yeah, well. You can give me lessons any time. Good job!"

The Sheriff's deputies arrived and arrested ponytail. I followed Robert to his office where I gave them all a statement. I explained to Robert about the guy trying to follow us into the reserved parking lot that morning, and then how he followed me into the stairwell and to the third floor. Robert pulled the report of the guard in the parking lot and got the license number and VIN of the white van. He gave that information to the sheriff's deputy also.

When it was just Robert and me, he asked me if the statement about watching my back meant anything. I reminded him of what Clark had said. He nodded and said, "Sounds like more than just a coincidence to me."

I agreed. "But, I don't understand why Clark would do something so foolish. If it was him, then he either has some powerful friends or he's a bubble off-center. If it was him, thank goodness he hired someone stupid to do the job. I don't think I could have taken a man that big who knew what he was doing."

"I think I'll let Detective Asimov know about this," he said.

"Robert, let's sit on this for a little while if you don't mind. Asimov didn't seem too interested before and all we have is a coincidental phrase to link Clark. Maybe this failure will discourage Clark if it really was Clark behind it all."

He nodded. "Makes sense to me. But take Clark's advice—watch your back."

"I will. Thanks for your help."

EIGHTEEN

I went to the cafeteria for a sandwich and gave this all some thought. *Based upon the admonition of Ponytail, there is no doubt in my mind that Clark was behind all this. But there has to be more here than I realize for Clark to behave so erratically. Either he has some severe psychological problems or I don't know everything about his relationship with Liz. In a very short time, I've grown to like her very much and care for her, but I think we need to talk.*

I returned to my office and completed the paperwork for our services that day. There was a knock on the door and Dr. Melbourne stuck his head in.

"Oh, good. You're here," he effused with a huge smile. He came around my desk and extended his hand.

"From the time you first came to my attention, I have liked you and admired you. I heard about what you did today. You are truly a remarkable young man. I'm very impressed that you are as capable outside your field as you are in it. I just wanted to thank you for your service to the hospital today—both in and out of the surgery theater."

He laughed.

"I just wish I could have seen you in action. The desk nurse who saw it all has spread the word. In her opinion, you are Bruce Willis and James Bond rolled into one man. And Robert Munoz has certainly praised you to Hospital Administration."

"You're very kind, sir. I was just lucky today."

"I understand you have had some training in self-defense. Was that military or your father?"

"Close. Our neighbor when I was a boy. He was a boxing champ and self-defense instructor in the Navy. He was a good instructor. He taught me and his son a lot."

"Well, good job," he said, and shook my hand again. As he was leaving, he paused, turned, and asked, "How well do you know Robert Munoz?"

"I just know him from the hospital. I like him a lot."

He nodded. "You might be interested in his background."

I had some time before I thought Liz would arrive, so I called Robert.

"It's Dub. Do you have a few minutes to visit sometime soon?

"I'm free now. Come on down."

I walked downstairs. His door was open and I walked in.

He saluted me. "My friend, your name is on the lips of everyone in the hospital today… and probably for the rest of the month, at least."

"Thank you. But, things could have just as easily gone the other way. I was lucky and had a good teacher."

"I watched you on the security footage. It sure looked like skill to me. How did you learn to move like that?"

I told him about Mr. McCain. I told him I also had some practical training in jujitsu when I was in college. I shifted gears.

"I wanted to talk to you a little bit about Clark, but Dr. Melbourne suggested I ask you about your background. He said I would be interested. What did you do before you came here?"

"Ah, Dr. Melbourne. There is a man who sticks by those he likes. I think a lot of him.

"In a nutshell, I went to the Point–West Point. I played tight end for Army. I was commissioned as an officer in the Military Police. I was with the MPs for three years, the first two of which were in the CID–Criminal Investigation Division. I did my third year with a tour in Afghanistan as a First Lieutenant leading an MP platoon that maintained compound and convoy security. I was set to attend Yale Law School and then move to the Judge Advocate Corps after Afghanistan. I had just been given an accelerated promotion waiver to captain, but the papers hadn't reached Afghanistan.

"I led my last convoy mission as a First Lieutenant the day before my promotion orders arrived. We were attacked. I took some shrapnel and a round in one thigh that did a lot of damage. I was flown home to Walter Reed. They fixed me up, gave me disability and discharge papers along with my captain's bars, and wished me well. I interviewed with the CIA, but they couldn't take me because of my disability.

"My dad is a doctor. He knows the Director here and Dr. Melbourne well. Shorthand version, the hospital security director was retiring and Dr. Melbourne suggested me for the job. I guess they liked my background, so here I am."

I liked Robert a lot and had certainly gained a new respect for him. And now I understood his slight limp when he walked.

"I'm impressed. Thank you for your service. I had no idea of what you did before coming here. That must have been a frightening experience."

"I came home. Some guys didn't. I was lucky." He shrugged. "That's history. The Army gave me a good education and good training. I have no complaints. I'm here and I have a good life."

"I assume you earned at least a Purple Heart."

He paused, sighed, and nodded slowly. "I was awarded a Purple Heart and a Silver Star. But they aren't worth the lives we lost that day." He paused and then chuckled. "And I also have a good conduct medal," he said in a humorous self-deprecating way that made me laugh.

I nodded somberly. I'm sure this guy was one hell of a good soldier and leader.

He shifted in his chair and asked, "So, what's on your mind about Clark?"

I told him about what Richard told me about take out from the deli. "I don't know whether that was just coincidence or the kid gave a subtle hint. Then, the thug this afternoon telling me I hadn't watched my back—the exact words that Clark used. That's two coincidences with the same guy at the center. What do you think?"

He leaned back in his chair and looked at the ceiling thoughtfully for a long moment. Then, he looked at me. "I'm just thinking out loud here, so bear with me.

"Coincidences disturb me. I didn't like them as an investigator. And I liked them even less in Afghanistan. Coincidences almost always seem to be followed by something unpleasant.

"Right now, all we have is speculation. Even if the guy is involved in drugs, why would he behave so stupidly just because you're with Liz? It isn't like she was his wife or had been his girlfriend for very long. Is there a correlation? Does he have some Rabbi in the criminal world who protects him when he does stupid things, so he thinks he can get away with them?

"Did the guy this afternoon intend to kill you or just scare you? I'd like to think he was just trying to scare you, but he could have delivered the message without waving his knife in your face if that was the case.

"For the time being, I think we should just be watchful. Let's see if the authorities get anything out of the guy who attacked you. Tell Liz to be careful and keep her eyes open."

I nodded. "What do you think of Asimov? He seems pretty nonchalant about what happened."

He nodded. "Yes. I thought so, too. But, maybe he's just overworked and our event was a small splash in a big pond. Let me ask Tim Carrell what he thinks. I'll keep you advised."

"Thanks, Robert. I appreciate your help. I find this very disconcerting and very… difficult to understand."

"You're welcome," he replied. "And Dub, my friends call me J.R. Feel free to do so." He smiled at me.

I laughed. "Thank you. I appreciate that. Thanks, J.R." I raised my eyebrows quizzically.

"Juan Roberto," he answered.

I smiled and nodded.

NINETEEN

I took the stairs to Jill's room. As I did, I wondered if I should start using the elevator until this enigma was resolved. As I passed the nurses station, the desk nurse stood and applauded, gave me a big smile and a big thumbs up. I thanked her. I quietly entered behind Liz and Vivian who were standing by the bed talking with Jill. Jill saw me and smiled. When she did, Liz turned.

She looked at me with wide eyes and began to tremble. She inhaled and her breath quivered in her throat. A few tears rolled down her cheek, then the tears came in buckets as she said through her sobs, "Oh, Dub. You could have been killed."

This was not at all what I expected when I entered the room. The fear and concern in her voice and the pain in her eyes stabbed my heart. If I had any doubt that she cared for me, it was gone. I stepped to her, gathered her into my arms, and held her. She held me tightly and cried.

All I could do was hold her, stroke her hair, and say softly, over and over, "Shh. I'm all right. Everything is all right." She had obviously heard about the day's adventure.

She cried herself out, reached for a tissue, and blew her nose. She looked me in the eyes, then kissed me in the most pleasant, gratifying way. "I'm sorry. I didn't mean to cry."

I kissed her back, held her at arm's length, and stupidly said, "Other than that, Ms. Lincoln, how was your day?"

She hit me in the middle of my chest–hard.

"It isn't funny," she said, then she started laughing. And we all joined in. "We haven't had enough time together yet."

"Oh," I said as I nodded. "When we've had enough time together, then they can kill me?"

She laughed and hit me in the chest again.

"You be careful," she admonished me seriously. "I don't want any more scares like that. Between Jill and you, it's a wonder I'm not a basket case."

She stepped back and Vivian hugged me as she said, "I'm so glad you are all right. What we heard was scary."

I felt a tug on my shirttail and looked down. Jill was pulling me to her and smiling. I bent and she hugged me as well as she could. "You take care of yourself. I want to get to know you better, as well." She hugged me again. "And thank you for taking care of Liz. She's like a sister to me."

I very gently hugged her back. "I'm looking forward to getting to know you better, too. Heal quickly."

When the word got out that I was in Jill's room, it seemed that everyone who was ambulatory stopped by to congratulate me. I hope that I was gracious to everyone. I'm not used to being the center of attention.

We visited Jill for a while until Vivian shooed us out. "I imagine the two of you need a little time together after today. You go now, and we'll see you tomorrow."

As Liz gathered her purse and briefcase, Vivian took my hand and said softly, "Please be careful. Richard told me that he told you about Phillip. I think it's pretty obvious that she cares for you. I don't know if she could recover from losing the second love of her life."

The reference to Phillip and the second love of her life surprised me. I guess Liz had talked to Vivian about me much more than I realized. I gently squeezed Vivian's hand.

"I don't intend to let that happen," I said with a grim smile.

TWENTY

Liz was quiet as we rode down in the elevator. As we walked to where she had parked my car, she silently took my hand, but still didn't say anything. When we were seated in the car, I asked if she wanted dinner. She shook her head and remained silent for a moment.

She turned to me and spoke softly. "I want to talk. I want to go somewhere quiet where we can talk. I think I'd like a glass of wine."

"A restaurant? Home? Where would you like to be?"

"Right now, I don't want to go home. There are too many memories there."

"My house? It's a beautiful evening. We can sit on the patio if you would like."

She nodded. "Please," was all she said.

When we arrived at my home, she asked if I would bring her suitcase in. I set it in the guest room.

"I have shorts and a top in my suitcase. Would you mind if I got comfortable?"

"I think that's a great idea. I will do likewise." She smiled, dug into her suitcase, and disappeared into the guest bathroom. I went to my room where I pulled some comfortable walking shorts and a Jimmy Buffet T-shirt from my dresser and changed clothes. She came into my room looking comfortable in white shorts and a white tank top. She had pulled her hair up into a ponytail. She looked wonderfully fetching… except for the strained look on her face and her sad, hollow eyes.

I pulled her to me and she silently laid her head against my chest.

I gave her a moment, then asked, "Red or white?"

Without looking up, she said softly, "White."

I took her hand and we walked barefoot to the patio. "You get comfortable and I'll be back with wine." She nodded.

I returned with glasses, an open bottle of a good chardonnay, and a chiller. She watched as I poured and handed her the glass. I poured for myself and sat, angled at ninety degrees to her. She took a sip and stared into the pool. I waited.

She turned to me. She looked agonized. She stared at me for a long moment, then softly said, "You could have been killed today, apparently because of me. Common sense tells me that we shouldn't see each other anymore."

I started to speak and she shook her head. "Let me talk for a minute." I nodded.

"I'm not a stupid person. That same common sense tells me that whatever harm has been done isn't going to go away if we stop seeing each other. But I don't understand what has happened. He was someone I dated for just a few months. I never slept with him. I never told him I had feelings for him. He was gone every other week. But the more that time passed, the more he seemed to become… obsessed with me.

"Early on, he gave me a pretty ring. I felt awkward accepting, but he insisted. He gave me a very expensive watch for Christmas. I tried to refuse and told him it was way too expensive, but he convinced me to take it. It was easier than arguing about it. Then, he tried to give me a car for my birthday. I flatly refused that. When we went out, it was always to someplace trendy and expensive. When he and I went with Richard and Jill, he insisted on picking up the check for everything, and that made them uncomfortable. It was like he was trying to buy my affection and their friendship.

"Until he came to the hospital and threatened you, I just thought he was a strange guy and I was glad that he was out of my life–or, so I thought.

"Do you think today was just a coincidence, or do you think he had something to do with it?"

I collected my thoughts, then told her everything that Robert–J.R.–and I had talked about and had speculated. I told her about Ponytail using the same words that Clark had used about watching my back.

"I think he had something to do with it, but, like you, I don't understand what is going on or why," I said.

She shook her head in agreement. "I understand the concept of stalkers and guys who are obsessed with a woman, but I don't understand that behavior taking him to the point of trying to harm you or kill you."

"I think he was probably just trying to scare me off, and I called his bluff."

"I'm not sure I can agree with you," she replied.

"Is there anything you can tell me about him that would help explain all this?"

"No. At first, he was nice. As time passed, he became more... not controlling, but obsessive.

He seemed to know a lot about business banking, but he always talked obliquely about politics and economics. I asked him where he went to college. He told me it was the school of hard knocks. He wouldn't talk about his childhood or his education. He told me that Jill and I were the only two college women he knew.

"It was obvious early on that we didn't have any basis for a serious relationship. I should have stopped it at the beginning, but..." She sat for a moment and I saw tears in the corners of her eyes.

"I need to tell you a story. I want you to know something about my life before you. I think I owe it to you to tell you."

I nodded. I was pretty sure of what was coming and I knew better than to tell her that Richard had already told me about Phillip.

My grandmother was killed in an auto accident when I was eight. It devastated my grandfather. He had a very hard time for more than a year. One day, he was at our home. Out of the blue, he asked me to sit with him. I did. He began telling me about my grandmother. I knew all this and started to tell him that I already knew. It was obvious that my mother knew that I was going to tell grandpa that I knew. Mom silently shook her head at me and mouthed the word listen.

I listened. My grandfather poured his heart out. He told me how much he missed grandma and how hard it had been dealing with her death. He told me about her as a girl and when he met her. He told me about dating her and falling in love with her and marrying her. He talked for a long time. Finally, he pulled me to him, tousled my hair, and thanked me for listening to him. He told me that I had helped him get a lot that was trapped inside him out and that it would help him move on with his life.

I don't know whether I helped, but I know that my grandpa was less troubled and more himself after that day. I realized that grandpa needed to talk and that if I had told him I already knew what he was going to tell me, I'm not sure if he would have gotten back to his old self that day. My mother told me the same thing.

Liz looked me straight in the eye.

"I met the love of my life early into my junior year at A&M. I fell head over heels in love with him. His name was Phillip Taylor. About the same time, Jill met Richard." She looked at me and I nodded encouragingly. She needed to talk. I was not about to stop her.

"The four of us became fast friends. Phillip and I became engaged two days before graduation. He was in the Corp of Cadets. He entered the army and was commissioned. He spent one year as an intelligence officer, then applied to Ranger School. He was at the top of his class. He completed jump school and was to make his final jump. Something happened that day. Before he pulled his ripcord, something–they think it was a bird–hit him in the face. The jump went bad and he landed all wrong. He broke his back and both legs. A broken rib punctured one lung. He was paralyzed from the waist down. He eventually died of his injuries.

"I was devastated. I had always known that something could happen to him as a Ranger, but I never imagined he could die in a training accident. Jill and Richard were all the support I had. Mother and Daddy were in South America. Mother came back for a month to be with me. I withdrew. I spent a year just working and sleeping. I saw no one except Jill and Richard. I received some counseling that finally began to break through to me. It was about that time that I met Damon, and I've already told you about that."

I nodded but said nothing.

"I knew I had to reconcile Phillip's death with my life and that I had to get back to who I had been before the tragedy–I had to move forward. ExxonMobil was a godsend. Everyone there was understanding and so accommodating, but I knew that couldn't continue much longer. When Damon asked me out, I accepted because I knew I needed to get back to a normal life. But I was eaten up with guilt. I felt as though I was betraying all that Phillip and I had together and all that we hoped to have.

"I never slept with Damon—not that he didn't try, but I couldn't. I would come home from a date with him consumed with guilt that I had betrayed Phillip.

"If you and I had met under normal circumstances, I'm sure I would have been attracted. We might even have found ourselves where we are now. But we didn't meet under normal circumstances. I got a crash course, a full immersion in the caring, compassionate man that Dub Wade is. Don't misunderstand or misinterpret what I'm going to say.

"That night was like being with Phillip. You weren't just a convenient substitute for him that night and that isn't how I feel about you now. I know the difference, but I saw in you that night all the wonderful strength and heart and compassion that the love of my life had given to me and everyone around him. It struck me as an act of God, or Providence, or whatever miracle can explain that kind of preternatural coincidence

"That's why I care so much for you, despite the short time I've known you. You and Phillip would have liked each other. The two of you have the same heart, and soul, and values. I know he would approve of us."

She raised her eyes to Heaven and said, softly, "I know that we have his blessing. I know he approves of you being in my life."

She kissed me gently. "I find it amazing that life brought you into my path. That first night, I needed what you gave me. I needed the comfort you gave me, and I was certain that I could trust you to understand that. I had finally come to grips with losing Phillip, and the day of Jill's accident, I had been confronted with the same fear–the fear that I would also lose the best friend a person could ever have. You were gentle and sweet and caring.

"It scared me, Dub. It was too good to be true—too totally impossible to think, to hope, that two such wonderful men would… find their way into my life and my heart.

"I'm sure you saw his picture in my room and have wondered. I want you to know who he is… was.

"When you rushed off to help with Jill the next morning, I was scared to death I would lose her until you told me that everything would be all right. I just knew I could trust what you said. Then, you walked into Jill's room on the doctor's arm and she told us you had been there, once again helping Jill. That sealed the deal. You were my hero.

"And now, I'm upset… scared because my hero could have lost his life because of me. I'm having a hard time dealing with that. I'm not superstitious. I know I'm not a jinx and I don't have bad juju. I don't think that I've somehow made God angry. But it sure seems like there has been an unfortunate string of circumstances that have affected three persons in my life about whom I care very much.

"So, there it is. I care. In a very short time, I've developed strong feelings for you. And I think you have feelings for me." I smiled and nodded affirmatively.

"Thank you for telling me about Philip. I'm sorry for the loss you have suffered. I will try to be the person you think I am. If we can sort this current mess out, maybe we'll get the chance to see where this relationship goes."

I stood, set my glass on the table, and reached for her. She set her glass next to mine, rose, and came into my arms. The hollowness that had been in her eyes was gone, as was the pallor in her face. I kissed her and she returned my kiss. We stood there for some time, just wrapped in each other's arms.

She looked up at me and said quietly, "One day at a time. Is that okay with you?"

I nodded.

This is good, Wade. This woman is the real deal. This woman has substance.

TWENTY-ONE

She nuzzled into my neck, sighed, and held onto me. Dusk was claiming the daylight and the only sounds were tree frogs beginning to chirp and a mockingbird in the distance. After a while, she looked up at me.

"What do you think we should do," she asked.

I think we should go to bed and make love.

"I wish I had an answer to that question. I think the only thing we can do is just what you said, take things one day at a time, be here for Jill, and see what happens. We'll go goofy trying to second guess what will, or could, happen."

"It may turn out that we're not good for each other," she said.

"We'll never know if we don't give it a chance."

She smiled and nodded, laying her head back against my chest.

"Why do you think he's so obsessed with you?"

She stepped away from me, took her glass, and sat.

"I'm just guessing here–woman's intuition, speculation, whatever. But I think he wants what I can give him that he doesn't have.

"He doesn't have a college education, yet he has an income-producing business. I'm guessing that the majority of the women in his life take their clothes off for a living or manipulate men to get what they want. I think he is knocking on the door of being able to have a respectable life and he wants someone who doesn't have an artificial bust line and who knows the difference between lie and lay. As I said, he told me that Jill and I were the only two college-educated women he knew.

"I think he thought he could buy respectability through me and his friendship with Jill and Richard. When I walked away, I burst his unrealistic bubble."

I nodded. "I agree. And for the same reasoning, I don't think that guy was trying to kill me. He was too inexperienced. I think Damon sent him to scare me, to scare me off. If he had meant to kill me or hurt me, he wouldn't have held the knife out toward me. He would have kept it in close to his body with his elbow bent in order to make a proper thrust."

"So, what do you think he will do next?" she asked.

"I'm no psychologist, but I think he will continue to be an irritant in the background. I don't think he is prepared to become violent, but I think we are going to have to watch for flat tires on our cars, and for him looking over our shoulders when we don't expect it. I think he will behave like a petulant high school boy."

She was quiet for a moment, then nodded her head. "I agree with you. I think that's a good assessment."

"One day at a time."

She nodded again.

"Do you think we should think about eating?"

I nodded. "In or out?"

"I'm too tired to go anywhere. Do you have any cheese and crackers to go with this wine?"

We raided the fridge and pantry and gathered thinly sliced ham, cheese, baby carrots, crackers, and cookies for dessert. We ate and talked easily about Jill, Vivian, Richard, Damon, RJ, and a dozen other things. I opened a second bottle of wine. Dusk became night and the air became cool, so we went into the house. She told me more about her childhood with Jill and I told her about my childhood.

As it got later, she yawned and mumbled, "I'm sleepy and I think I've had one glass too many of wine."

She smiled coyly and asked, "May I invite myself into your home? I don't want to go home."

To say I was overjoyed would be a monumental understatement.

TWENTY-TWO

A week passed with nothing noteworthy. RJ's man, Tim Carrell, had checked on the guy who came after me. Carrell told RJ that Ponytail had a long history of charges for assault and battery and intimidation, but only two convictions for assault. He often hired out for strong-arm work that didn't require a lot of independent thought. The van was his and there was nothing that led past Ponytail. His name was Hector Gomez.

The only thing Gomez would say was that he wasn't going to kill me that day. RJ said Gomez was only supposed to scare me. Gomez said he was paid by a guy who called him, met him later at a bar, and paid him in cash. He said he didn't know the guy, he didn't know where the orders came from, and he couldn't identify the guy who paid him well enough for the authorities to discover who he was. At least, that was his story and he was sticking to it.

No one posted bail. A grand jury indicted him for assault with a deadly weapon based upon the hospital video, so he was sent to a holding facility outside Huntsville near the prison pending trial.

On Wednesday of the next week, Clark called Liz at work and asked her to have lunch with him. She said no and he argued that it had all been a misunderstanding. He asked her to meet him and talk. She asked about what and he said he wanted to see her. He said he knew they could work things out. She said she was happy with her life just as it was now and his retort was, "That guy won't always be around."

She asked what he meant by that and he told her that he had warned me once to watch my back and that I wouldn't get a second warning.

On Thursday, I talked to RJ about Clark. He asked me if I knew anything about guns. Both my dad and Mr. McCain taught Carter and me about guns and how to shoot safely and accurately. I've had a concealed handgun permit for some time. I told him that. He said he wanted to have the Director list me on the roster as a special employee in his security department. He said, with a smile, that he had a pretty convincing argument. He said the salary would be nominal, but I would have the authority to carry a handgun on the premises, and I would be covered by the hospital's general liability insurance policy. I liked his idea. It became official, but not general knowledge, the next Monday.

RJ told Tim Carrell everything and instructed Carrell that, in RJ's absence, Carrell had the authority to give me any assistance or information I needed. I liked Tim; he was a good guy. And I appreciated RJ's confidence in me.

TWENTY-THREE

John Candelero summoned Bobby Duvall to his office on that same Thursday. Candelero had known Duvall when Duvall and Damon were kids. He liked Duvall. Like Damon, Bobby called Candelero Uncle John. Duvall often judiciously apprised Candelero of pertinent information about Damon and his business dealings. Duvall knew it was Candelero, not Damon, who would take care of him in a pinch. Candelero frequently asked Duvall what was going on that he should know about. In that way, Duvall could always say that Uncle John asked about this or that and that he wasn't going to lie to Uncle John.

When Damon was young and dumb and first making good money, he decided he wanted to keep a couple of prostitutes on the payroll for himself. Bobby tried to discourage him, but he persisted. Bobby told Candelero who summoned Clark. He told Damon he had heard that he was trying to recruit prostitutes and told him they didn't run whores. When Damon told Candelero that they were for himself, Candelero told him he was brainless.

"Forget that adage about, if it flies floats or fucks, rent it," he had said. "Whores fuck for money and whores talk for money. That's the quickest way for your business to become common knowledge. Whores can't keep their mouths shut. Get your pussy just like the rest of us."

"I heard my nephew made a scene at that hospital up in The Woodlands a couple of weeks ago," he said to Duvall. "What was that all about?"

"He's trying to buy respectability, Uncle John. He wants to be legit and wants a woman who can give him respectability. This woman has a college degree and a good job. She dumped him after she found out he was fucking a different girl in every city where we have delis. She's seeing some doctor at the hospital now. Damon went up there to try to make up with her and she told him to get lost. This guy was there and Damon got hot and threatened the guy."

Candelero thought for a moment, then said, "Ah. Now I understand. That's why Hector was arrested. Damon sent Hector to scare the guy. Right?"

"Yes, sir."

"I owe Hector an apology. I thought he had gone off the reservation and I was going to let him hang himself. Now I know that Damon put him up to it. Hector isn't too bright, but he always knew when to keep his mouth shut. I gather that's what he is doing now."

"Yes, sir."

"Damn. This is as stupid as when he wanted to hire whores!" He looked at Duvall. "And he threatened this guy in front of witnesses?" he asked incredulously.

"I wasn't there, but that's my understanding, yes sir."

"Thanks, Bobby. Keep me advised if he does anything else stupid."

"Yes sir, Uncle John."

TWENTY-FOUR

On Friday morning, Jill's traction system was replaced with external stabilization. She made it through the weekend with no problems and was released the next Tuesday morning, three weeks after the accident. Vivian had found a ground-floor apartment close to the hospital and a good therapy center that was associated with the hospital. For the next three weeks, therapists would come to the apartment for Jill. If she was approved at the end of that time, she would go to the therapy center for physical therapy and would be transported by the center's van.

Liz stopped to see her everyday day after work and I went with her every time that I could. We both went to visit and have lunch with Jill and Vivian each Sunday. Richard flew home every third weekend.

That week and the past week had been busy for Liz. She had a lot of work that needed catching up, so we didn't see each other much during those weeks, but we talked each evening and spent each weekend together. Jill was now settled in with her mother. We had more no contact with Clark and it had been two weeks since I was attacked. I was beginning to think we had heard the last of him.

We had planned to take a pizza to Jill's Friday evening and visit with her and Vivian. As I was retrieving my keys in order to pick up Liz, my phone rang. Her number showed on caller ID.

"Hi," I answered. "I'm on my way to pick up the pizza and you."

"Dub. Damon is parked in front of my home. What do I do?"

Her voice was filled with apprehension.

"How long has he been there?"

"I don't know. I just walked into the living room and saw his car outside."

"Stay on the phone. I'm on my way."

Her home was less than ten minutes away. I drove as fast as I safely could. Fortunately, there were no police cars on my path. When I arrived, he was gone.

She was waiting at the door as I went up her front walk.

"He just drove away. He must have seen me through the window with the phone in my hand."

"Are you sure it was him?"

"Yes. It was his Land Rover. I recognized his license number."

"Why would he show up now?" I wondered.

"This is the third time this week," she replied.

"Why didn't you tell me?"

"The first time, I wasn't sure. The second time, he drove off as soon as I saw him. I didn't want to sound like the boy who cried wolf."

"Has he ever said anything? Or done anything?"

"No. He was just sitting there in his car each time."

"It's too bad you don't have a gate at the entrance. I'll call RJ tomorrow. I imagine he will tell me we should file a stalking report."

"Okay." She took my hand. "May I stay with you tonight."

"As someone near and dear to me said recently, 'Oh, please, don't throw me in that briar patch.'"

She laughed. The levity helped.

Liz quickly packed a bag with clothes for the next day. As she closed her bag, she looked up at me and I could see apprehension clouding her face.

"Should I be concerned?" she asked

I wasn't sure what to say. "Be concerned enough to be cautious. As I've said, I think he is behaving like a petulant schoolboy. Keep your eyes open and stay alert."

She nodded wordlessly.

We picked up the pizza and went to see Jill. It was a good evening. Jill's spirits were up and Vivian was rested and happy. Jill said her physical therapy was going well, but her stamina was short. She told us she and Vivian had settled on an attorney to handle her case and that they were pleased with the man they had chosen. We had a nice evening together and left around nine-thirty. I drove to Liz's home and she asked why.

Damon's black Land Rover was parked in front of Liz's home.

"That's why," I replied. "And now you have a witness."

We didn't stop; I continued to my home. Unless he knew where I lived and followed someone through the gate, we wouldn't see him again tonight.

Inside, I poured us each a glass of zinfandel and she sat close to me on the couch. "What do we do," she asked.

"Let me talk to RJ first; but, I think you should file a stalking report. Otherwise, we should forget him for the evening and enjoy our time together."

She set her wine on the side table and cuddled close to me. "Good plan of action," she whispered as she pulled my head toward her and slipped her tongue between my lips. Half an hour later, we retrieved our wine and picked up where we had started, except that our clothes were now piled on the floor next to the couch and we were both wet with perspiration.

We finished our wine and she led me to bed, where we had wonderful seconds.

TWENTY-FIVE

We woke late on Saturday morning to the sound of gentle rain falling outside the window. I pulled her to me. She snuggled into me and we kissed. She rose and peeked through the shutters.

"What would you like to do today?" I asked as I took in the sight of her warm smile smooth breasts and exciting body.

"It's raining. I think we should stay in bed for a while," she said with a mischievous smile as slid back into bed, reached for me, and kissed her way down my torso.

Two hours later, we woke again and I asked the same question. She again peeked through the shutters. Closing the shutter, she smiled coyly and said softly, "Still raining."

This time, I kissed my way down her torso and we again made love until we were worn out. We went back to sleep to the sound of the still pattering rain. I woke at two o'clock, quietly rose, stepped into my boxers, and made coffee.

A few minutes later, she padded quietly into the kitchen, naked and sleepy-eyed. She kissed me and asked, "Is it really two o'clock?"

I nodded, handing her a cup of coffee. She disappeared down the hall and came back wearing panties and the polo that I wore last night. I frowned.

She smiled and said softly, "Don't frown. I'm not finished with you yet."

I grinned happily.

We sat at the table, staring out the window at the still falling rain, sipping coffee. "Do you think it will ever stop raining?" she asked.

"I don't know, but the guy next door called and asked me what a cubit is?"

She laughed, thought about it, and laughed harder. "I like your sense of humor, Wade," she said with a laugh.

"Funny," I replied. "I like yours, too."

I kissed her. "As a matter of fact, I think I like everything about you."

"Whoa, Cowboy," she said. "We hardly know each other. You may be premature in your assessment."

"You're right. I need to get to know you better before I make such a broad declaration."

"Would that be know in the biblical sense?" she asked with a coy smile.

"I like the way you think, woman," I replied with a chuckle.

She laughed, set her empty cup on the table, took my hand, and said sweetly, "I agree. We need to get to know each other a little better."

I chuckled. We spent another two hours getting to know each other better. It was wonderful.

At five p.m., we decided it was time to eat. The rain had stopped and the sun was peeking out. We rose and showered.

"How shall I dress," she asked.

"What do you want to do?"

"I'm perfectly happy crawling back into bed with you, but you have to feed me first."

"Damn, woman. Are you always this demanding," I asked with a chuckle.

"Only when I'm hungry."

I pulled her to me. "This has been such a wonderful day. I think I know the perfect way to feed you and end the day."

She kissed me, and chanted, "Tell me, tell me."

"Let's run by your place and you get fresh clothes. Then, I think we should return to Coco's."

I could see in her smile that I had made a good suggestion. She pulled me to her, kissed me, and replied, "Excellent suggestion, my dear. Excellent suggestion."

I dressed and we drove to her home. I fully expected to see the Land Rover parked nearby, but it wasn't. She dressed in a pretty sundress and sandals, fixed her hair and makeup and we left. While she got ready, I called to make a reservation.

"Here or there, tonight?" she asked.

"Your choice," I said.

"I'm not going to let him scare me away from my home, but may we be at your home tonight?" I nodded.

We arrived at Coco's. When I made the reservation, I asked if Sofie was working that night. She was and I asked that we be seated at her table. She was waiting when we arrived and whisked us to our table. "It's so nice to see the two of you again. We've missed you. I'm glad there was another date."

We thanked her. Liz told her there had been some drama in our lives that kept us busy for a couple of weeks, but that we had returned as quickly as we could. We chatted briefly with Sofie, ordered, and sat back.

I looked up as Sofie brought our drinks and saw Samuel Linz behind her. He welcomed us warmly and was enthusiastic about seeing us again. He remembered our names and said he was really glad to see that we were still together. We chatted with him for a few minutes and he excused himself.

Liz looked at me and said, "You know. I like this place. And I feel at home here."

I agreed. We decided we would come often and bring friends.

Dinner was served and it was superb. We talked and teased and laughed and thoroughly enjoyed ourselves. At one point, Liz looked at me with a happy smile.

"This has been a wonderful and unusual day. I've never spent an entire day in bed when I wasn't sick. I think we've learned something about ourselves together today, and I like what I think I've learned. Perhaps we should do the same thing again every so often." She laughed, but I could see her eyes were serious.

I started to make a smart quip, but the look in her eyes belayed my first inclination. I was quiet for a long moment as she gazed at me. "I think you've made a good suggestion. I think we've found something that is becoming very good. And I think I like rainy days."

She smiled coyly and said softly, "As do I. I will never forget today."

We finished dinner and dessert, said good night to Sofie and Samuel, and drove to my home. We held hands the entire way.

I poured a small glass of wine for each of us and we sat quietly for a while. I think we were both musing over the day, and the pleasure we had given and received. I know that was certainly what was in my mind.

She looked pensively at me. "Dub, are you okay with the memories of Phillip?" she asked.

I nodded. "Thank you for putting me in such good company."

She gazed me and nodded. Very softly she said, "Phillip was my past and I loved him with all my heart. Now, you are my present."

I nodded my head silently and smiled understandingly.

Liz rose and peeked out the shutter. "It's raining," she said suggestively.

I took her hand and we walked to the bedroom, continuing where we had left off earlier. Later, as we lay together, I asked her, "Was it really raining?"

She smiled coyly and said softly, "I'm sure it was."

She giggled and I laughed. She cuddled close to me. We kissed and fell asleep easily.

TWENTY-SIX

Sunday morning came with bright sunshine and the promise of a beautiful day. We drank coffee by the pool, then made breakfast.

"What do you want to do today," I asked as we were making the bed.

Would you show me again how to hit your speed bag?"

Surprised, I said, "Sure." I looked at her and saw a look of apprehension cross her face. "Anything else?"

"Maybe you could show me how to defend myself."

I smiled and wrapped her in my arms.

"I think that would be a good idea," I said as I kissed the top of her head.

We went into the bag room and I walked her slowly through the rhythm and sequence of the speed bag. I put on a pair of hand pads and held my hands up at chest level and a foot apart.

"Slowly. Fist first, then come back with the outside of the fist, your right hand on my right hand, then back against my left hand; then the same thing with your left. Not hard. Just get the rhythm. Five times with each hand, then take a break."

It isn't hard to get the rhythm when the bag isn't bouncing. The hard part is timing the backhand to the bounce of the bag. She ran through the sequence five times and did pretty well. I worked with the change in position of her fist from strike to backhand and told her to try again.

This time was better. She tried the sequence three more times and did very well.

We took a break and I got her some water. Then, I wrapped her hands since I didn't have gloves small enough for her, and I moved her in front of the bag. I explained the difficulty that the moving bag would create and explained that she had to control her strikes to control the direction and bounce of the bag.

I ran through a quick sequence myself and explained that I wasn't just hitting the bag, but that I was driving it in a specific direction to control the bounce back. She watched closely and I saw her nodding her head.

I had her make one strike at a time, right hand, then left hand, and told her to observe where the bag hit the platform and how it bounced back. We worked until she could control her drive and make the bag hit the same spot on the platform each time. Then we worked on one strike and one backhand. When she had the sequence down pretty well, I gave her a break and water. Perspiration was beginning to leave a sheen on her face, arms, and chest and her bikini top was wet.

"Okay, now put it together. Work at your own pace and don't get frustrated. It shouldn't take you too long to get it. Don't start too slowly because your hands have to be ready to hit the rebound of the bag each time. Try to build a rhythm."

The first few attempts were as awkward as one would expect. No one can just step up to a speed bag and run through a sequence without a lot of practice, but she was getting the hang of it after ten minutes. We took a break and I made sure she took some water. She tried again and began to get some rhythm and consistency. I didn't want her arms to be too sore on Monday, but she was close.

"Feel like a few more?" I asked. She nodded and gulped some air.

Five more minutes and she had the hang of it. The bag seldom got away from her. I stopped her.

"Oh, that's fun," she effused with a huge smile on her face.

"It is. I know, but if we don't stop, you are going to have a hard time lifting your arms tomorrow. We'll practice again in a day or two."

I gave her a bottle of water and we sat.

"How do I use that to protect myself? No one is going to stand still and let me hit him repeatedly like that bag."

"You're right. First, some things to know, then some things to do.

"Things to know." I held up my index finger.

"First: Never hit anyone on the jawbone or head with your fist as you see in the movies. The mandible is the hardest bone in the body and the forehead is one of the hardest. Your hands and wrists are too small. You'll break your hand. Don't hit his mouth because his teeth could cut your hand.

"Use what you just learned to first hit the nose or the eye socket or the temple. When you make contact, carry through just like with the bag, then swing your backhand with the outside edge of your fist against the temple or nose. Same thing on the other side. It will stun him and probably give you time to run. The whole time, you should be screaming for help.

"Second: Despite what you have always heard about the groin, it is too easy to block a kick or a knee to the groin. Instead, stomp on his instep as hard as you can. Then, either hit his nose or stomp the other instep or kick the side of the knee joint.

"Third: Immediately scream, fight back, and run. The first second is the most critical. Most assailants don't know what to expect, but they generally don't expect immediate retaliation. Take advantage of that second of indecision when he is surprised at your response.

"Fourth: Bite–particularly ears, lips, nose, neck, and fingers, but bite with the intent of biting completely through whatever it is you are biting. Be that aggressive. If you can bite the jugular vein in his neck, do so. If you have to bite on the body, bite hard and deep enough to tear flesh loose.

"Things to do." I held up the other forefinger.

"Let's talk about action/reaction and physics. The first lesson of judo is to use the other person's strength and weight and motion against him. Let me show you.

I told her to grab me any way she wanted. When she did, I pushed her backward. She immediately reacted by moving forward to counter my push.

"That reaction is what you will use. And it works both ways. If you push and he moves toward you, pull him around you and off his feet. If you pull and he moves away, follow his motion and run right over him. In most cases, turn your hip into him when you counter. It gives you a fulcrum if he moves toward you and you can flip him over. If he moves away, it is a force to drive him away from you and then you over him.

I showed her by example several times and had her then use my reaction to her advantage. She learned that concept quickly.

Then, I explained the weakness of the opposing thumb and how to break any grip by moving against the thumb rather than the hands and fingers. Again, she learned quickly.

"Don't ignore the element of surprise. As I said, in that first second, he won't know what you are going to do so he isn't prepared. Surprise him—scream, bite, kick, and run away as fast as you can. Remember, if he has a gun, a stationary target is easy to hit. A moving target is difficult to hit with a handgun, especially if the target is running away. Don't run in a straight line. You may be hit, but odds are you will be missed or only wounded. If you just stand there, the odds are greater that you will be dead."

She looked pensive but nodded for me to continue.

"When you hit someone in self-defense, even with the boxing sequence, use the heel of your hand, fingers extended on the strike, and always the outside of your fist on the backhand. Aim for the nose primarily, then the temple or the larynx, then the sternum, then the locked side of the elbow, or your heel to any side of the knee. When you hit someone with the heel of your hand or the side of your fist, try to hit in a full swing through your target—don't stop at the point of contact.

"And, use any weapon you can get your hands on. A ballpoint pen, a bottle, a chair, a knife or a fork. Strike for the eyes, the temple, the throat. You will hardly ever be able to stop someone by striking at his heart with a fork or knife, but you can kill someone by striking him in the temple or throat with a fork or knife or any hard object.

"Just keep your wits about you and remember that it is you or him. Don't be squeamish. If you can bite off an ear or a nose, or gouge out an eye, you have gained a distinct advantage.

"One of the most basic and effective weapons the average person can carry is a metal Sharpie marker pen. Drive it into an eye or the temple and you win.

"But your best weapon is to scream and run. Some persons will tell a woman to pretend to faint and collapse in a heap. There is some merit to that, but it leaves you helpless and in his grasp. I don't recommend that tactic unless you are in his firm grasp and you can't strike him. Then collapsing like a dead weight may have some merit and may buy time for help to arrive.

"Do not let him get control of you. Do not let him force you into a vehicle or a secluded area, even if he threatens to harm you or kill you. Scream, run, fight back. "

I kissed her on the forehead. It was a segue. "One last move."

I turned toward the bag and smashed my forehead into it. She jumped in surprise.

I turned to her. "Head butt. Your greatest close-range weapon. Your forehead, just below your hairline, is one of the hardest bones in your body. If you can head butt someone in the nose with real force, you can inflict a great amount of pain and produce a lot of blood. Most people are scared when they see their own blood, and they pause for a second, which provides a good opportunity for another head butt or a blow with the side of your fist. Just remember to aim for the base of the bridge of the nose, which is cartilage, not bone. Don't aim for the other guy's forehead or chin, which is just as hard as yours.

"Practice your head butt, too."

"Lesson over. That's enough for you to absorb at one time."

I expected an effusive thank you with bewildered eyes. I was surprised. Liz sat pensive and quiet for a long moment. She finally looked up at me and said evenly, "I don't know that I have ever received so much understandable and practical advice in such a short time. Thank you, Dub. Will you work with me until I have the basics mastered?"

I do love intelligent individuals. No squeamishness, no hesitation, just a certain statement that she could master this. It was easy to understand why a Ranger would fall in love with her.

"Any time you want and as often as you want. Your safety is important to me, pretty lady."

She beamed and pulled me to her. "May I do the speed bag one more time?"

I laughed out loud and watched her run through the sequence without a miss. The rest of the day, out of the blue I would get related questions such as: if I hit with the heel of my hand, are my fingers bent or straight; if I bite, do I use my front teeth or try to get him back into my big teeth?

How can one not appreciate a woman with that much grasp, grit, and determination?

TWENTY-SEVEN

obby walked into Damon's office Monday morning. He hadn't seen Damon since Wednesday of last week, even though Damon had been in town all week. He left the report for the past week on Damon's desk and turned to leave. As he did, Damon walked in.

Hey," Bobby said, "How was your weekend?"

"Lousy. She was with that guy all weekend."

"She? You mean Liz."

"Of course. Who else would I mean"

"How would you even know? What are you doing, following her around?"

"Just checking," Damon said. "This guy is really pissing me off. I guess Hector didn't scare him much. And I paid him a thousand dollars just to scare the guy off. He owes me a grand. He didn't do his job."

"Jesus, Damon. The guy kicked Hector's ass. And now, Hector's looking at prison time. All because you're thinking with your dick."

"He didn't do the job."

"So? What are you going to do now? Do you think you can kick the guy's ass and scare him off? The word I heard was that he looked like he knew how to take care of himself."

"Well, if I can't have her, he ain't gonna have her either."

"What are you talking about? Are you thinking of killing her? Or him?"

"Neither. I'm going to sell her."

"You're gonna what?"

"I'm going to sell her."

"To who?"

"I know a guy who buys women."

"For what? Body parts?"

"No. He buys good looking women and girls and sells them to rich guys in the Middle East and some other places."

"Ragheads?"

"Ragheads, Muslims, Russians, Chinese, Japanese, even some white guys. Depending on the girl, he'll pay up to fifty thousand, sometimes more. He sells them for four to five times that much."

"You're crazy."

"No. He's crazy, but he makes money. And he can make her disappear without a trace."

"Why don't you just have him make the guy disappear?"

"Because I'd have to pay him to do that. He'll pay me for her."

"Are you serious?"

"You're damn right, I'm serious. She shut me down. She ruined my plans to get ahead. I'm going to make her pay. And that asshole doctor, too."

"Why would someone pay money like that for a woman? What do they do with them?"

"They sell them to really rich guys who want to own a beautiful woman. Or they just fuck them. They get them strung out on drugs or fear or promises of going home and fuck their brains out. After a few years, the women get to looking bad, their skin ages, they don't eat right and they start looking old. So, the guys sell them to some pimp down the line and buy a new girl. Hell, they've got money. It's no big deal for them. It's mostly oil money or drug money."

"Damon, this isn't like selling a dime bag of weed in a takeout lunch. You're talking serious crime and serious prison time."

"Nah. They can make it happen and leave no trail. No risk and it will show her she can't treat me that way. All I have to do is deliver her."

"So, they don't kidnap her; you have to do that?"

"It depends on the girl and what they think she's worth. But, yeah. They pay on delivery. Unless they think she's worth a bundle; they charge a lot if they have to grab her."

"How do you know about this?"

"There are some things you don't know, my friend. Those girls I fuck in Austin and San Antonio… and here. They're whores. They work for me."

"Jesus Christ! How do you know they're whores? I mean, what do you mean they work for you?

"Just what I said. They work for me."

"How do you manage that?"

"It's easy. I started a few years ago. You find some girl who has nothing but her looks, or who thinks her daddy doesn't give her enough money. You chat her up and get close to her, flash some bills, and a Rolex. She tells you she needs money for a new iPhone, or concert tickets, or some bullshit.

"You tell her that you will loan her the money, but she has to pay you back because the money is for your sister's college tuition or your mother's surgery or some shit. You make her promise to pay by a certain date.

"One of two things happens–they pay or they don't. If they pay you back, you compliment them on being trustworthy and dependable and tell them to let you know if they ever need to borrow some money again because you trust them to repay you. You just keep leading them on until they can't pay when the money is due. Usually, right away they can't pay.

"They're girls. When they can't pay, they turn on the charm. Eventually, they offer to fuck you a few times instead of paying you. After a time or two, you tell her you know a guy who wants to fuck to her and he'll pay her, and you can set it up. Either way, she now fucks for money. After that, it gets easier.

"High school girls are easy because they think money grows in Daddy's pocket and on trees. The problem is, you're dealing with statutory rape, so you have to be careful.

"College girls and girls under twenty-five are best. Especially the ones who want things and have to work for their spending money. You just run the same game on them. They're all on the pill, so it doesn't take long to convince them to work with you. Next thing you know, you've fucked them and they now work for you."

"You're serious?"

"As a heart attack. I've been doing this for three years now. I get all the pussy I want and make money to boot. I don't act like a pimp and I don't treat them like whores, so they're cool with the arrangement. I'm just the guy who helps them out."

"So, what does all this have to do with the Barton girl? How can you sell her?"

"A year ago, this big guy comes in the deli one afternoon when things are slow. He tells me he knows about our little weed business on the side. I think that he's in the Russian mob and I'm being warned off. Instead, he tells me he works for a guy who is always in the market for really high-end girls with exceptional looks. We talked a while and he told me his boss will pay good money, big money, for the right girls. They aren't looking for teeny boppers. They want college girls and above. He told me his boss sells to big money guys around the world.

"At first, I thought he was just bull-shitting me because it sounded so outrageous, but he convinced me that he was serious."

"You haven't kidnapped anyone or sold anyone, have you? I mean, that's some serious shit!'

"Not really. I gave him a girl who was becoming a liability and she disappeared. But I think Barton is a good candidate."

"What do you mean disappeared?"

"I never saw her again."

"So, when you kidnap her, you're going to tell her why and what's going to happen to her?'

"Yes. I'm going to show her she can't just dump me like that. Uncle John told me he's going to get Hector a lawyer and get him out of jail. When he's out, Hector can grab her and we can get her to the guy."

"Damon, you're not thinking good."

"Why do you say that?"

"You were seeing the woman. She dumped you for the doc. Hector tried to scare the doc off with a knife and got himself arrested for assault and attempted murder. Hector kept his mouth shut, but the cops know the whole story except who hired Hector. And everyone knows Hector works for you. I'm amazed they haven't brought you in just based on that knowledge. They can put it together without any trouble.

"Uncle John may get Hector a lawyer, but the thing happened in a hospital, for Christ's sake. It wasn't like an argument in a bar that goes unnoticed. If that girl disappears, who do you think will be the first guy the cops go to?

"You need to let sleeping dogs lie, my friend. You have been very lucky so far."

As if on cue, Damon's cell phone rang. He looked at the caller ID. "Speak of the devil," he said and answered.

"Hi, Uncle John,' he said brightly.

"Damon, I want you to come to see me. And bring Bobby with you. Now." Candelero hung up.

Damon looked at Bobby. "Uncle John wants us both, now."

TWENTY-EIGHT

Candelero's secretary walked Damon and Bobby to his office. They entered quietly and took seats. He was reading a document and didn't look up, just waved his hand at the chairs in front of his desk. Candelero kept a large coffee pot in his office that was always full. Without looking up, he asked, "Would one of you get me a cup of coffee?"

Bobby rose quickly and responded. As Bobby placed the cup on the desk, Candelero looked up. Bobby could see the hard look in Candelero's eyes. His eyes returned to the document for another minute or two. He signed with a flourish and looked up.

"My lawyer, Saul Stein, is going to represent Hector. He told Saul quite a story." He looked right at Damon. "He says you sent him to scare the guy. He said your words were, `I mean, really scare the guy.' Is that true?"

"Yes sir, but–"

Candelero cut him off. "Did you tell him to use a knife?"

"No, sir."

"Did you tell him not to use a weapon?"

"No, sir."

"What did this guy do that made you want to scare him so bad?"

"He took my girl away from me."

Candelero mused, never looking away from Damon. "So, is that like he stole my candy," he said in a little boy's voice, "or like he stole ten grand from me," he asked evenly.

Oh, fuck! Damon thought. *Don't fuck this up. Don't make him mad.*

"She was my girl. She was pretty important to me."

"How long had you been seeing her?"

"About a year, I guess."

"You sure about that?"

"I guess it was more like four months."

"Were you engaged?"

"No, sir."

"During those four months, were you still fucking the girl in San Antonio?"

"Yes, sir."

"And the one in Austin?"

"Yes, sir."

"Fuck," Bobby thought. *Now he'll know I tell Uncle John what he does.* But that thought was quickly dispelled.

"Does it surprise you that I know about those women?"

Damon was quiet for a moment and his eyes flicked toward Bobby before he answered. "Yes, sir. I guess it does."

"Damon, you're my sister's kid. Bobby has been your best friend since Juvie. I know everything the two of you do. Everything! Guys who know the two of you tell me what I need to know."

Bobby breathed a silent sigh of relief.

"Why is this girl so important?"

Damon was again quiet for a moment. "Because she's respectable. And I want to be respectable. I want to be somebody in this city."

"Well, at least you're moving up from wanting to hire prostitutes. What was your grand plan that this guy fucked up for you?"

"I was going to marry her and have a kid. I was going to start contributing to political things. I want to be County Commissioner one day. And I want to turn the deli and dope sales over to Bobby."

Candelero stared silently at Damon for a long moment, then spoke. "Isn't it for me to decide what Bobby does and who takes over if you move up?"

"Well, yeah, Uncle John. I just meant that I was going to suggest to you that Bobby take over. He knows the business and does a great job."

"I see," Candelero said evenly. "And how soon do you plan to do all this?"

"If this guy hadn't butted in, I was going to date her for six months, then give her an engagement ring."

"It's my understanding that she broke it off with you because she found out about the girl in San Antonio. Is that right?"

Damon was slow to respond. *Don't lie. He knows the truth*, he thought. "Yes, sir."

"Were you going to continue banging women in other cities after you married her?" Candelero looked directly at him. "Be honest."

"Yeah, probably."

"The press just loves dirt and scandal. Do you think the press wouldn't learn of your flings and make it public knowledge?"

"I can keep it quiet."

"Yeah. Just like you did with the girl in San Antonio," Candelero said derisively.

He stood. Damon and Bobby started to stand, but he motioned for them to remain seated. He walked to the coffee pot, refilled his cup and stood, his back to them, looking out the window. He spoke without turning.

"Damon, you were in juvie because you didn't use your head. You both were. Because you're my nephew, I gave you a job and taught you a trade. You make a lot of money selling sandwiches these days. Until recently, I thought you had learned how to handle yourself–how to stay off the radar.

"When you told me about wanting to put whores on your payroll, I put the brakes on that because it wasn't smart. But, at least, I understood where you were coming from.

"I've had to remind you more than once not to attract attention to yourself. The Blacks and the Hispanics tolerate us because they don't understand how much business we do. And they don't know about the farm in Colorado. But don't kid yourself, they know how much a new Range Rover costs. And they know how much that place you live in costs.

"But you've really fucked up this time. Hector is looking at a minimum of five years. Saul is going to cost us ten grand to get the attempted murder reduced. Actually, Saul is going to cost you ten grand because you sent Hector on a shit for brains job. It would have been stupid, but fixable if you had told Hector to rough the guy up in a dark parking lot one night. But this took place in a public hospital in front of at least one credible witness who saw the knife. And it's on film!

"What the fuck were you thinking? The cops know Hector works for us. They know you had been seeing the girl. They know the girl is now seeing the doctor. They know you're my nephew and they know what your business is. If Saul can get this pled down to one count of assault, we can probably keep the lid on this. But this is the kind of case a young prosecutor is going to want. Hell, they know someone hired Hector to do what he did. If some hotshot young prosecutor starts leaning on Hector and investigating, he's going to wind up with his feet on your desk reading you your rights.

"And when he gets through with you, somewhere in all the investigation and questions, it's very possible that our little take-out order business is going to come out. And you know where that's going to point? Right at me.

"So, for right now, this is what you're gonna do. First, you bring me ten grand for Saul. Second, you pay Hector's wife three grand every month until he's out and back on the job. Third, you and Bobby get the marijuana out of the take-out business until I tell you I think it's safe to bring it back in-house. That doesn't mean we stop doing marijuana business, but we don't do it out of the shops for a while–and we don't let profits slide. Fourth, you stay away from that Barton girl and the doc. Fifth, use your head and keep a low profile. Don't threaten anyone, don't beat your chest, don't flaunt your money, and don't offend anyone, especially women."

He turned and looked directly at Damon.

"If this blows over, we'll talk about your future. If it doesn't, your future will be in a cell next door to Hector. Do you understand me?"

"Sure I do, Uncle John. But Hector–"

"Don't even try to go there. Hector tried to do what you paid him to do and you didn't use your head.

"Man up, Damon. You fucked up!"

He turned back to look out the window and said over his shoulder, "Get me ten grand for the lawyer and get three grand to Hector's wife by five o'clock today. Tomorrow, I want to know how you're going to get the take-out bags out of the delis and maintain distribution. And by the next day, I want it done. Am I clear?"

"Yes, Uncle John."

"Get out of here and make it happen."

Damon started to say something, but Bobby stopped him and led him out of the office.

TWENTY-NINE

When they were seated in Damon's car, he smacked the steering wheel hard with both hands and shouted, "Fuck! Just fuck! I can't believe Uncle John just did that to me."

He started the engine, backed abruptly out of the parking space, and peeled rubber the length of the parking lot, shooting into traffic unexpectedly in the path of a FedEx truck and forcing the FedEx driver to slam on the brakes.

"Easy, man," cautioned Bobby. "Getting us killed isn't going to solve the problem. Let's go back to the office and figure this out."

When they reached the office, Bobby excused himself to make a couple of phone calls before they got started. He took his cell phone to his car and called Candelero.

"Uncle John, it's Bobby. I didn't want to ask a lot of questions in front of Damon, but can you help me understand about the marijuana. Do you mean everywhere, or just here in Houston?"

"I'm glad you called, Bobby. I was going to call you. You're the only one over there with a working brain. You need to know that we are expanding our marijuana business, which is why I can't have the trickle we run through the delis come to the attention of the cops. So, we're going to stop that for the time being in Houston. Austin and San Antonio will continue for now. We're building a distribution system to move marijuana into the states where it's legal. That system is almost ready to begin operation. We're also building a system to distribute it statewide here and into Louisiana. I wasn't going to say anything yet, but we're close enough for you to know. I'm thinking of moving you out of Damon's operation and you are going to be an integral part of the distribution system here.

"For right now, this is what I want. I want Damon to stew for a while. I want him to spend time thinking about what I told him and I want him to come up with a plan. I don't care what it is, but make him do the work. I want you to come up with a separate plan to get it out of the Houston shops and maintain distribution if we need to. You let me know what you come up with, but keep it to yourself. We'll talk about it later.

"But make him come to me with his plan. He's going to whine and bitch, but he is going to have to come to me and ask for help. He needs to get his head and his priorities straight. I'm serious about what could happen if some go-getter prosecutor takes this on. When he realizes he can't do what I told him and calls for help, I'll tell him what I just told you—but make him come up with a plan for the Houston shops. Don't give him your plan."

"You and I will talk soon about my plans for you.

"And I want you to keep me informed about the girl. I know Damon; he isn't going to let it go."

"No, sir; he isn't. He told me he wants to sell her and he says he knows a guy who buys pretty white women and sells them to rich guys."

There was a long pause. "You're serious?" Candelero asked evenly.

"Yes. That's what he said. He wouldn't tell me who the guy is, and maybe he's just blowing smoke, but he was pretty twisted up when he told me, and I think there really is a guy who buys women. I think he's going after her and the guy."

"Do your best and keep me informed about everything. He will realize he is going to have to come to me with the same questions you had, but let him stew until he realizes that."

Bobby returned to Damon's office and they brainstormed the problem the remainder of the day. By three o'clock, Damon had proposed three stupid and impossible plans. He finally realized that he needed to ask for help. He called Candelero. He was told what Bobby was told, but not that Bobby was making a plan of his own. He was also told to advise Candelero of his plan and to get approval before putting it into action and to hold off implementation until he was instructed to do so.

Damon relayed the conversation to Bobby and said they could talk tomorrow, now that they had some breathing room. Bobby admonished him not to delay getting a plan to Candelero, but Damon said he was hungry and wanted to get laid.

"How are you going to do that," Bobby asked.

"I got a piece that will fuck me crazy for dinner and drinks at a fancy restaurant."

Bobby shrugged. "Don't leave Uncle John hanging, and get the money to him and Hector's wife," was his only response.

Damon gave him the money to deliver to Candelero and to Hector's wife.

THIRTY

My boss, Tom Barrow, called Monday morning, May 29. He asked if I had dinner plans. I said that I did not, although I had hopes of seeing Liz that night. He asked if I was seeing anyone special. I told him I was dating someone very special to me.

"Have dinner with my wife and me at Brennan's this evening. Bring your special lady. I'd like to meet her and I'd like for my wife to meet you."

I called Liz, relayed the invitation and she agreed. I called Tom back and confirmed dinner at seven o'clock.

We looked in on Jill at the end of the day, then drove to the restaurant. We arrived, were seated on time, and introductions were made. We ordered drinks and chatted. When the drinks came, Tom looked at me and raised his glass.

"I had a nice visit with Dr. Melbourne last week. I understand there was an unpleasant event at the hospital and that you diffused the situation singlehandedly. He was quite effusive in his praise of what you did. Apparently, your praises have reached administrators at some of our other hospitals."

"*Oh, shit,*" I thought. *I probably should have told Tom. My bad.*

"Congratulations," he said. "I had two calls from hospitals asking about our services and each caller mentioned you by name. We can't beat publicity like that. Tell me about it."

I recounted the event and downplayed it as well as I could.

When I finished, Liz added, "Everyone at the hospital knows what happened and who Dub is." She put her hand on my arm and smiled. "He's the local hero."

"What was his purpose in attacking you," Tom asked.

When I hesitated, Liz said, "A man who I dated for a brief period didn't want to accept that I no longer wanted to see him. Dub came to my rescue after an unpleasant scene and that man sent the other man to threaten Dub. But, the second man failed in his mission."

'We're glad he did," Tom replied. "We're very glad he failed. We have some plans for Dub, which is why we're here tonight."

We ordered and over dinner, Tom explained that I was being given more responsibility and a raise. He explained what that entailed and I was pleased. When the business was out of the way, he and his wife, Sharon, told us a little about themselves and we chatted amiably.

After a while, Tom touched my arm. "There is a guy across the room who has been staring a hole in you all evening." He described the man and asked if I knew him.

Liz and I turned to look and she inhaled sharply. Damon Clark was sitting across the room with a stunning blonde; and he was staring at me, a malevolent look on his face. He raised his right hand, pointing his index finger at me with his thumb extended, like a gun. Then, he dropped his thumb as if he were firing the gun. I shook my head in disgust as I stared back at Clark, then turned to Tom.

"That's the man about whom we were just talking. He is the one who threatened me and who we believe sent the fellow to scare me, but we have no proof. He has also been stalking Liz."

I shook my head.

"This is just too coincidental. He couldn't have followed us here or known where we would be. What are the odds that we would both be in the same restaurant at the same time?"

I wanted to confront Clark, but my better judgment prevailed. I excused myself and called RJ. I quickly explained what had happened and that we had all seen it. "Do you have any suggestions?"

He told me he would call me back. Two minutes later, my phone rang.

"Do you have a business card with you?"

I said I did.

"Have your waiter give it to the Maître d' and tell him a man will come in shortly asking for you. Someone will be there in a few minutes to take care of things."

I did as instructed and explained to Tom, Sharon, and Liz what I had been told. We ordered after-dinner drinks and waited. Five minutes later, the Maître d' came to the table with a man in a suit. The man introduced himself as Sergeant Ford, asked me to describe Clark without turning to look at him and to describe what Clark had done with his hand. He told me that Clark would be leaving in police custody. He said he would call me tomorrow about filing a formal charge and making a statement.

Ford followed the Maître d' to Clark's table where he was presented with his check and quietly escorted from the dining room. His date followed him out, a bewildered look on her face.

"I'm impressed," Tom said. "That was handled very well. Once again, you demonstrate why we have confidence in you. I hope this is the end of his nonsense."

I called RJ on the way home and thanked him. I was told Clark would be charged with making a terroristic threat. He said I would have to file a formal complaint tomorrow, which I did. He also told me that Damon's actions didn't rise to the level of a terroristic threat, but it would work to inconvenience him for a while. RJ suggested keeping my gun with me for a while.

RJ also suggested that Liz file a stalking complaint, which she did the next morning. I later learned that two waiters had separately seen Clark's motion with his hand and had reported the incident.

I looked at Liz as I drove. Her face bore a strained look. I took her hand.

"Are you okay?"

"Not really. I'm scared, Dub. I'm afraid he will try again to hurt you."

I tried to reassure her, but I don't think I was successful. She slept the entire night pressed tightly against me.

PART 4

THIRTY-ONE

On Tuesday, May 30, bond for Clark was initially refused because the charge was a terroristic threat, but his lawyer was quickly able to get the threat charge reduced. He pleaded, posted a bond, and paid a fine and court costs–and learned William Wade's name. However, charges were still pending arraignment on the stalking complaint, so he wasn't released. On Thursday, he posted a bond on those charges and was released. On Friday, he took a deal on misdemeanor stalking. He paid a fine of one thousand dollars plus time served plus thirty hours of community service.

Clark immediately went to his office. Bobby was there doing paperwork.

"I gotta make a call," Damon said. He tapped a contact in his phone, called a number, and identified himself. The line went dead. Five minutes later, the phone rang. He answered and a soft voice said, "You called."

"Yeah," Clark said. "I still want to do that thing, but I want to add another job."

He looked at Bobby. "Give me a minute will you. Make us some fresh coffee."

Bobby nodded, picked the empty coffee carafe, and went out.

"What kind of job," the voice asked.

"I want a guy removed."

'We don't do that."

"Okay. Then, I'll get the girl and bring her to you, but I want you to get the guy. I want him worked over real good. Bring him back to me, and then I'll wrap a chain around him and dump him out by an oil rig. My guy who could do that is headed to prison. I just need a little muscle."

"How much is real good?"

"I want him pissing down his leg and crying for mama."

"The girl is still a flat fifty grand to you if I like her looks, but the guy will cost you two grand. Give me an address. When we're done, we'll tell you where he is. You get him. If you want pick-up and delivery, it's an extra three thousand dollars."

"Take it out of the fifty."

"It does not work that way. Five grand up front with pick-up and delivery."

"Okay. When can you take her?"

"Get me some good pictures of her. If she's young and beautiful, it will take me a week or two to market her. Get me the money by five o'clock today for the guy."

Damon paged Bobby. When Bobby called, Damon told him he wanted Bobby to deliver something for him by five p.m.

"What's going on?" Bobby asked when he arrived.

Damon hesitated, then looked at Bobby for a long minute. "Sit down," he said. "I guess it won't hurt to tell you. I know you can keep your mouth shut.

"I'm going to get rid of that bitch, Liz, and her friend."

Oh, fuck, thought Bobby. He was silent for a moment, then asked evenly, "How are you going to do that?'

"Like I told you, I'm gonna sell her. I know a guy who will give me fifty grand for her. It's all set up for next week.

"And they'll do a number on the doc, too. Then I'm going to take him out near the oil rigs, wrap him in chains and drop him overboard. The rigs dump kitchen garbage overboard and there are always sharks swimming around the rigs. If anyone finds part of him, there won't be enough to identify him."

Bobby shook his head. "Man, I still don't think this is a good idea. There is too much to link you to them if something happens. If Uncle John finds out, he'll go ballistic. He's already unhappy with you. You know that.

"It's just what I said the last time and what Uncle John said. The cops can tie you to her and the guy with no trouble. It's not a long step to tie you to Uncle John and he doesn't need that kind of publicity. He's about ready to increase the marijuana business here. You need to stay low-key."

At that moment, Damon's phone rang. He looked at the caller ID and said, "Speak of the devil."

He answered and said, "Hi, Uncle John. Bobby and I were just sitting here talking about you."

"Damon, I just learned that you were arrested and charged with two stupid offenses. And you didn't call Saul. Why not?"

Saul Stein was John Candelero's attorney for everything, and Damon knew it. He didn't call Stein because he was trying to keep Candelero from learning what happened.

"Aw, you know, Uncle John. Saul is pretty busy and I thought I'd handle this myself. It's no big deal."

"Wrong. It's a very big deal. You were charged with making a terroristic threat. First, I know what you did and that shouldn't be considered a terroristic threat. That can be a federal felony. If they charged you with that, it's because you're on the radar of someone with some juice. Second, even though the charge was reduced, you're now on a federal watch list. Third, that stalking charge is going to get a Protective

Order issued against you within the week, so you will be in the system for that. And fourth, you just reinforced your unfriendly connection with that girl and her boyfriend. You should have sent them a bottle of wine and smiled a lot. If anything happens to either of them, you'll be the first person the cops look for."

"Relax, Uncle John. It was only a coincidence that we were in the same place at the same time. I assure you, they aren't going to be a problem in the future."

"They are already a problem. Saul will take over the charges against you as soon as I hang up. You keep your head down and your nose clean." He paused. "Jesus Christ, Damon. Start using your head!"

He hung up.

"What was all that?" Bobby asked.

"Uncle John is mad again, but he'll get over it."

"What's he mad about?"

Damon summarized for Bobby.

"Hell, I didn't know they were going to be in that restaurant at the same time I was. I go there a lot; I've never seen him in there before."

"Bro, you need to start using your head."

Bobby unknowingly repeated what Candelero had just said.

"You need to forget about selling the girl–or doing anything to her or the guy. You would be the first person the cops looked at when she went missing."

"Yeah. I guess you're right. I don't want to be in that position. I'm going to san Antonio and get laid."

When Bobby left, Damon called the number again and left his name.

Five minutes later, the phone rang and he answered. The soft voice said, "You called?"

"Yeah. Listen, about those two things, I need to put that on hold for a while."

"I heard you had some problems. I think it's probably better that I stay away from you for a while." The line went dead.

He went home to pack. As he was getting ready to leave, there was a knock on his door. He looked out the window and saw a constable on his front porch.

"Fuck me dead," he said as he went to the door and opened it.

"Damon Clark?" the officer asked perfunctorily.

"Yes, Officer."

He expected to be arrested. Instead, the officer handed him a sheaf of folded papers.

"Mr. Clark, this is a temporary restraining order. You are not to come within one hundred fifty feet of Elizabeth Barton or her residence, her place of employment, or her vehicle or any place in which you know that she is. You are not to contact her except through her attorney, whose information is in those papers. You are ordered to appear in court next Tuesday to determine if a Protective Order will be granted. The time and place are in those papers. Failure to abide by this order and/or failure to appear will be grounds for arrest. Do you have any questions?

"No."

"Do you understand what I have told you?"

"Yes. I understand."

"Please tell me what guns you own and gather them for me."

'What?" Damn shouted.

"Sir, you cannot possess firearms while a restraining order or Protective Order for family violence is in effect. Please get your weapons now."

"But she isn't family. I only dated her."

"Your lawyer can explain that to you, sir."

"I don't own any weapons." He didn't say why.

"Thank you, sir." The officer turned and left.

Damon slammed the door, cursed loud and long, and flung the papers across the room. "Fuck her. Just fuck that bitch!"

He left the papers where they had fallen without reading them and drove to San Antonio.

THIRTY-TWO

A week passed without event. I accompanied Liz when she appeared for the hearing for the Protective Order, which went smoothly. Damon Clark appeared with a lawyer and only spoke when the judge spoke to him. He avoided all eye contact with Liz and me.

Jill was healing well and in good spirits. Vivian planned to remain in Houston a little longer. I was enjoying my new responsibilities. Liz and I were together almost every night. We had dinner at Coco's and thoroughly enjoyed ourselves and the environment. Every weekend, we practiced her self-defense moves. She was back in the rhythm of her job and up to speed on her project. Life was good.

Then, I got a call from a county prosecutor, Arvin Choksi. He said he had reviewed the file on Hector Gomez and he asked me several questions. He came across as a competent guy, so I explained what I could and offered my thoughts and supposition. He listened and paused me often enough that I knew he was making notes. He mulled over what I had told him for a long moment, then asked, "What can you tell me about Clark?"

I told him everything I knew, including about the incident at Brennan's and the coincidences of what he said to me and what Gomez said. I told him about the Protective Order for Liz.

"Anything else?"

I thought for a minute, then told him about what Richard had told me about the take-out business and the boy who died of the overdose. That seemed to get his attention. "Have you told anyone else about this?"

"I told Robert Munoz, Director of Security at the hospital. A detective named Asimov came out and talked to me about Gomez. I thought about telling him, but he didn't seem too interested in my complaint."

Choksi said he knew Asimov, but nothing more about him. He was quiet for a moment, then told me he would get back to me and thanked me for the information I had given him.

I called RJ to give him a heads up that he might hear from Choksi.

THIRTY-THREE

Arvin Choksi had five years of experience as a prosecutor, having come to the office directly from law school. He wasn't yet a seasoned prosecutor, but he was smart and diligent and had the trust of the District Prosecutor and the District Attorney. The Gomez case was assigned to him. He immediately saw the dead-end of information and it aroused his suspicion. He reviewed his notes from his conversation with William Wade, and he reviewed the file carefully. On Monday, June 5, he called Vastian Asimov.

He had never met Asimov but knew of him by reputation. The word was that Asimov was a problem solver, not assigned to a single division. Asimov said he would stop by the Prosecutor's Office later and discuss the Gomez file. He arrived at three o'clock.

As Asimov arrived, Choksi's phone rang. It was Janice Evans, the District Prosecutor, who advised him that Asimov was coming to see him. Choksi said that Asimov had just arrived and was told to sit tight until she arrived. When she arrived, introductions were made all around and Evans invited everyone into a conference room.

"We're informal when we're in the office," Evans advised Asimov, "so unless you have an objection I'm Janice, this is Arvin, and may we call you Vastian?" Asimov agreed.

"Good. This is a meeting that we anticipated having soon, but Arvin's diligence got ahead of our anticipation." Looking at Asimov, she said, "It is my understanding that you have some background information of which we need to be aware."

He nodded and began. "Let me give you some of the background first.

"Hector Gomez is a small-time thug who works for John Candelero. Candelero is a local businessman who owns two vehicle dealerships in Houston, three used car sales companies, and a large salvage parts and inventory business. Gomez runs a team of thieves who steal vehicles and vehicle parts. The vehicles usually end up in Mexico, occasionally on Candelero's lot, or stripped for parts. Parts are then comingled with legal parts in Candelero's salvage business and sold. Gomez also does strong arm and collection work for Candelero.

"John Candelero is the son of Damon Candelero, a wealthy man in Dallas who owns auto dealerships in Dallas and Fort Worth. We have no information that Damon Candelero is not a legitimate businessman. John Candelero has a business degree from Southern Methodist University and says he came to Houston because he likes the weather better here than in Dallas. His businesses in our city have made him a substantial millionaire.

"When Colorado began to show signs of wanting to legalize marijuana, John Candelero bought five hundred acres of land in southern Colorado. He now raises marijuana on that land and sells most of it in Colorado. Last year, he reported an income of five million dollars from the sale of marijuana.

"Six years ago, John Candelero opened a delicatessen, which has become a lucrative franchise chain in Houston, Austin, and San Antonio. Those shops are well positioned near schools and major business districts and are very popular with students and millennials. The popularity of the chain rose significantly when dime bags and marijuana cookies and cupcakes became part of the menu for carryout orders. We have information that some marijuana is sold out of the shops also. The delicatessens are ostensibly run by Damon Clark, the nephew of John Candelero.

"Damon Clark has a significant juvenile record, mostly auto theft and assault. He is moderately intelligent but dropped out of high school. He obtained a GED. Damon Clark has a second in command named Bobby Duvall. They met in high school and spent a lot of time together in juvie. Duvall has one juvie offense for auto theft and a major offense for possession with intent to distribute. He was caught with two bricks of heroin.

"We haven't moved on either Candelero or Clark because, quite frankly, they have been small fish. Candelero has been investigated a few times for stolen goods, but we've never been able to prove anything worth pursuing. The amount of marijuana moving through the delicatessens is probably more than we estimate, but everything is in small quantities and we could probably only prove a few sales.

"A few months ago, a teenager overdosed and his father thinks the drugs came from the delicatessens. We did some background investigation and don't believe Candelero is moving anything stronger than marijuana, at least at this time. The dead boy may have gotten marijuana from the delicatessen, but we don't think the drug or drugs that caused his overdose came from Candelero or Clark.

"That brings us to recent events. We have information that John Candelero has purchased land in Montgomery County, Texas, and in Louisiana on which he is going to construct storage buildings for marijuana that he intends to bring in from Colorado. We also have information that he is connected to a group that intends to build a distribution network from Colorado to Nevada, Oregon, and eventually to Washington, all states that have legalized marijuana. We are working with the FBI to thwart the efforts to move marijuana out of Colorado and to shut down all of Candelero's illegal activity in Texas before he becomes a big fish.

"He was in on the ground floor in Colorado when marijuana was legalized. He owns five hundred acres on which he legally raises marijuana and hemp. It has quickly grown into a very profitable business for him.

"Marijuana grows much like tomato plants. A marijuana plant needs nine square feet to grow properly. On one acre of good land, one can grow more than forty-eight hundred marijuana plants. At an average market price of two thousand dollars per pound, an average acre yields an income of one million two hundred thousand dollars in round numbers. There is very little processing needed to prepare marijuana for the market and little to no effort needed to put it to use. The only problem for growers of legal marijuana is growing competition that affects the economics of supply and demand. Lawful production can easily exceed lawful demand; therefore, alternative markets are necessary.

"Candelero is now a major producer in Colorado, but he also smuggles small amounts of his product into Canada, Texas, and Louisiana. And, transportation across state lines is still illegal everywhere.

"When his sister asked him to do something for her son, Damon, he agreed. He set Damon up in a small delicatessen, taught him the business–which he had learned from his father–and they have grown the business into several shops in Houston, San Antonia, and Austin. The shops quickly became popular and trendy.

"That popularity has been enhanced in recent years by the fact that marijuana quickly became an expensive staple–either in dime bags or in the form of brownies or cookies–of many carry out orders from their various delicatessens for those who had a need and the money and who could be discreet about their source.

"We have a task force that is working to gather sufficient hard evidence on Candelero that we can use to prosecute him. That is one reason I am here. We have discussed this matter with the FBI and with the District Attorney. We believe Hector Gomez will give us a wedge into Candelero's organization. We will be following his case closely in hopes of offering him a plea bargain for information. We don't believe his intent was anything other than to scare Wade away, but we are asking your office to vigorously pursue the assault and attempted murder charge for the leverage it will give us against Clark and Candelero.

"This is what we have at the moment, and most of this you know from the Gomez file."

Asimov recounted the events and circumstances surrounding Elizabeth Barton's brief relationship with Damon Clark up to and including the belief that it was he who commissioned Gomez to attack William Wade, as well as his stalking charge brought by Ms. Barton. "We believe that Ms. Barton is nothing more than a victim and has no relationship to any activity being investigated except Gomez's attack on Wade."

"We have information from an informant that Clark is developing noticeable signs of megalomania and is threatening to harm either or both Barton and Wade. We're prepared to work with your office to the full extent on this matter."

Choksi looked at Evans with a questioning gaze. He was certain the case would be taken from him.

Evans understood his look. "Don't worry, Arvin. This is your case. I'm your backstop and right hand. The second reason I'm not taking this case is that we fear that putting me on the case would tip our hand. But the first reason is that we believe you can handle this. I think the fact that you got ahead of the curve by already talking to Wade shows your tenacity and ability to do what will be needed to prosecute this case the way it needs to be handled."

Choksi grinned his thanks and looked at Asimov. "Wade told me he thought you didn't seem very interested in his case when you came to the hospital to interview him."

"I'm sure he did. I couldn't say much then. We knew about the Gomez thing, and his relationship to Candelero and Clark, but I didn't want to draw any conclusions in front of Wade."

"Okay," said Choksi, "so my job–our job–is to build a strong case against Gomez and go after him with a pointed instrument. Your job is to build a case against Candelero. Who is going to protect Barton?"

"Good question," Asimov responded, impressed that Choksi understood the need for the question. "At this point, we have some weight from the Protective Order, but that also works against us because she now has court protection–for all the good a piece of paper can do. Not trying to be funny, but we think Wade is a pretty good first line of defense for her. He handled Gomez pretty well. But we are trying to be mindful of her safety as well. For the time being, that's about the best we can do."

"Do you have any concerns for the safety of Gomez," Janice asked Asimov.

"From what I've seen of Candelero, I think he is just a greedy guy who thinks he found a way to make tax-free money. I don't think murder is in his wheelhouse. I think just the thought of a murder charge would scare the pants off him. Clark on the other hand, I don't know."

THIRTY-FOUR

On Friday of that week, Arvin Choksi called me and asked me to again go through the incident with Gomez in careful detail, especially anything that Gomez said, which was precious little. Richard came to Houston that afternoon and we had dinner with him, Jill, and Vivian at Vivian's. It was great to see him. He and I talked about the Gomez incident and I brought him up to date on what I knew. On Saturday, Liz and I had dinner at Coco's and were welcomed like family.

Another uneventful week passed. Liz and I were still visiting Jill regularly and she was improving. She could get out of bed and into a wheelchair, and she was receiving daily physical therapy. She had asked her boss to send her some work because she was bored and worried about her job. Vivian planned to stay another month if things continued well with Jill.

I had to go to New Mexico on business for two days. Liz called me while I was gone and told me she thought she had seen Damon's Land Rover down the street from her house twice, but she wasn't certain it was actually his vehicle. I told her where I kept my binoculars and told her to get them and check the license plate if she saw it again. If it was him, I told her to call the Sheriff.

THIRTY-FIVE

Bobby walked into Damon's office on Monday morning, poured himself a cup of coffee, and sat down. "Uncle John called me and I'm going over there. Do you have anything for him that I can take or pass on?"

"No. I haven't heard from him about my plan to stop moving marijuana in the shops. Let me know if he says anything about that"

Bobby nodded. "Are you staying away from the Barton girl like he told you?"

Damon paused. "Yeah, but I really want to talk to her. I think if she would just listen to me, she would understand that we could be good for each other. I could give her things women want and we could have a kid."

"Yeah, but do you love her?"

"I love my mom. I don't love women, but I sure like them. You tell a woman you love her, she's got you by the throat for the rest of your life."

"Why her? You met one educated woman; you can meet another. There are more out there"

"Yeah, I know. But she got under my skin. I don't like that she just dumped me. It's like I lost and she won."

"Damon, you were fucking two other women and she knows about one of them. Women don't like it when you do that."

"I know; I know. But I still want to try talking with her."

"Leave her alone, man. You could get arrested for even contacting her."

"Yeah. I know you're right. It's just that…. You know…"

"Yeah, I know. You're thinking with the wrong head." He shook his head. "I'm going to see Uncle John. Leave the woman alone," Bobby advised as he left.

Damon sat at his desk and pondered. After a while, he called Liz Barton. He got her voice mail.

"Liz, this is Damon. Please don't hang up; listen for just a minute. I didn't call to cause a problem. I'd just like to talk to you. We can do it someplace public where you feel comfortable. Let me know."

~~~

Bobby was shown into John Candelero's office. Candelero greeted him warmly, offered him coffee, and led him to a conference table in his office that was covered with paper, maps, and photographs. They sat and Candelero appraised Bobby.

"Bobby, I've known you for ten years now. I think I know you pretty well. I want to talk to you like a Dutch uncle for a few minutes."

Bobby nodded. "Sure, Uncle John."

"You know what goes on in my businesses, both good and bad, as it were. Except for the marijuana in the delis, I've kept you and Damon away from anything that could get you into real trouble. You both had a rough time in juvie and I don't think either of you wants real trouble with the law again. You had…, what, a couple of stolen vehicles, some truancy, and a little drug bust." Candelero had no idea of the true facts of Bobby's drug arrest and conviction, and Bobby had never enlightened him.
~~~

"Tell me what you want to do with your life. You're a bright guy and you handle yourself well. And you're street smart. What do you want to do?"

Bobby sat quietly for a moment. "I want to make money–big money. That's not easy to do when a guy only has a high school education and no special skills. I want to sow some wild oats, then find a pretty girl who will stay pretty, and have a son. I want a nice home and a nice life and I'd like to visit Australia and New Zealand before I get too old. I'd like to be able to save enough money that I don't have to worry when I get old." He paused and looked thoughtful. "At this stage of my life, that's pretty much it, Uncle John."

Candelero watched him thoughtfully for a moment. "I set Damon up in business for my sister. Her shit for brains husband is in the wind, and she and Damon aren't ever going to get any help from him. My father will take care of them and leave them in good shape when he dies. I've done all I'm going to do for them.

"Damon doesn't get it. He wants to be somebody, but he thinks he can do that by buying respect and marrying the right girl. That's his big plan. He doesn't have what it takes to be successful.

"You do. I've talked a little with you about the marijuana business. I've given this a lot of thought. My father got me my first dealership and I owe him for that. After that, I've built what I have with no one else's help. I don't have a best friend or a business partner that I trust. I know I operate on the edge a little, but it's profitable and I don't think it's big enough to draw a lot of attention.

"I've mentioned to you what I want to do with the marijuana business, but I haven't told you much. I don't even know how much you know about my businesses. Did you know that I own five hundred acres in southern Colorado and that I legally grow marijuana on all five hundred acres?"

"I knew you owned a piece of land there, and Damon told me that the marijuana came from Colorado, but I didn't know you owned that much land or that you grew the weed there."

"Marijuana is legal in Alaska, California, Colorado, Maine, Massachusetts, Michigan, Nevada, Oregon, Vermont, and Washington and the District of Columbia. Medical marijuana is legal close to us in Louisiana, Arkansas, and New Mexico. The big problem is that it is illegal to transport it across any state line. I've been able to bring enough into Houston under the radar to supply our delis in Houston, Austin, and San Antonio. I've been working on how to build a delivery system to the west coast and into Texas, New Mexico, and Louisiana that can avoid detection. I'm working with some businessmen in California and we're about ready to go on a couple of big cities on the west coast.

"Now, I need to get the system in place over here. I've leased some warehouse space north of us in Montgomery County with an option for a long-term lease, if this works out.

"If it does, I want you to run the operation in Texas, New Mexico, and Louisiana. I need someone I can trust. If you want to stay clear of any involvement, I will understand and no hard feelings. We could go to jail if this doesn't work out. Think about it for a few days. If you think you want the job, I'll explain my plan to you. Until then, what you don't know can't hurt you.

"If you don't want the job, then I have another proposition for you."

THIRTY-SIX

Liz called me and told me about Damon's message. She told me that she didn't call him back either Monday or Tuesday. She was adamant that she wanted him out of her life and was not going to return his call. She was busy with a work project, so we just talked Monday and Tuesday by phone. On Wednesday, we visited Jill and ate out afterward.

I had a late morning on Thursday, so I followed her home after dinner. She parked in her garage and I parked on the drive behind her. As I got out, I looked up and down the street. A black Range Rover sat by the curb a block away. As I exited my car and stood up, I heard the Range Rover start and watched as it pulled from the curb and drove away.

"That was him, wasn't it?" she asked.

I didn't think she had seen the Range Rover.

"I don't know. I couldn't see inside and couldn't read the plate, but it was odd that it drove off when I got out of my car."

"What should we do?"

"We can't prove it was him. Keep a log of dates and times. He will eventually slip up. Maybe one time, we'll get a plate number. If you can, take pictures if he shows up again."

Inside, she dropped her purse heavily on the kitchen counter and sighed deeply.

"You okay?" I asked.

"Frustrated, angry… maybe a little apprehensive. I'm glad you're here. I'm glad you saw it, too."

I put my arms around her and hugged her to me. She nestled for a minute, then said she was going to change into something comfortable. I was still in scrubs. She looked at me and said, "I think I need some scrubs, too. Those look pretty comfortable."

"They are," I grinned and said hopefully, "and they come off really easy, too."

"Prove it," she said with a laugh as she took my hand. I proved it to her–actually she proved it for herself, and made my day.

The next day, Liz called me just before lunch. "I had another phone message from Damon this morning. He said he wants to talk to me and asked me to call him. Do you think if I called him and told him that I never want to talk to him again, it would stop him?"

"Did you keep the voice messages?"

"I erased the first one. I haven't erased this one yet. Should I start keeping them?"

"Yes. But don't call him.

"I think you should have your lawyer call him. I know your Protective Order was done by the District Attorney's office. Do you have a lawyer?"

"No. I have a Will that was done by Mother and Daddy's lawyer. He is the only lawyer that I know."

"Let me make a couple of phone calls," I said. I walked to RJ's office and asked him what to do.

"If you and she want action, call the DA's office. If you just want to warn him off, I can ask Tim to have someone at Houston Police call him and tell him how the cow ate the cabbage."

I opted for door number two.

Tim called me ten minutes later. "I had a friend call Clark. Clark swore that Liz was mistaken. My friend told him that she had a picture of his car and Clark said all black Ranger Rovers look alike. My friend told him he was lucky she hadn't asked for an arrest warrant to be issued and advised him not to come near her."

I thanked Tim and called Liz. I explained what I had done.

"Thank you," she said with dejection in her voice.

"Keep the messages and take pictures. That should be enough to get him arrested, if that's what it is going to take to get his attention."

"I will," she said with the same dejection in her voice.

"Can you get tomorrow off?"

"I think so; we're at a lull right now. I'll ask and call you right back," she replied hopefully."

Five minutes later, the phone rang. I answered and heard a happy, "I'm all yours."

"The weather is supposed to be beautiful this weekend. Take your pick: Moody Gardens and Galveston or Austin or San Antonio."

"I'm not up for a long car ride. I would love Moody Gardens and Galveston."

I made reservations and we had a wonderful weekend of sun, sand, and relaxation. We enjoyed IMAX 3D, walking the Strand, the railroad museum. We spent two hours in the Bryan Museum of Texas History and had a wonderful dinner at Gaido's.

THIRTY-SEVEN

On Friday, Bobby called Candelero and was told he would be in a meeting until noon. The secretary said that Candelero told her to tell him to come to the office at noon if he called. He went to Damon's office and flopped into a chair. Damon looked harried.

"What's up," Bobby asked.

"Nothing. Everything's good."

"You don't look like everything's good. Is there a problem?"

"I can't get Liz out of my mind. I called her and was really polite. I asked if she would talk with me and offered to meet her someplace public. I got a call back–from a fuckin' cop."

"Man, I told you. Forget her. Think, Damon. She never slept with you. You only spent three or four months with her. You fucked around on her and pissed her off. Move on, man. You keep this up and you're gonna step on your dick big time!"

"Yeah, yeah. You don't understand."

"What don't I understand."

"She shut me down," he shouted. "She dumped me. I never had a woman dump me before. I gave her nice things. I took her nice places. I took care of her friends. And I get told to fuck off!" His face was red and his voice was at full pitch.

"I don't know what else to tell you, man. You need to move on."

Bobby stood. He was tired of Damon's whining. "I need to check some things. Then I have to see Uncle John."

"What for?"

"Don't know. I was just told to come at noon." He left Damon's office.

At noon, Bobby was ushered into Candelero's office. After greetings, Candelero asked, "Have you had enough time to think?

Bobby nodded. "If I like what I hear, I'm in. What are my options?"

"I think Damon has about passed his potential and his value to me. I'm seriously thinking about giving him a severance package and taking the delicatessen business away from him. If I do that, I'll sell you the business on a long-term note at a decent interest rate, if you want it. You forget about what I just told you. It would be your call whether you continue the takeout side business or not. The delicatessens were a good business investment.

"It would be your chance to go clean and have the life you described to me a few days ago. Quite frankly, my long-term goal is to grow the marijuana business legitimately, then sell it as a public offering. I want to have a good life and retire happy, just like you.

"I believe that you have always been straight with me, Bobby. You're the son I never had. Damon has always been an albatross. You have always been an asset. I want you to have the life you want, whichever path you take."

Candelero could have cut the look of amazement on Bobby's face with a knife.

"You're serious, Uncle John?"

"I'm serious, Bobby. Do you need a little more time to think?"

Bobby was quiet for a long moment. Finally, he said, "Yes sir. That's too much to think about right now. I need some more time."

"I can give you three weeks. Think about it. Make the right decision for you."

"Yes, sir." Bobby got up to leave and hesitated

"Uhh… Uncle John, I think you should know that Damon is getting, well… weird about the Barton girl. He has violated the protective order and a cop told him he would be arrested next time. He brought up selling her again and I tried to cut that short. He's upset because she dumped him and he says he has never been dumped by a woman.

"I don't want any part of human trafficking. That woman has done nothing to Damon that he didn't bring on himself. I'm at a loss about what to. I don't know the girl, but I don't want to see anything bad happen to her because of Damon."

"Are you just concerned or do you really think he will do something stupid."

'It's just my opinion, but I've watched Damon for more than ten years now. I think he has slowly been unraveling, and it's happening faster lately. When you first set him up, he seemed happy and grateful. But he's gotten full of himself. It's like he thinks everyone owes him something. That stupid job he sent Hector on is a good example. He put a simple-minded man in harm's way for no good reason other than to show us that he could do it. Now, he says he knows a guy who sells women. He sounds serious about getting rid of the Barton girl.

"If he keeps up like he's going, we are going to have a lot of people looking our way, if they aren't already."

Candelero looked thoughtful. "Thanks, Bobby. Thanks for telling me. You're right. Let me think about this… and call me if you think he's going to do anything stupid very soon."

"Yes, sir, Uncle John."

PART 5

THIRTY-EIGHT

We returned from our weekend in Galveston, rested and happy. I had enjoyed myself, and I know Liz enjoyed the weekend. She slept well and ate well. We teased and talked and laughed a lot for three days and I think it was just what she needed. She had called Jill Sunday and begged off our Sunday visit that day. Of course, Jill understood and gave us positive reports on her progress.

We weren't ready for the weekend to end, so Liz stayed with me Sunday night. I took her home early Monday, June 12, then drove to the hospital for a ten a.m. surgery. After surgery, I went to my office in the hospital. There was a voicemail from RJ asking me to call him and one from Liz. I called RJ first.

"Hi. It's Dub. What's up?" I asked when he answered.

"Are you in your office?"

"Yes. I just finished surgery and was going to get some lunch."

"Sit tight for a minute. I'm coming your way."

I left my door open and called Liz. She answered on the first ring. "Dub, Damon was just here, in the building about fifteen minutes ago."

"What happened?"

"He went to the front desk, told the receptionist that he was here to take me to lunch, and asked what floor I was on. She called me and told me his name. I put her on hold, called security, and quickly explained that he was in violation of a Protective Order and asked for help.

"I clicked the line back to the receptionist. She told me he said that if I wasn't coming, he was leaving–and he did, just ahead of the security guards."

"Are you all right?"

"Yes. A little scared."

"Let me call you back in a minute. RJ is coming up and I have a funny premonition that what he is going to tell me is related to what you just told me. In the meantime, call your security officer and ask him to make a report to the Sheriff."

I clicked off as RJ and Tim Carrell walked in, shutting the door behind them. They looked solemn, so I rose and we shook hands. "Is something wrong?" I asked.

RJ nodded.

"Damon Clark was in the hospital earlier, asking to see you," RJ advised me. "He wanted to know where your office was. He seems to think you're a doctor.

"The receptionist recognized him from the picture we put in her logbook. She called Tim and told him about Clark. He told her to stall the guy and she did."

Tim spoke. "I went down and introduced myself. He was very cordial. He said he was a friend and wanted to take you to lunch. He sounded sincere, like it happened every day. I told him you were unavailable and that he wasn't allowed on hospital grounds without prior authorization.

"He gave me a hard look and asked if you were that fucking important.

"I said you were. One of my guys walked up and we took him by the arms and escorted him to his car. His only comment was that he just wanted to have lunch with you. He drove away without further incident."

"What time did this happen?"

"About ten minutes ago."

I looked at RJ and Tim and just shook my head. "Liz just called me. He tried the same thing at her office just before he came here. I told her to have security make a report to the Sheriff."

"Good," RJ said. "We've made a report also. There isn't much else we can do at this point."

"What can they do to him?" I asked.

Tim replied. "Normally, forty-eight hours in jail and a fine of one thousand dollars for violating a protective order, but he has two violations within an hour. My guess is ten to twenty days in jail and a fine of twenty-five hundred dollars. He could get as much as a year in prison with two violations back to back like this."

"We need to figure how to keep you and Liz safe until this idiot is out of commission," RJ said. "Would you like for me to call ExxonMobil security and talk with them? Then we can talk."

"Most certainly," I replied.

RJ called from the switchboard phone in my office. He explained to Stan Pulanski, his counterpart at ExxonMobil, who he was and about Liz and me and the Protective Order. He said that he believed both Liz and I were in possible danger from Clark and that he wanted to suggest some steps each employer could take to avoid physical confrontation at both locations. Pulanski was aware of Clark's visit to the company and welcomed RJ's suggestions.

Fifteen minutes later, RJ hung up and looked at me. "This is our suggestion. There will be an arrest warrant out for Clark, so the priority is to inform all security personnel and familiarize them with Clark and his picture.

"When Liz arrives at work and departs, she will notify security and they will escort her to and from her vehicle or the front entrance if she rides with you. It will be suggested to her that she eat lunch on campus until this is resolved and that she always eats with a friend. It will also be suggested that she program 911 and company security into her phone and have it with her at all times.

"The suggestions are the same for you. Keep your eyes and ears open as you move around the hospital and parking lot.

"The Sheriff should have confiscated all of Clark's weapons when he was served with the Protective Order, but we can't be sure. Keep your weapon as close as possible at all times. You are officially part of my staff now, so there is no problem with you carrying here, just try to keep it concealed. Don't carry in the operating rooms.

"I know you can defend yourself, but don't take any unnecessary chances.

"You and Liz need to work out some strategies for when you aren't at work. Do either of you live in a gated community?"

I told him that I did.

"Not being presumptuous, but I suggest the two of you live at your home for a while. Does he know where you live?"

"Not that I am aware of, but I'm sure he could easily find out."

"Does Liz know anything about self-defense?"

"As a matter of fact, she does. We've been working on basics for three or four weeks now."

RJ laughed. "Why does that not surprise me?"

Tim asked if she knew anything about handguns.

"Good question. I don't know. But I will teach her what I can as soon as I can."

They left and I pondered for a while.

How did a little thing like this get so out of hand? This guy isn't playing with a full deck. And your first job is to keep Liz safe.

I called Liz and she told me that their Head of Security had explained the call from RJ and had briefed her on what RJ told me. She also told me she had been given a parking pass to the executive floor which had limited access by pass only and an elevator that worked only with an employee ID containing an authorized chip. She said her new ID would be in her hands before the end of the day.

I went to the cafeteria for lunch and then to surgery for an afternoon heart bypass surgery.

I met Liz outside her building and drove her to her car, then followed her home where she packed some clothes. After a weekend of hotel and restaurant food, we decided to cook in. She was apprehensive early in the evening, but we had a couple of glasses of wine and I let her talk. She finally relaxed a little. We ate and sat outside by the pool for a while, then went to bed. I took her hand and she slept close against me all night.

THIRTY-NINE

D amon Clerk had enough experience as a juvenile criminal to know that there was now an active warrant out for his arrest. He thought to himself. *This is all her fault. If she would just let me explain, we could fix everything. She's smart. I can explain that I'm better for her than the doc and this will all go away,* he thought.

Monday afternoon, Damo drove from the hospital to one of his uncle's used car dealers and rented a sedan, leaving his Land Rover with instructions to store it inside and keep it clean for a week or two. He knew he couldn't go home for a while, so he found a hotel that rented efficiencies by the week and paid cash for two weeks. He drove to the mall and bought fresh clothes and toiletries. He didn't give the delicatessens a second thought. He knew Bobby would take care of things.

Warrants for his arrest were immediately issued and officers appeared at both Damon's office and his home, but he wasn't there.

Bobby was at the office when the officer came. As soon as the officer left, he called Candelero, who asked if he knew where Damon could be. Bobby had no idea. Candelero told him to take over the delicatessens and to ensure that things ran smoothly.

"Try to find him and call me when you do," Candelero directed.

Bobby called Damon's number and he answered right away.

"Where are you?" Bobby asked. Damon told him.

"What the hell did you do? Cops were here with a warrant for your arrest."

"I tried to talk to Liz and to her boyfriend. They wouldn't let me see either one of them," Damon said as if he had no idea why. "They have pissed me off now."

"They who?"

"Liz and the guy. Hell, all I wanted to do was talk. If she would just talk to me, we could get this all resolved."

"How are you going to get it resolved?"

"Like I told you, I'm going to explain to her why I'm better for her, that I can give her anything she wants."

Bobby thought before he spoke. "Damon, she doesn't trust you. I don't think things are as important to her as trust. I'm sure she is a great girl, but I think you pissed in your Wheaties, man.   You need to find another girl and get back here to your business. Uncle John's lawyer will work all this out for you."

"Yeah, I don't need Uncle John preaching to me now. She has really fucked things up and I have to make her understand that. She has to withdraw that Protective Order."

"Well, what if you can't convince her?"

"Then I'm going to sell her and get her out of my life."

"Damon, just leave the girl alone. Why do you want to sell her?"

Damon had been conversational until that question, but his voice rose to an angry shout. "I told you, Bobby. She shut me down. She dumped me and no one dumps me!"

"Okay, okay," Bobby responded placatingly. "I understand, man. So, what are you going to do?"

"I'm going to give it a couple of days to cool off. Then I'm going to make her talk to me. If she doesn't want to make all this go away then I'm going to sell her. And I'm going to dump that doc in the gulf."

"Okay," Bobby said calmly. "Stay in touch. Let me know if you need anything. Let me know if you need any help taking care of things."

"Sure," said Damon, again calm. "Thanks, man. I knew I could count on you. Listen, don't come here. They will follow you. I'll talk to her and then let you know." He said it like they were just deciding where to go for dinner.

Bobby called Candelero, told him where Damon was and that Damon was again talking about selling the girl and killing her boyfriend.

"I think he is serious, Uncle John. He's off the rails. We need to do something. That girl is a person. It's not like a car that he wants to replace. We can't let him do that to her. We can't be anywhere near that kind of bad act. It will blow back on us somehow."

"I know, Bobby. You said he was going to give things a couple of days to cool off."

"Yes, sir. That's what he said.

"Let me think about this."

Bobby, too, thought about it. He knew he had to do something, but decided to give it a day before he made a decision.

Candelero called him the next morning and told him to come to the office. He said he didn't want to talk on the phone. Bobby made sure the delis were covered and left immediately.

He sat in Candelero's office as Candelero paced. Looking out the window for a long moment, he spoke without turning.

"I have thought about this constantly since we spoke. I've decided. And I've made your decision for you, at least for the time being.

"Damon has become a liability. Since I can't send a bolt of lightning to take him out and I'm not getting close to a murder charge, this is what we're going to do.

"I want you to take over the delis. The offer to sell is open for as long as you want. I want out of that business. It's yours if you want it. If you don't, we'll sell it.

"I know I should sell what I have in the marijuana business, but I think there is long-range potential there if I can just avoid stubbing my toe until the laws change.

"I'm going to get Damon out of the picture and he has given me the perfect way to do that. In a way, it's a little poetic given what he wants to do to the girl. I'm going to have him committed."

Bobby squinted his eyebrows in confusion but remained silent.

"I've already talked to Saul. He is going to contact the DA and tell him that he has a person who came to him with knowledge of a planned murder and human trafficking crime of two separate persons. That person will be you. Saul is going to get a promise of immunity for you. Then, you are going to tell about the girl and the doc, and that Damon, on his own nickel, ordered Hector to attack the doc. We'll get Hector to back you up and trade that for a reduction of his sentence.

"We get Damon off the street and out of our hair. And we protect the girl. And maybe we can help Hector a little, as well. Life goes on smoothly and I will be quietly working in the background on the weed business. Can you live with what I described?"

Bobby thought for a moment. "Sure. That's ingenious, Uncle John. I like the irony in it." Bobby laughed. "Yeah. I'm in. Let me think about the long-term marijuana business. What do I do?"

"Wait for Saul. When he is ready to start the ball rolling, we will call you. In the meantime, stay in contact with Damon and try to keep him away from the girl–and the cops– until we're ready for them to take him."

He ran his hand through his hair. "Jesus. My sister is just going to have to live with this. I wouldn't do this if I didn't think the kid was out of control."

FORTY

Bobby went back to what was now his office and thought. *You lucky son of a bitch. This couldn't be any better if it had been written in a book.* He got a Corona and a lime wedge from the fridge, sat with his feet propped on his desk, and continued to think, trying to imagine any unforeseen problems that could arise from all this. He couldn't think of any.

He called Damon. "Hey, just checking on you. You doing okay?"

"Sure. I'm sitting here watching NFL highlights and thinking about Mexican for dinner. Do you want to meet me at Pappacito's at five o'clock?"

"Sure. Listen; I talked to Uncle John. He says to stay where you are and sit tight. I've got the delis covered. He's going to get Saul to work on making all this go away. He specifically said to leave the girl alone. He means it, man. He is not happy. He says Saul can take care of things if you just stay low and quiet.

"Oh, and I'm going to bring you a burner phone. We're going to get you a new one in case the cops take the old one. They don't need to see your call log. I'll set the new one up in my name until this blows over, then we'll change it over to you."

Bobby made it sound like it was Candelero's idea and Damon didn't protest.

"See you at five."

Bobby hung up and tapped in a number he knew from memory. It was answered and he said, "It's Duvall. I need to meet."

"Where are you?"

"At the Woodlands office."

"There is one of those Top Golf super driving ranges on IH 45 near the High School. Meet me at the top level at three."

Bobby ate lunch and bought a phone for Damon. Just before three o'clock, he arrived at the golf center, paid his admission, and went to the top level. At three o'clock, the elevator door opened and Vastian Asimov stepped off.

FORTY-ONE

When Bobby was fifteen, he and Damon stole a car. It was a prank. It was a new Mustang that a friend's parents had just bought. The parents were out of town and the friend invited a group of kids, including Bobby and Damon, to the house for a party. The friend took his girlfriend for a joy ride in the new car. When they got back, she was all over him. He hung the keys on a hook by the door and took the girl upstairs.

Damon quietly lifted the keys off the hook and beckoned Bobby. Damon was flying high and speeding. He ran a stop sign and hit another car. No one was severely injured, except for the two cars. In the end, the boy's father pressed charges for auto theft. Damon was charged with grand theft auto and driving under the influence. Bobby was charged as an accomplice. Saul did his best, but Damon served eight months and was on probation until age eighteen. Bobby was given probation until he was eighteen.

From that time, Damon was constantly running on the edge. He was never a good student, but he wasn't stupid. Saul got him out of two misdemeanor charges and got a burglary charge dismissed plus a misdemeanor drug charge.

Bobby was a solid B student and had never gotten into trouble until that day. His parents were both dead and he was raised by an aunt who worked long hours as a waitress. The experience scared Bobby and he tried to stay out of trouble, but he remained friends with Damon.

When he was seventeen, a friend called Bobby and said he had left his car at his girlfriend's house, which was near where Bobby lived. He told Bobby the keys were under the dash and asked him to bring the car to where he was partying with a group of friends.

Bobby found the car and the keys with no trouble. On his way, he rolled through a stop sign and a light show appeared behind him. When he couldn't produce the title and proof of insurance, the officer ran his information. The accomplice charge and probation came up. The cop searched the car and found two bricks of heroin in the trunk. Bobby was immediately arrested.

At the time, Vastian Asimov had just been promoted to Detective. It was he who questioned Bobby and handled the case. The owner's fingerprints prints were confirmed as being all over the drugs, but no prints from Bobby. The owner admitted that Bobby was only driving the car at his request and had nothing to do with the drugs and no knowledge of them being in the car.

Asimov took a liking to Bobby and pushed hard for a small fine and probation, which was granted. But the probation was for ten years. Asimov pulled some strings and got himself appointed as Bobby's probation officer.

Bobby and his aunt lived on the edge of a bad part of the city, and he saw things and heard things. He passed information to Asimov that helped Asimov's career. When he was nineteen, Bobby witnessed a murder. He refused to talk to anyone but Asimov. They worked together and Asimov fed Bobby information as he got it. Bobby watched and listened. It was Bobby who eventually learned the identity of the shooter, but he would only tell Asimov. Asimov broke the case, which was a huge boost for his career, notwithstanding that he was a very capable detective.

About that time, John Candelero had seen the same thing in Bobby over the years of his being Damon's friend that Asimov had, and he took

Bobby into the legitimate side of his parts business. When he started the deli business, he assigned Bobby to help Damon.

~~~

Asimov walked to Bobby, sat across from him and asked, "What's up?"

"You aren't going to believe what I may have for you." Bobby began at the beginning with Damon and Liz. He told about the reason for Hector's attack in the hospital and Damon's continuing obsession with Liz. He explained Damon's repeated threats to sell Liz and kill her boyfriend. He explained Candelero's plan to have Damon committed.

"Uncle John is going to have his lawyer come to someone downtown and tell them that we have information about the attempted murder of the doctor and about human trafficking of the girl. That someone is supposed to be me. Can you work it so you're the person who investigates?"

Asimov nodded. "So, all you have is Gomez rolling on Clark, and a statement by Clark that he is going to sell the girl and that he knows someone who knows someone who traffics in women?"

"I think I'm going to have more than that. I overheard one of Damon's conversations with the guy. Damon called the guy and just gave his name. A few minutes later, the guy called him back, but I didn't hear the conversation."

"And?" Asimov asked.

"Damon is holed up in a hotel. He knows there is an arrest warrant out. He violated a protective order big time. I'm going to meet him at five for dinner. I bought a burner phone and told him Uncle John wants me to get rid of his phone in case he gets arrested. I'm going to trade him phones at dinner. If I've guessed right, there will be a record of his calls to the guy.
~~~

"I know he has made at least two to the guy who will sell the girl, and I know the date and time of one of them. The last one, I'm pretty sure he told the guy to hold off for a while. Can your guys go through his phone and pull off all the numbers he's called in the last month or so?"

"Yes, but that's a lot of work."

"I have an idea that might work. If your guys can pull off the numbers and eliminate the obvious ones, I can use Damon's phone to call the other numbers and imitate him. If the guy calls back, I pretend to be Damon and tell him I want to do it now. I think I can pull it off. Damon and I kind of sound alike sometimes. If I can confirm, then your guys can go to work on the phone number and find the guy."

"It might work. Do you think you've ever met the guy? Would he know your voice?"

"No, idea, but it's worth a try. I don't want to see anything happen to that girl. Damon is just pissed at her because she found out he was fucking around on her and she dumped him.

"And it's not just fucking around on her. He told me he is running prostitutes and has been for a while now. That's who he was fucking; not just some girlfriend he had in another city. The girl doesn't deserve what he wants to do to her. And he has told me twice now that he is going to take the doc out to a rig, wrap him in chains and throw him overboard."

"He isn't a doctor, but he does work in operating rooms."

"Whatever. The threat is real. Can you protect the two of them?"

"If we can prove something, then maybe yes. Until then, they are on their own. Get me the phone and let's see what we can find. But if you reach the guy and tell him you want to go ahead, you are dumping the girl into the grease until we can get permission to protect her. I suggest you tell them you want to hold off"

Bobby nodded. "I'll call you when I leave the restaurant."

"Okay. Anything else?"

"Uncle John is set to get big-time into marijuana."

"We know about the marijuana farm in Colorado. Is that where the stuff comes that you sell in those takeout bags and at the deli?"

Bobby looked surprised.

"I know all about it. And the cookies. You stay away from the weed." He shook his head.

"There is just never enough money for some guys. He'll slip up and lose everything he has. Don't let him get you caught up in that stuff. Stop selling it in the shops. If you get another drug charge, I can't help you."

"I'm going to take over the delis when Damon is gone and we're going to stop the carryout stuff. Uncle John told me I could stop the carryout marijuana traffic and that I could buy the delis at a low interest rate from him. This is my ticket out. I can't believe it."

Asimov smiled. "I'm glad for you, kid. You've had your share of bad breaks. You only have a year left on your probation. Stay away from the weed and don't be in the wrong place at the wrong time again."

Asimov stood. "Call me when you have the phone. It would be nice to put a dent in the human trafficking business in this city."

FORTY-TWO

Bobby arrived at the Mexican restaurant and found Damon already at a table with a beer. He was surprised. Damon appeared calm and cool, even though he knew there was an arrest warrant out for him. They exchanged greetings, ordered, and munched chips and salsa.

"You look relaxed," Bobby observed. "I'd be pretty nervous if I were in your shoes."

Damon shrugged. "It's going to be all right. She's going to waive the cops off and everything will be to be fine."

"Have you talked to her? Did she tell you that?"

"No. But I'm going to talk to her. I'm sure she will understand when we talk."

"What is your plan?"

"We're going to talk tomorrow night. I'm going to her house and we'll talk."

"Okay. That's good," Bobby said. "I hope you work it out. That would be best all around."

Bobby raised a finger. "Oh, yeah. Give me your phone."

Bobby put the new phone in its box on the table for Damon.

"Here is your new one. It's all set up. You just have to program it. "

"Okay, Thanks. I'll just trade SIM cards."

"Whoa. Don't do that. If the cops confiscate your phone and you trade SIM cards, all your old calls and contacts will be on this phone. That's what Uncle John doesn't want to happen."

Damon thought for a minute, then agreed.

"Give me a sec to copy a few numbers I need."

He grabbed a napkin and scrolled through the phone until he found what he wanted and wrote it on the napkin, which he folded and put it in his pocket.

Bobby dropped the old phone into his pocket.

They had another beer and ate. Bobby said he had to go.

When he got back to his office, Bobby scrolled through the phone history on Damon's phone. He found a strange number that didn't look familiar. He checked outgoing calls and that number was on the date he remembered. There was also an incoming call on that date. *No harm in trying.*

He pressed the call button. The phone rang twice and was answered with silence.

"Damon Clark," Bobby said. Remembering what he had seen and heard Damon do, he hung up.

The phone rang four minutes later. Bobby answered and heard silence. "I want to hold off on that thing we talked about," he said tentatively.

The line was silent and he thought he had done something wrong. Then a patient voice said, "Get me pictures of the girl. I'll sit on it for the time being." The line went dead.

He called Asimov. "I have the phone number. I found the number on his phone and tried it. It was the right number." He explained what he had done and the response he got. He gave Asimov the phone number. "If you still want the phone, let me know."

Asimov called back fifteen minutes later. "Put the phone in an envelope and leave it with my name and title at the security desk in the

Allison Tower of Anadarko Petroleum. I'll pick it up. I'll get someone working on the phone number. You did well. I'm glad you didn't paint a bulls-eye on the girl's back." Asimov hung up.

Bobby went to sleep that night worried that he had set a deadly game into motion, but knowing he had done all he could to help.

FORTY-THREE

On Tuesday, June 13, Damon was parked down the street from Liz Barton's home at six-thirty a.m. When she didn't drive out of her driveway by eight-thirty, he left. He returned at four-thirty and waited until eight o'clock. She did not come home.

He went to his office and let himself in. He quickly noticed that Bobby had taken over his office, but it wasn't of concern to him. He turned on his computer and went to the internet where he found the county property tax records. He found property owners named Wade, then by process of elimination began weeding out names outside the Woodlands area. He culled all but four male names. He pulled up a people search application and entered the four names. One was obviously too old, one was probably too old, the other two were possibles–both were William Wade.

He pulled up the online hospital directory of physicians, but the only Wade was a woman. He googled the two addresses of the William Wades he had found. The first William Wade was on the golf course in the middle of The Woodlands. The other William Wade was in a pricey subdivision not far from the hospital. Of course, it could be in the next county, Montgomery County, but he figured the doc would be close to the hospital. Or he could be in an apartment, which would be a problem for him to discover if that were the case.

On Wednesday, Damon drove to both addresses. The first Wade lived in a large, two-story home with a pool and an expensive-looking jungle gym with an attached slide in the back yard. He apparently had a wife and children. Damon moved to the next address. This William Wade lived in a gated community. He could not enter. He thought about it.

The age is right. The residence is in the right economic range. It's a gated community. She is probably afraid of me, so she is probably staying with the doc since she doesn't appear to be at her home.

He was parked across the street from the entrance to the gated community Thursday, the next morning at six-thirty. He knew that her work hours started at eight a.m. He sat, watching. At seven-thirty five, he saw a silver Porsche Cayenne followed by her white BMW stop at the gate. It looked like the doc in the Cayenne and he could see Liz at the wheel in the BMW. He caught what he could read of her license plate number as they went through the gate. Damon pulled into traffic behind the two cars. The Cayenne followed the BMW to Liz's building where she turned into the parking garage and the Cayenne turned away back into traffic.

Isn't that nice; he walks her to school.

She had pulled into the contract-only entrance. Damon entered the Visitor Parking side and drove every floor, Contract and Visitor, to the top and back down. He saw too many white BMWs to even guess which was hers and didn't see any with the partial plate number that he had observed. When he got back to the first floor he saw a ramp for underground parking that was marked RESERVED ONLY and blocked by a metal gate controlled by a card reader. He found a space, parked, and took a chance that the garage wouldn't be patrolled. He entered the elevator, but couldn't get to the lower level without a security card, so he walked down the ramp and walked the aisles. Bingo! There was the partial plate number on a white BMW.

Damon returned at four-thirty. He parked on the street, walked to a bench outside the entrance to the parking garage, and sat. He wore sunglasses and a baseball cap, and he had a newspaper in his hand. He sat as if reading the paper and watched the garage. At five-fifteen, the Cayenne turned into the circular drive in front of her office building. A minute later, a white BMW with Liz driving pulled up the basement parking ramp from the Executive Reserved level and out of the parking garage. It followed the Cayenne into traffic. Damon smiled to himself as he quickly retrieved his car and followed them to the gated community he had found the day before. He waited until they were in, then followed the next car to the gate, and drove inside. He quickly found the address.

He decided the best time would be around seven o'clock after most residents were home from the office and settled in for the evening.

He went for dinner, had a couple of drinks, and drove back to the office. It was empty and he didn't see Bobby's car anywhere. He let himself in. He printed an address label for Wade's address with the word CONFIDENTIAL in capital letters below the address, and a return label with the address of Methodist Hospital-Woodlands. He put them on a large manila envelope, into which he slid a dozen pieces of blank typing paper. He opened the safe and removed a Glock nine-millimeter pistol. A thought struck him and he picked up a clipboard. He typed a list of random names numbered one through twenty, which he clipped on the board. As an afterthought, he picked up a delivery slip from the messenger service used by the deli chain.

He went to a discount store where he bought a plain, black ball cap, black pants and a black golf shirt, a black jacket and some dark sunglasses. He looked around and picked up a clear gel athletic mouthpiece to disguise his mouth and voice. He bought twenty-five feet of cotton rope, a roll of duct tape, and a medium-sized black backpack. He returned to his hideaway and watched some television while he contrived and scribbled assorted signatures for the first eighteen of the twenty names he had typed. The nineteenth name was William Wade. He filled out the messenger service slip in Wade's name with the hospital as the sender and went to bed.

At four o'clock on Friday, Damon dressed in his black clothes, packed the pistol, rope and duct tape in the backpack, picked up his hat, sunglasses, and jacket, and left. He bought a sandwich, fries, and a drink on his way to Wade's subdivision. At five-ten p.m., he followed a car through the gates, where he parked near the entrance in the lot of the community clubhouse. At five-twenty, the Cayenne came through the gate followed by the BMW. Damon ate in his car and read a book, moving twice between then and six forty-five to avoid being conspicuous. He put on the hat, jacket, and sunglasses, and laid the envelope, clipboard with the list and delivery slip on the seat next to him with the backpack.

At six fifty-five, Damon drove onto Wade's driveway. He inserted the mouthpiece, put on his cap and sunglasses, exited his car. He slung the backpack over one shoulder, picked up the clipboard and envelope in hand, and walked to the front door. He checked but didn't see an eye for a video doorbell. He rang the bell.

PART 6

FORTY-FOUR

Liz and I arrived at my home around five-thirty, Friday evening, June 16. We parked in the garage and walked into the house. As she passed the speed bag, she gave it a quick right-hand jab and laughed as it bounced off the backboard with a solid thump.

"Who would have thought that I would learn to use a speed bag and enjoy the workout," she said as she followed me into the house.

"I'm impressed. You've gotten pretty good with that little bag. Maybe we should enter you in some lightweight competition."

She laughed. "I like my nose just where it is, thank you. But I do enjoy the workout."

She dropped her briefcase just inside my study and started toward the bedroom. "It was a long day," she said as she walked down the hall. "I want to get out of these clothes and veg for a few minutes."

I was still in my scrubs.

"Wine?" I asked as she went into the bedroom.

"Oh, yes. You read my mind."

I poured two glasses of chardonnay and carried them to the bedroom as she walked out of the dressing room in bikini panties and bra, with a tank top and shorts in hand. She laid the top and shorts on the bed and I handed a full glass to her.

"Wine for the fetching wench."

She laughed and took a sip. "Why, thank you, my love. You are so sweet."

"My pleasure," I said as she set her glass on a nightstand and kissed me.

I took her in my arms and returned her kiss, probing with my tongue and she responded. I stepped back and gave her an appraising and obvious leer.

"May the girls come out and play."

She smiled coquettishly as she reached back and unhooked her bra, slowly removing it as I watched. She dropped it on the bed, took my wine and set it on the nightstand, then took my hands. She stood on tiptoe and nuzzled my neck, then probed my mouth, as she took my wrists and placed a hand over each breast.

I stroked her nipples and she probed my mouth again. When I leaned down, taking one nipple into my mouth, she arched and moaned.

She stood on tiptoe again and whispered against my ear, "I want you, but I want some wine and dinner first, and then a shower. It was a long hot day and I want to be fresh for you."

"Some say that anticipation is half the pleasure," I responded.

"I'm glad you think so," she said with a giggle. She stepped back and handed me my glass, as she softly said, "I'll make the wait worth your while." Her smile said it all, and I knew she would.

She pulled on her shorts and, sans bra, slipped into the tank top. She quickly brushed her hair out and pulled it up in a ponytail. I held her wine out to her and asked, "In or out?"

"Patio. It's too nice to be inside."

We sat and talked. We refilled our glasses and enjoyed each other's company for a while longer.

"Salad or cook," I asked.

"Salad tonight and grill tomorrow?"

"Works for me."

It has been what… three months. And we're so compatible. She's an amazing girl, Wade.

We finished outside and went to the kitchen. She made a salad as I set the table and poured iced tea. We ate and cleared our dishes. It was nearly seven o'clock.

"What are you going to do?" I asked.

"I want to call Jill. Then…" she paused and gave me a winsome smile, "do you think it's too early for a shower?"

"Not at all. Let me check my email quickly and I'll join you. I think a shower is in order for me as well."

She laughed as she walked toward the bedroom. "See you in the shower," she said with a giggle.

I went to my study and started the computer as the doorbell rang.

I looked out one side panel and saw a beige Toyota sedan parked on the drive. A man was standing a respectful distance from the door. He wore dark sunglasses and was dressed in black pants, a black shirt, a black jacket, and a black cap. He had a medium-sized backpack slung over one shoulder and was holding a clipboard and a large envelope with labels on it.

He held up the envelope and said, "Delivery for William Wade from…." he looked at the envelope, "Methodist Hospital."

He sounded as though he had a mild speech impediment. I could just read my name and address on the envelope label. He held up the clipboard and I could see a page with several names and signatures, with two names lacking signatures at the bottom.

"You have to sign for it, please."

I opened the door. He stepped to me, handed me the envelope, then handed me the clipboard, and stepped back. I tucked the envelope under one arm took the clipboard. I didn't see a pen. "Do you have a pen?" I asked.

He looked at the clipboard in surprise. "Oh, I must have dropped it somewhere. I'm sorry. Do you have one?

"Sure," I said and stepped back into the room turning toward my study.

He stepped into the house, wedged his foot against the door, reached inside his jacket and withdrew a semiautomatic pistol.

"It's okay, Doc. You don't have to sign it."

When he called me doc, the hair went up on the back of my neck. I turned to look at him as he stepped inside, staying out of reach, and closed the door. He removed his hat and sunglasses, and a sports mouth guard from his mouth.

Way to go, Wade. You just got suckered like an amateur. Your hands are full and Liz is back there naked.

I heard Liz's voice from down the hall. I could see that he heard her voice and knew approximately where in the house she was. He looked down the hall toward the bedroom. Her voice continued and I realized that she was talking to Jill. I didn't hear the shower, so I knew that, thankfully, she was still dressed.

He nodded toward a wing chair across the room and said quietly, "Sit in the chair. Put your hands under your butt and sit on them. Stretch your legs out in front of you and cross your ankles.

He was too far away to reach and I had Liz to worry about. I put the envelope and the clipboard on the coffee table and did as he said.

He nodded toward the hallway.

"Get her out here."

I started to yell to her that Damon was here in hopes that she would tell Jill to get help, but I heard her say goodbye before I could speak. I did the next best thing in hopes she would call 911.

"Liz, Damon is here,'" I said loudly.

I heard her coming down the hall. Damon stepped back against the wall as she stepped into view and said, "I'm sorry. What did you say."

I saw that she was still holding her phone.

Well, shit. So much for 911.

Then, she saw Damon holding the gun and screamed.

FORTY-FIVE

Damon did something surprising. He told Liz to stand with her back against the wall and not move. She looked at me and I nodded. She did as he told her. I didn't understand what he intended to do. He pulled his phone out of his jacket pocket, tapped it one-handed, and took two pictures of Liz. Then, he told her to stand on her toes and reach toward the ceiling and not move.

What the hell is that all about?

She looked at me again and I nodded. She did as he told her and he took two more pictures. He told her again not to move as he stepped closer to her and took two face shots. Then, he pocketed his phone. All the while, he maintained his grip on the pistol.

He told Liz to close the shutters in the living room. She did so without a word.

He reached in his backpack and pulled out two short coils of rope and a roll of masking tape, which he laid on the table between them. He told her to tape my mouth. She refused. He threatened to shoot me and I nodded my head to her.

She took the tape, tore off a section, and put it over my mouth. When she finished, he tossed her one coil of rope, telling her to tie my hands. She did and he tossed her the other coil and told her to tie my crossed ankles together as they were. He held the gun menacingly and I nodded to her.

We were up the creek and the paddle was floating away.

When she had tied me as loosely as she could without being obvious, he told her to sit in the matching wing chair. She did.

What he did next again surprised me.

"Would you like something to drink," he asked her as if she were a guest in his home.

Confused, she repeated him questioningly. "Something to drink?"

"Sure. We need to talk. I thought you might like something to drink."

She still looked confused. "No, thank you. Would you like something?"

"Maybe later," he replied conversationally.

He sat on the couch facing the wing chairs across a coffee table. To the right of the couch was a loveseat that faced the fireplace and formed the base of a horseshoe with the couch and the chairs. I was in the chair to Damon's right; Liz in the chair to his left, by the fireplace.

"It's been a while since we've seen each other," he said. "You look well."

Liz was silent.

"How is Jill," he asked as if he had just stopped by to inquire about her health.

I saw a thoughtful look cross Liz's face. She looked at Damon and replied conversationally, "She is healing nicely. It was a terrible accident, but we're optimistic that she will have a full recovery."

She smoothed her hair back, and asked, "How have you been?"

"Good," he said. "Good. Business has been good. This thing with the Court has become a real pain, but we'll get to that.

"I guess you're with the doc now?" He nodded toward me. "Is that right?"

Lis nodded. "Yes. That's right."

"Yeah, well, that's what I want to talk to you about."

"If you really want to talk, please put the gun down. I don't think a conversation at gunpoint is going to be very fruitful."

He paused. Then, another surprise as he said, "Sure," and laid the pistol on the couch cushion next to him.

"Better?" he asked.

She nodded. "Yes," she said firmly.

"We need to talk," he said. "You never got to know much about me. I think you should know who I am."

He conversationally leaned toward her and began talking.

"My grandfather is Damon Candelero. He lives in Dallas and owns car dealerships. He is a millionaire. His son, my uncle John Candelero lives in Houston and owns car dealerships. He is also a millionaire. Uncle John set me up in the delicatessen business. He learned the business when he was in college. He owned a delicatessen here in Dallas while he was in college, then came here and built it up to three. He's a great guy.

"My mother is a good-looking, rich, spoiled brat who spent a lot of time at SMU, didn't graduate, disappointed grandpa, and got knocked up by the quarterback of the football team, who had about as many brains as those footballs he threw. He got hooked on drugs and no one knows where he is."

In summary, Clark spent the next half hour extolling himself, painting himself as a lost boy whose father abandoned him and whose mother didn't care about him. He recounted his life from the age of three to date. Liz listened patiently without interrupting him. When he finally ran out of family history and his life, he started on the delicatessens and how successful they were. He told Liz how much he made each year and on and on. I was surprised at the income generated by those delicatessens.

She finally asked him what his point was.

"I'm trying to make you understand how good I can be for you. I can give you anything you want. We can have a big home and a kid or two. I'm going to be someone in Houston, maybe in Texas. I have plans and I want you to be part of them."

"Why me, Damon. We barely know each other."

"That's why I'm here. I want you to know who I am and how good I can be for you. I can give you anything you want."

"Damon, I don't want a man who can be good <u>for</u> me. I want a man who can be good <u>with</u> me, together with me. You've shown me you aren't trustworthy. I don't want a boyfriend who has a girl in every city and I certainly don't want a husband who is a philanderer."

"But…"

"Damon, there is no but. We have nothing in common. We had a few dates. You were off every other weekend with a woman in another city. We have no common interests. We have no foundation for a relationship, let alone a marriage. I'm sure you know many women who would be very happy to have a relationship with such a generous man."

"You can't just dump me like that," he whined.

"Damon, I didn't dump you. There was nothing to dump. You cut your own throat with Melissa in San Antonio and whoever it was in Austin, not to mention whoever else you were seeing in Houston."

"I wasn't seeing anyone else in Houston."

"Oh, nice," Liz retorted. "There was one city in Texas where there wasn't someone else"

I saw his face flush and his eyes grew hard.

"You're a cold fish. You're not even worth my effort," he shouted angrily.

"Then leave. Why are you even here?"

"Because we could be good together. I could be good for you," he shouted.

"Damon, you aren't listening. I'm not interested. It's that simple."

"You can't just dump me like that, you fucking bitch," he screamed, red-faced as he bolted off the couch and around the coffee table in a quick heartbeat.

Her reaction was priceless and impressive. Liz, apprehension but no fear on her face, stood to meet his attack. She took one quick step away from him, her eyes watching his hands, as she readied to defend herself.

His first mistake was thinking this was like the movies.

"You bitch," Damon shouted again as lunged toward her, grabbing the front edge of her tank top in the center with his right hand and pulling down hard. Surprisingly, it didn't rip, as I'm sure he thought it would.

Two things happened in quick succession. One bare breast was momentarily fully displayed and Damon was distracted. Like any guy, he looked–and didn't see her hand coming at him. His momentum and the effort he exerted had caused him to pull himself slightly into her as she deftly drove the heel of her right hand into his nose as firmly as if she had struck the speed bag.

I heard the simultaneous wet crunch of cartilage and his painful yelp as a spout of blood burst from his nose. His head swung to his right as she drove through just as I had taught her, then backhanded his nose again with the edge of her fist. He yelped again and she grabbed his right hand that was caught in the neck of her top, pulled him to her, and head-butted his bloody nose. He wailed and cursed as she immediately dropped her head to his right hand and bit into his thumb like a bull terrier. I saw blood seep around her teeth.

He cried out and jerked backward, pulling his hand free, which threw him off balance. He flailed like he was swatting mosquitos. As he struggled to regain his footing, he crashed backward into the coffee table, grabbing Liz's hair as he fell and pulling her with him. She fell on top of him, hitting him in the nose again as she went down and rolled to her right.

He yelped in pain again.

"You bitch," he screamed as he lashed out at her with a fist, catching her on one side of her face before he hit the edge of the coffee table.

She yelped in pain, scrambling up and away from him as he grunted and grimaced with the pain. He struggled to rise after Liz, but she was quicker than he. She pushed herself up and saw it at the same time I did.

The pistol was still where he left it, on the couch cushion. She spun around him toward the pistol, grabbing it by the handle as she turned toward him, sidestepping to her right, away from his attempt to rise–and amazed me again.

She flicked the safety off, smacked the base of the magazine with the heel of her free hand, racked the pistol, ejecting the round that had been in the chamber and seating a fresh round. She swung the pistol into line with his center mass as he tried to rise and lunge at her. Fortunately, he lunged away from me to get around the table to her.

She fired once.

He grunted with the impact of the shot, and then howled in pain as I saw spreading blood stain his left waist. He grabbed his wound, lurched, and stood dazed for a second, almost as if he couldn't believe she had shot him. Then, he glared at her.

"You fucking bitch. You shot me," he yelled with disbelief. "I'll get you for this," he shouted, as he turned and stumbled for the door.

"Stop," Liz shouted.

"You won't shoot me in the back," Damon yelled over his shoulder as he disappeared through the door.

Liz flipped the safety on and came to me. I just stared at her. She later told me that she had never seen such a huge, lopsided grin as I wore.

We heard his car start and peel out of the driveway.

It was obvious that Liz was wired. She was a bundle of energy. Her hands were shaking and her arms were twitching and swinging randomly.

She was trying to move in four directions at one time and she couldn't focus her gaze. And my first thought was, *RJ should have seen that.*

"Let me lock the door. Then I'll untie you," she gasped.

As she untied me, she began shaking all over like a leaf. I knew it wasn't fear. She was experiencing a bona fide adrenalin rush. I stripped the tape off my mouth as she pulled the ropes free. She grabbed me, pulled me to her with the strength of a bear, and ran her tongue down my throat.

"Do you think he'll come back," she asked hoarsely.

"No. He is wounded. You have a gun. He doesn't."

"Oh my God, I feel as though I'm going to explode, like the top of my head is going to come off and my heart is going to come out of my chest," she moaned.

"It's the adrenalin," I told her. "You're wired and you're going to be wired for a while–until it wears off."

"Then take me to bed," she moaned. "Wear me out!"

My thought, exactly!

She dropped the gun onto the couch, grasped one wrist, and drug me down the hall. In the bedroom, she quickly stripped me with shaking hands, then herself, breathing heavily the whole time.

She gasped a quick, "Oh, God, Dub," as she pulled me down on top of her, greedily fed me into her, and we made love like it was rutting season. She was on a mission and I was along for the ride–and what a ride it was! She moaned and mewled eagerly as she writhed and squirmed against me with a purpose.

She came in a great burst of sound and passion, gripping me tightly, as though she expected me to try to escape. She gasped, groaned in emotional release, and still in a frenzy, again pulled me to her. She peaked a second time with gusto, wrapping her legs around me and grasping my shoulders single-mindedly, gasping for air until she finally drew a long, deep breath, then another and exhaled as slowly as if she were dying.

When she finally began to come down, she said softly, "Hold me. Just hold me."

I did. We were soaking wet from perspiration, and she still quivered from the effects of the adrenalin and her breaths still came in little, urgent gasps.

After a minute, she looked up and into my eyes as she asked earnestly, "Do you think we should call the sheriff now?"

I couldn't help it. I roared with laughter!

She looked perplexed until the irony of what she had said hit her, and she quickly joined in the laughter. I could see on her face that the laughter had just taken some more of the last of the sharp edge of the adrenalin rush off her nerves.

"Get dressed, Joe Louis. I'll call."

As we were dressing, I saw flashing lights in the street. I called 911 and was told that there had already been a report from our subdivision of a gunshot and a car was on the premises. I told the dispatcher I could see it. She took my information and said another car was on its way.

I left the gun where Liz had dropped it. I marked the ejected shell and the empty casing as Liz poured two glasses of wine. Damon's fingerprints had to be all over the spent casing and the rounds in the magazine.

As we waited for an officer to come, I looked at her and shook my head. "Where did you learn to handle a pistol like that?"

"Phillip. He was in the Corp of Cadets and he was a Ranger. He knew all about guns. He taught me about pistols shortly after we started dating. We shot often at a range outside College Station. We also shot skeet and he taught me how to shoot a deer rifle. He even gave me a handgun."

"I was impressed. I was really impressed that you had been taught to rack an unfamiliar gun rather than chance trying to fire on an empty chamber."

She looked at the gun. "I just racked it without thinking. Habit."

"Lady, I hope you are never mad at me."

"Rumor has it that you know how to take care of yourself. I just had two good instructors."

The doorbell rang and we spent the next two hours with police officers, then detectives.

We told everything just as it happened–except the very last part. We walked them through the sequence of events. As Liz was explaining about shooting Damon and him running out, one detective scanned the wall behind where Damon had been.

"Slug is in the wall; it went through him." He dug it out.

Liz told about the pictures. When she was asked how she had overpowered Clark, she complimented me as her instructor.

They collected the gun, the spent slug, the ejected casing, took pictures and said good night.

FORTY-SIX

When everyone was gone, I drove Liz to the hospital, where an ER nurse checked her. She had the beginning of a black eye and a big blue bruise on her cheek below the eye, and a large bruise on the heel of her right palm. The nurse gave her an ice pack for each and the ER doctor gave her a mild pain reliever.

As we drove home, she took my hand and asked, "Did I embarrass myself?"

It took me a second or two before her meaning sunk in.

"No, ma'am! You handled yourself like a pro. That was one class A, bona fide, big-league adrenalin rush. And they usually always happen after a barroom brawl. You did not embarrass yourself. You earned that rush."

"I've never experienced anything like that."

"Well, at least you knew what to do with it. That was incredible sex!" Which was really the basis of her question.

Out of the corner of my eye, I could see her smirk and then grin from ear to ear. She leaned toward me, kissed my cheek, and said brightly, "Yes. It was, wasn't it?"

We laughed heartily.

"Dub, who is Joe Louis?"

"Joe Louis was one of the greatest heavyweight boxers of all time. He was the world heavyweight boxing champ from 1937 to 1949. He was known as the Brown Bomber. He is best known for two fights with Max Smelling, a German. In the first fight, Smelling beat Louis in twelve rounds. In the second, Louis won by a knockout in the first round.

"Really," she mused. "I like that," she said with a giggle.

"Why do you think he took those pictures of me?"

"No idea. That didn't make sense."

"What do you think he intended to do with us? He had to have had some plan or objective in mind."

"He had a gun, but he didn't seem that intent on using it. Maybe he was just trying to scare you into submission and scare me away from you—and the latter isn't happening!"

"Nor the former," she said emphatically. "I think he has some serious emotional problems. He went from Jekyll to Hyde without any warning."

"Yeah. I think a psychiatrist could make a case study out of that guy."

I set the home alarm system and checked all the doors and windows, just in case. She cuddled close to me in bed and asked, as she rolled me onto my back, "Should we rest on our laurels or see if we have any adrenalin left?"

Silly question.

FORTY-SEVEN

Damon Clark was in pain. He carefully maneuvered into the slow lane and drove cautiously. He pulled onto the shoulder once because his vision was blurred and he had to wait until it cleared. He drove carefully to his rented apartment. Inside, he swallowed a shot of bourbon and called Bobby, who answered sleepily.

"Bobby, it's Damon. I need some help, man"

"Uh, yeah, sure. What do you need?"

"I've been shot. I don't think it's too bad, but I need gauze, alcohol, antibacterial ointment and tape. Can you bring me some?"

"'Yeah. Where are you?"

"The apartment." Damon gave him the address. I'll leave the door unlocked."

He hung up and called the number. It rang twice and was answered with silence.

"Damon Clark," Damon said clearly. "I had to get a new phone. He recited the number and hung up."

The phone rang and he answered.

"I want to do this thing now.'

There was a brief pause. The voice asked, "Are you sure this time?"

Damon didn't register the underlying meaning of the question. "Yeah."

"Do you have pictures?"

"Yeah."

"Text them to this number. I'll let you know."

Before the line went dead, Damon quickly said, "What's your name?"

There was a long pause. "You can call me Marco."

"Okay, Marco. I'm out of commission for a while. You'll have to get the girl. Forget the guy for now unless you can take it out of my fifty thousand, but get the girl."

"What do you mean, 'out of commission'?"

"I'm going to be arrested, but I need to lay low for as long as I can."

"What did you do?"

"I went to the girl's house. I did a stupid thing and she shot me."

"Did you harm her?"

"No. Just scared her."

There was another long pause.

"All right," Marco replied, "but this time only."

Damon gave Liz's name and address and where she worked. He texted the pictures, then laid his head back, closed his eyes, and passed out.

Bobby arrived and found the correct unit. He let himself in and saw Damon. "Holy shit!"

He checked to see if Damon was breathing, then called John Candelero.

"Uncle John, I'm with Damon. He's been shot and he's passed out in a chair."

"Is it bad?"

"It looks like it went through the fatty part of his left waist. It looks pretty bloody, but I don't think it hit any vital organs. His shirt is soaked. And it looks like someone beat his face pretty good, too."

"Call 911. Whatever he has done, we'll use it to our advantage. Keep me advised."

Bobby punched in 911.

He noticed Damon's phone on the arm of the chair and looked at it. He started to pick it up, then better judgment prevailed. He tapped the screen with his knuckle and the sent message screen popped up with three pictures attached, all of a woman who looked like the description Damon had once given him of Liz Barton.

"What the hell," he muttered.

He left the phone as it was, not wanting his fingerprints on it. He called Asimov and quickly explained about the shooting and the texted pictures.

"I'll wait for the report to come in and see who is working the call out. Don't touch the phone. I'll look at it when it gets in here," Asimov advised.

Two sheriff's deputies and an ambulance arrived at the same time. Damon was loaded onto a gurney and into the ambulance as the deputies interviewed Bobby. They asked for Damon's name and he told them. One deputy nodded to the other and the other went outside.

Bobby told what little he could. One deputy carefully put the phone in a plastic bag, which he sealed. He was asked if anyone else knew.

"I called his uncle, who is his only family here in Houston."

"Who is his uncle?"

"John Candelero. Is it okay to call him and tell him where Damon was taken?"

"The officer nodded. "Methodist Hospital in the Woodlands."

Bobby called Candelero and conveyed the information.

"Saul and I will go to the hospital. You go home when you can. I'll call you later," Candelero instructed him.

The second deputy returned. "He has a juvie file and an outstanding warrant for two violations of a protective order. Lady's name is Elizabeth Barton. There is a report that Clark came to her home earlier, tied up her boyfriend, and assaulted her. She shot him and he ran."

The first deputy asked if Bobby knew Elizabeth Barton. "I have never met her. Damon dated her briefly several months ago. I don't know anything about the protective order except that it's out there. And I don't know anything about what happened earlier. I was asleep when he called me. He told me he had been shot, but he didn't say who shot him or why. He was passed out when I got here."

"Did you ever hear him make threats toward the woman?"

Bobby didn't know what to say until Candelero's plan popped into his head. He realized this was the perfect opening. "Yes. He threatened to hurt her and her boyfriend."

"Did he say how?"

As the question was asked, Vastian Asimov walked in in the door, and Bobby breathed a sigh of relief.

"I'll take it from here, guys. Tell me what you have."

FORTY-EIGHT

Asimov went outside with the deputies who relayed what Bobby had told them. The deputies left and Asimov returned.

"Good," he said. "They don't know about the threat to sell her. As you called, a report came in that Clark had invaded a home where Barton was staying tonight and she shot him. The report of your call came in. I figured I needed to get out here right away.

"Now, I want you to tell me everything you told me before about selling her and the threats made by Clark. Tell it as if I had never heard it before and remember what you tell me this time, not what you told me before. We never had a previous conversation."

Bobby did as he was instructed and Asimov took notes, nodding his head as Bobby talked. When Bobby finished, he said, "There's something else, something new. Look at his phone."

Asimov pulled on a latex glove and removed the phone from the evidence bag.

"Tap the screen," Bobby instructed.

Asimov did and the three pictures and the text appeared. "This must be Barton. Nice-looking girl." He looked closer at the screen, then at Bobby. "Holy shit! Am I seeing this right? The message indicates he texted these to someone and my guess is to the guy who is supposed to buy her!"

Bobby nodded. "That's what it looks like to me. That should help your case at both ends, shouldn't it?"

"You bet your ass it will. This is good. This is really good, Duvall. You did well."

"Thanks. I called that number like we talked about and told the person to hold off for now."

"This text may have started it up again, but we have no way of knowing."

Asimov nodded, dropped the phone into the evidence bag, and put it in his pocket.

"And one more thing you should know."

Bobby told Asimov about Candelero's plan to get Damon arrested and committed. "He wants me to do exactly what you want me to do."

Asimov grinned. "Sometimes things do work out right! Let's hope there is something in this for you, as well."

He patted his pocket to ensure he had the phone.

"Okay. I'm going to close this place up. You go home. I'll call you when we need you. Get in touch if there are any problems." He paused. "Does Candelero know about any of this?"

Bobby nodded. "He knows about the shooting, but he doesn't know about the pictures."

FORTY-NINE

By the time Damon's wound, as well as his nose, had been assessed and treated in the emergency room, John Candelero and Saul Stein were standing at the nurse's station outside the ER. Saul had left a phone message for the District Attorney and faxed to him a letter of representation for Damon Clark, both communications bearing an admonition that Clark was not to be questioned without Stein or an attorney in his firm being present.

Damon was moved to a secure room, handcuffed to the bed and an officer was stationed outside his door. When all the hospital staff were out of the room, Candelero and Stein were allowed in for ten minutes alone with Damon.

Stein looked at Damon, spoke with him, and verified that Damon could understand him and was coherent.

"I only have ten minutes. Listen carefully and answer my questions as briefly as you can. Don't lie to me and don't make up shit," Stein admonished.

"Where were you when you were shot?"

"The doc's home. Liz was there with him."

"Who are Liz and the Doc?"

"Elizabeth Barton, an old girlfriend, and her boyfriend, a doctor named Wade."

"How did you know she was there?"

"I had been following her. I always knew where she was."

"How did you know she was there that night?"

"I followed them there from her office."

"Where is his home?"

Damon told him.

"Is that a gated community?"

"Yeah."

"How did you get in?"

"I followed someone in, then pretended to be a delivery guy to get him to open the door."

"Did you threaten him with the gun?"

"I showed it to him and told him to sit in a chair."

"Did he?"

"Yeah."

"Why were you there?"

"I wanted to talk to her about getting back together and dropping the protective order."

"Were you in violation of the protective order when you went there?"

Damon was silent, then mumbled something unintelligible.

"We don't have time for bullshit, Damon. Were you in violation of the protective order when you went there?"

"Yeah."

"Did she have a gun?"

Again, Damon was silent until Candelero ordered him to answer.

"No."

"But you had a gun?"

"Yeah."

"And she took it."

"Yeah."

"Did she shoot you with your own gun?"

Damon looked embarrassed. "Yeah."

"Did she have a gun of her own?"

"No."

"So, you went there with a gun. She was unarmed, and she shot you with your gun. Is that right?"

"Yeah."

"How did she get your gun?"

"I laid it on the couch. She got it before I could get it."

"Did you verbally threaten her life?"

"Not really. She told me she would talk to me if I laid the gun down. I did and she got it."

"Did you struggle over the gun?"

"Not really. I grabbed her before she got the gun. Then, she hit me and got the gun, and shot me. I ran out of the house."

"So, do I understand you correctly: you went to her home with a gun, you laid the gun down and were no longer a threat to her, then you struck her, she struck you back, got your gun and shot you with it?

"Yeah."

"Did you send Hector to threaten the doctor?"

"I just told him to scare the guy away from Liz."

"What instructions did you give Hector?"

"I don't remember. I just told him to scare the guy so that he would leave Liz alone."

"Did you ever threaten the doctor?"

"I told him to watch his back, but I never straight out threatened him."

The pain killers they had given Damon began to take effect about the time that the deputy told them their time was up.

They agreed to meet at the hospital at nine the next morning.

PART 7

FIFTY

On Friday, June sixteenth, Marco looked at the pictures on his phone. He stared at Liz's figure, arms upraised, and a defiant look on her face. Her breasts stood out, full and firm against the fabric of her top. Her upraised arms caused a band of firm, tanned flesh to show above the waistline of her shorts. He stared at the smooth, tan skin and imagined what was just below it.

Nice. Very nice. It's too bad I will never get a chance to have her. She should bring a good price.

Marco re-routed the pictures of Elizabeth to a number he knew well. He waited ten minutes, then called the number.

The phone rang at the other end and a woman's voice answered softly in Russian, "Da?"

"Etoh Marco," he replied in Russian. Then, in English, "Did he receive the pictures?"

"Yes. He was pleased. His instructions are to arrange for nude photographs of her as soon as you have her. As soon as he gets final approval from the buyer, we will give you transportation arrangements. Do not damage her; it took two weeks for the bruises to heal on the last woman. Get her drugged before she can struggle."

"Okay. Clark says he will be out of commission for a while and wants us to take the fee for the guy out of his cut of the sale. I said yes.

We can sell his heart or liver or kidneys. If the buyer doesn't want her, she will easily sell to someone else. She is very beautiful."

"I will tell him. What about the blonde model?"

"I am ready to go on her, but I think we should wait. She is either gaining weight or is pregnant. Either way, she is not going to be marketable."

"I will tell him."

Marco pondered Clark's call over the weekend. On Monday, he called his lawyer and told him that he needed to know everything about Damon Clark.

An hour later, he learned of the protective order against Clark, that he had been arrested for illegal possession of firearms and malicious trespass with more charges to come, the details of the incident at Wades' home, her address, the address of Dub Wade, and the name of Clark's lawyer. He also learned that Clark had a sealed juvenile file.

"Keep me up to date on any additional charges against him, and especially if my name or the name Marco appears in any of his statements or his file."

He considered the situation. Clark had his assumed name and his phone number, but not his real name nor any personal information about him. Clark had the name of the girl.

It might be better to pass on this girl, but half a million dollars is a lot of money, he thought. *I'll make my plans, but wait to see what happens by the end of the week.*

FIFTY-ONE

John Candelero called Bobby on his way to Saul Stein's office Saturday morning. He brought Bobby up to date as well as he could and instructed him to focus solely on the deli business until further notice. He asked what Bobby knew about Liz Barton.

"Until last night, I didn't know much more than I have already told you. He dated her for about three months, fucked around on her and she dumped him. After she did, he seemed obsessed with her. He thought she would be his ticket to respectability if he could just get her to marry him. He doesn't love her; he just wants her for what he thinks she can give him. So he sent Hector to scare the doc off. He threatened to get even with her and to dump the doc offshore somewhere. I learned last night that he plans to have her kidnapped and sold."

"Sold? What do you mean, sold, Bobby?"

"He told me he knows a guy who buys women and sells them to rich guys. I don't know any more than that, but that was what he said he was going to do when I talked to him last night. What do I do if the cops ask me about any threats he has made. I don't want to be an accessory to human trafficking."

"Let me talk to Saul. I'm going to meet him now. I'll call you when we are finished."

When they were seated in Stein's office, Candelero brought Stein current on what Bobby had told him. "What do I tell Bobby?"

"Let me think and talk at the same time," Stein responded. "On the positive side, this about covers our plan for Damon. The DA can charge him with violating a protective order, kidnapping, illegally possessing a firearm, fraud, criminal trespass, threatening bodily harm, physical assault, and battery. There is nothing I can do for him except plead insanity or try to get a reduced sentence. The boy is going to prison for this. I see no way around it.

"If he talks too much, he could endanger your businesses. I think you are well enough insulated that the worst you would get would be a slap on the wrist, maybe minor charges as an accessory for trafficking in stolen goods, and a drug charge for the marijuana in the delis, but we can withstand that. I see no way you can be tied to his plans for the woman and her boyfriend.

"I won't let him near a plea bargain that would incriminate you or me in any way. And he can't afford a lawyer with the stroke to get him out of this. As far as you are concerned, I intend to tell him he is going to have to pay his attorney fees because I can't have your name associated with this. So, he will have to accept what we can do for him and take his lumps."

"Tell him he has to cover the first fifty thousand. If it goes over that, I'll pick it up."

"Frankly, I don't think it will. A jury will never see this. I'll try to get us in and out as gracefully and expeditiously as I can."

"Thanks. I agree with what you've said. I've been contemplating getting on the wrong side of the marijuana business for more than two years, but I gave everything a lot of thought last night. I make a nice income from the legal marijuana I grow in Colorado, the car dealerships are profitable. I could deal with the hit from stolen cars and auto parts. And what we make in the delis brings in a nice chunk of change. What we make from selling a little marijuana was good for Damon and Bobby, but not worth the chance of it going south for me.

"It may be time to go straight. I have enough to live comfortably–very comfortably–the rest of my life. And I've offered to sell Bobby the deli business."

Saul nodded his head. "It seems we've talked our way to a happy ending as far as Damon is concerned. But, we need to think about the girl. If his threat is just bravado, we can shut him up pretty quickly. But, if he has actually set the wheels in motion, we need to be very careful. I don't want to see a young woman sold into a life of sexual slavery, but I also don't want to look like we tried to cover anything up. Unless he tells me about his plan, then we're better off if we don't do anything.

"If I can get Damon to talk to me about his plans, I can ethically report it to the authorities since Damon was in the process of committing or intended to commit a crime and/or intended to further the crime or to cover it up. I will see what he has to say this afternoon."

FIFTY-TWO

Monday morning, June 19, Vastian Asimov met with Janice Evans and Arvin Choksi regarding the events of Friday night at the home of William Wade. Evans asked Asimov if he had anything he could add to his report or that he could add about what they knew of Clark's involvement in the Gomez case.

"As a matter of fact, I do. I have a confidential informant who knows Clark very well. He has informed me of two facts that we should know—and of a planned crime that we need to address. My source tells me that it was, in fact, Damon Clark who solicited the attack on Mr. Wade. My source said that the intent was not to actually harm Wade but to scare him away from Ms. Barton. Barton dated Clark briefly, learned that he was cheating on her and ended the relationship, which Clark did not handle well.

"My source also advised me that Clark wanted some revenge or retribution on Barton for dumping him. He told me that Clark told him he intended to sell Barton and to kill Wade and dump him in the Gulf wearing chains."

At that moment his phone rang and he excused himself to answer, saying this was a call he was expecting would be helpful to Evans. He spoke for only a long moment, asked that the information be emailed immediately to Evans's office, hung up, and turned to Evans and Choksi.

"Bear with me. We need to do this in sequence, I think. Last night, at the scene, I found Clark's phone sitting on the arm of the chair he had apparently been sitting in. The phone was on and I tapped the screen. Up popped photographs of Barton. As you saw in my report, she reported that Clark had made her stand, told her how to pose, and had taken pictures of her. The pictures clearly showed her figure and how attractive she is. Barton told me she had no idea why Clark made her do that, but that she complied because Wade was bound to a chair and Clark threatened to shoot him if she did not comply."

The computer on Evans's desk chimed and Asimov asked her to check her email. She did.

"It's from the lab. Clark's fingerprints are all over the gun and shell casings in the magazine. Barton's prints are on the handle and trigger only. The email says to tell you that they are still working on the phone numbers on the phone, and are concentrating on the number to which the photographs were sent. And there are photographs attached, which…," she paused as she brought the attachments up… "are of Barton just as you described," she said as she swiveled the monitor toward Asimov and Choksi. The photographs were as described by Asimov and showed serious tension on Barton's face, as well as her beauty and figure.

Asimov nodded and said, "These pictures were texted to a cell phone number that we are trying to identify. It is my opinion that the person at that number was either a buyer of Barton or someone who was going to kidnap and then sell Barton.

"As we all know, human trafficking has become a significant problem in our city, and in the past fifteen months, we have lost far too many young women who have simply disappeared without a credible trace. I think Clark's phone may be the lead we need to build many of our missing person cases and get a threat out of our jurisdiction.

"I don't know if Gomez has any relevant knowledge, but I think we need to lean heavily on him and Clark, and scare the shit out of both of them."

Evans called Saul Stein and advised him that she wanted to interview Clark at one o'clock Tuesday afternoon and Gomez thereafter. Stein agreed.

FIFTY-THREE

Liz and I received calls from Janice Evans, the District Prosecutor, on Monday morning. She asked us to meet with her that afternoon and we agreed. Liz's bruises and a black eye were obvious.

Interestingly, when we arrived Arvin Choksi was there, also. Evans told us that Choksi was handling my case involving Hector Gomez and that she would be handling Damon's case with Choksi's assistance since it appears that Damon Clark was a significant figure in both cases. She noted the fact that she had read the transcript of my recorded statement to Choksi and that she had read the report of Detective Asimov of the events of last night. She advised us that she would like to take a statement from each of us about both the Gomez and the Clark cases that day and that we could not be together during the statements. When she told us that it would probably take the rest of the day and into the evening for both of us, I booked a room for us at a nearby hotel that night.

I knew Liz would be nervous and I wanted her to get it behind her, so I suggested she go first. Evans agreed. When Liz was finished, Evans had an officer drive her to the hotel and he returned with me. I finished at seven-thirty. As I was leaving, Evans asked if we would join her for breakfast the next morning. She said she would meet us at the hotel at eight-thirty.

I called Liz and was driven to the hotel. It was a very long day for both of us, but we agreed that we had told virtually everything we knew about the two incidents and Clark.

When I knocked on the door, she opened it for me. I was concerned that she might be upset, but she greeted me with a warm smile, pulled me inside with her, and fell into my arms. We kissed and held each other as we both decompressed. Just as I was about to suggest the perfect solution for stress relief, there was a knock at our door and an announcement of Room Service. I opened the door and was greeted by a young man with a cart bearing a chilled bottle of champagne in an ice bucket and a plate of apple slices, cheese, and crackers.

"I thought we could both use a glass of champagne and I thought you might be a little hungry," she said knowingly. She was right on both counts.

We drank champagne, munched, talked of the day, avoided talk of either of the incidents that had consumed our day, and teased convincingly. We skipped dinner for a later room service snack. We stripped, hung our clothes to air out, and let some of the wrinkles ease, showered, and made love long enough to leave the day way behind us. We fell soundly asleep, naked and warm against each other.

The next morning, we were in the restaurant with full coffee cups when Evans entered. I poured coffee for her as she sat and announced that her department would take care of our hotel bill. We ordered and talked easily through a pleasant breakfast, learning that she was a single mother of a daughter who was a cheerleader and in the National Honor Society. When the plates were cleared, she asked for another carafe of coffee and looked at us seriously.

"We are concerned that before Clark was arrested, he may have set into motion some act against the two of you. We are investigating and at the moment, I cannot say much more. Without some hard evidence, we can't authorize protection for you, but I want to stress to both of you to keep your eyes open and avoid being in situations where you are alone until we know more. If you see anyone who looks threatening or who acts suspiciously, don't hesitate. Dial 911 and tell the operator to get a message to me immediately.

"For the next week or two, I suggest you stay in the gated community and go only to work. I suggest you have your groceries delivered. Tell the heads of security at your jobs what I just told you, give them my name and number and be vigilant. We should know within a week if there is a reason for concern."

Evans turned to me. "Mr. Wade, I have a question for you. We want to discuss a plea bargain with Mr. Gomez on this case in hopes of learning more about Clark's plans concerning Ms. Barton. Would you be willing to drop your charges, or agree to minimal punishment for him if he can be helpful to us?"

"I never believed that Gomez intended to harm me. I think he was a witless pawn for Clark. I have thought that since he walked out of the stairwell into the hallway behind me," I replied. "No problem. I will agree to anything that helps put an end to what Liz is going through right now."

She thanked me and told us she would be in touch.

FIFTY-FOUR

On Monday morning, June nineteenth, Saul Stein spoke with Janice Evans. He listened carefully as Evans listed the charges against Damon Clark, which included assault with a deadly weapon, unlawful possession of a weapon, kidnapping and unlawful restraint, trespass, malicious trespass, battery, three counts of violation of a protective order, violation of probation and several other minor and/or ancillary causes of action.

"What are we looking at?" he asked.

"My initial thought is twenty-five years. Except for the fact that he didn't fire the weapon, I see no mitigating factors here. That's all I can tell you right now, although I have been given an indication that there may be a pretty heavy charge coming down soon that could skyrocket what we will ask for."

Stein merely nodded. He already had a good idea of what was coming.

He met with Damon Clark early Monday afternoon in a secure room at the jail. Damon was handcuffed to a ring on the table and Stein didn't ask that the cuffs be removed. When Clark was seated and the deputy had closed the door behind himself, Stein just sat, wordlessly looking at Damon.

When the silence finally became uncomfortable for Damon, he looked at Stein and demanded, "Well, say something. You aren't being paid to stare at me."

Stein nodded. "That's right. I'm being paid to pull a rabbit out of the hat for you, but the problem is, Damon, there is no rabbit. You're on the south side of assault with a deadly weapon, unlawful possession of a deadly weapon, three counts of violation of a protective order, kidnapping, and I'm not sure how many counts of parole violation–just for starters. And I cannot find a mitigating circumstance anywhere in this whole mess. I'm at a loss for something to say, other than what I just said."

When Damon didn't respond, Stein continued, "But, perhaps you can enlighten me. Please tell me that you have some argument, however small, for mitigation."

Again, Stein stared wordlessly at Clark until the silence again became uncomfortable for Clark.

"Come on, Saul. You know the cops are just trying to use all this to get to my Uncle John, to get me to tell them all about his business. I don't want to be forced to do that just to get out of this mess."

For a third time, Stein stared wordlessly at Clark until the silence again became uncomfortable for Clark.

"Come on, Saul. You aren't going to let that happen."

"A little early to show your hole card, isn't it Damon?"

"Look, I don't know enough about Uncle John's business to be a threat to him."

"I know that, Damon. That's part of my job. So, why would you even intimate that you would talk about his business to the cops?

"You're a spineless turd, Damon. If it hadn't been for the testimony of the other kids at that party, you would have let Bobby take all the heat for that stolen Mustang joyride you took back when you were a snot-nosed kid. And now you're telling me that you'll talk about your uncle's business just to get a break for yourself.

"Maybe we should talk a little bit about your business, instead. You sent a harmless simpleton to threaten a man when you didn't have the balls to do it yourself. Now Hector is facing prison time for your poor judgment."

"I didn't tell him to pull a knife on the guy in front of witnesses!" shouted Clark as he tried to stand and was stopped by the ring to which his wrists were shackled.

"And you didn't tell him not to, either, did you?

"We know all about your temper tantrums. We know about the little co-ed whores you run."

"Fuckin' Bobby and his big mouth," shouted Damon.

"And we know about the one you beat so bad she needed medical care in an emergency room. And the one you threatened with a gun."

"How… " Damon stammered, then shouted, "I never threatened any of them with a gun. Bobby is lying!"

"Why do you think Bobby told us any of this? Your uncle knows everything you and Bobby do, and so do I. Too many people know you, Damon, and know what you do. John Candelero didn't get where he is by being oblivious to what goes on around him."

"It has to be Bobby. No one else knows what I do."

"So you don't deny what I just said. You just deny that someone other than Bobby told us. Is that it?"

"So, what the fuck does all that have to do with the charges against me in here?" Damon shouted.

"Sit down and listen, and I'll explain to you.

When Damon sat, Stein spoke. "Damon, you've been getting too big for your britches for a long time now. You're unraveling. You act as though you are superior to those around you; you show signs of a persecution complex; you don't demonstrate clear rational thought processes.

"Because you haven't taken all that has happened seriously, going back to your juvie probation terms, because you haven't looked seriously at the legal consequences of your haphazard and shortsighted thought process, you have turned a small snowball into an avalanche and it is coming down on you. And there is only one way to stop it.

"You are going to plead temporary insanity and you are going to work hard to make that defense believable. You will do some time in a mental institution, but you won't do twenty-five years in prison. You need to get on board quickly because I have reason to believe that there may be some federal charges out there waiting in the wings. You need to be *non-compos mentis* before those charges hit the fan.

"You're the crazy one, not me! What the hell are you talking about."

"I hear you're trying to sell a woman into a life of slavery and prostitution."

"What the fuck are you talking about?"

"If you want to trade information about someone or something to help your case, your uncle John isn't the one you want to be talking about. Tell me about what you intend to do to the Barton girl. That information is the only bargaining chip you own that is worth anything."

"You're crazy!"

"No, Damon. You're the crazy one; crazy to even consider such a scheme. If you tell me about it, I can get you ahead of the curve and use the information to your advantage. Otherwise, you're going to be part of the problem, not the solution, and you aren't going to like where that takes you.

"I'm going to leave now and give you some time to think about this. Your little costume party in front of the Barton girl and her boyfriend, and being shot by her with your gun, should get a good laugh from the jury when they consider the question of sanity.

"And you can be sure that story will get around the prison in no time once you're in."

With that, Stein summoned the deputy and left Damon to think while he went to meet with Gomez.

FIFTY-FIVE

On Tuesday, June 30, Stein arrived as Gomez was being moved into an interview room. Gomez was handcuffed to the table and left alone for thirty minutes, while Evans discussed the options she had for Gomez.

When they were finished, they went to interview Gomez.

Evans talked first, advising Gomez that his attorney had asked for a meeting and that she and Stein had discussed a plea bargain.

"Mr. Gomez, I will get right to the point. This is a meeting to discuss a resolution to this matter. What I say cannot be repeated in front of a jury.

"Having said that, we do not believe that you intended to harm Mr. Wade. We believe you were sent to simply scare him away from Ms. Barton. If you will tell me everything about Mr. Clark's instructions to you concerning Mr. Wade and Ms. Barton, and if you will testify at trial against Mr. Clark, and if you will give us a written statement under oath of what your testimony will be, I believe we can make you an attractive offer."

Gomez listened, then looked at Stein, who nodded and asked Evans for a few minutes to visit with Gomez. When Evans was gone, Stein moved his chair close to Gomez.

"What do I do, Mr. Stein?"

"Listen to her and watch me. There are allegations that Damon is planning to sell Ms. Barton. Have you heard anything like that?"

Gomez was quiet for a minute. "I was in the office one day several months ago. I heard around that Damon was pretty angry at her because he said she dumped him. I asked him how he was doing and he said that he was going to sell the bitch to some ragheads who would show her who was boss.

"I asked him what he meant and he said it was nothing and not to worry about it. But it didn't sound like a joke or just nothing when he said it."

"Is there anything else you can tell me about his plans for Ms. Barton?"

"No, sir. We didn't talk a lot."

"Do you know anything about him tricking or forcing girls to be prostitutes or anything like that?"

Gomez was quiet for several minutes. When Stein finally prompted him for a response, he said, "I heard a story at the deli once. There was a girl who was pretty mouthy and gave Damon a hard time sometimes. There was a rumor that she fucked Damon and would fuck for money. I don't really know whether she worked as a whore or not, but…"

Stein nodded for him to continue.

"I heard him say one time that she was nothing but trouble and he was going to make her disappear, that he was going to give her to some guys who could straighten her out. I never saw her again after that, but I don't know what happened to her."

"What was her name?"

"Carla, I think. I didn't know her last name."

"Anything else I should know?" stein asked.

Again, Gomez was quiet for a moment. "After he told me to scare that doctor, he told me that if scaring him didn't work, he was going to get rid of him and the girl both, but he never explained what he meant and I didn't ask him."

Evans returned and Gomez gave her a complete recorded statement under oath of everything he had told Stein in return for a disposition of time served and one-year probation.

FIFTY-SIX

On Wednesday, Gomez was released. Stein met with Damon and told him that Gomez had given a statement about the attack on Wade. Damon swore at Gomez and called him a liar.

Stein asked him if he had thought about what they talked about on Monday.

"I'm not going to say I'm crazy. Uncle John is paying you to get me out of this, not to get me locked up in a crazy house."

Stein nodded and began putting papers back in his briefcase. He paused and looked up at Clark. "You had a girl who worked for you whose name was, I believe, Carla. Whatever happened to her?"

"Oh, she quit. Moved away, I think."

"Did you give her the last check when she quit or did you mail it to her?"

"I don't know. What does it matter?"

"Just wondered if you had an address for her?"

"Don't know."

"What was her last name."

"I don't remember," Damon answered cautiously.

"No problem," said Stein. "I'm sure our accountants will have her information and we will have employment records. I'll get the information from them."

With that, he picked up his briefcase and said, "Oh, by the way, why did you take pictures of Ms. Barton the night you assaulted her and Wade?"

"I just wanted her picture."

"What did you do with it?"

"I guess it's still on my phone. It was no big deal."

"Is that why you threatened them at gunpoint—to get her to pose for you?"

Clark stared sullenly at Stein without speaking.

"Think about what I've told you," Stein admonished.

After he left, Damon sat with a sick look on his face.

PART 8

FIFTY-SEVEN

The week passed with no news from Evans. Dub and Elizabeth continued their routine at the end of each day, Dub following Liz from her office to his home. On Friday afternoon, June twenty-third, as Liz walked from the elevator to her car, she noticed that the company security man who normally met her at the elevator wasn't there. She looked about but saw no one who appeared threatening. As she started toward her car, she heard her name called. She turned and saw a large, bald man behind her.

He held out a folded piece of paper, smiled disarmingly, and said, "You dropped this, ma'am."

She looked up at him, taking the paper and stepping away from him toward her car. He remained motionless as she unfolded the paper. On it was typed in boldface, WE HAVE WADE. MAKE NO OUTCRY AND GET IN THE VAN WITHOUT RESISTANCE. HIS LIFE DEPENDS ON YOUR COOPERATION. At that moment, a white van with an opened sliding panel drove next to her and stopped.

She looked at the man, surreptitiously crumbled the note into her palm, and dropped it behind her as she quietly stepped into the van. As she sat, she glimpsed a motionless man wearing hospital scrubs in the seat behind her in. His head, which was covered with a black, cloth bag, lolled to one side. He looked like Dub. The large man followed her into the van and closed the door. As the van drove away, he pulled a cloth bag from his pocket and said, "I'm going to put this bag over your head and tie your hands. Don't resist." As soon as the bag was on her head and her hands were bound, she felt a needle prick in the side of her neck and quickly passed out.

A similar scenario had played out in the parking lot of Methodist Hospital with Dub Wade as the abductee twenty minutes earlier.

~ ~ ~

As Stan Pulanski, head of security at ExxonMobil Woodlands, was making notes for the upcoming week, he heard a tap at his door. He looked up and saw a middle-aged woman whose face he recognized, but whose name he could not remember.

"Mr. Pulanski, I'm happy to find you still here. We've not met, but I am Constance Malawi. I am the Internal Audit Manager. I just saw something that… just didn't look right. I thought you should know."

"Please come in," he said as he motioned her to come in and sit. He put his notes aside and pulled a notepad closer to him.

"I park in the executive lot in the basement of the garage. As I was walking to my car, which was parked on level B, I heard a male voice call out, 'Ms. Barton, you dropped this.' I looked without really thinking why and saw a large, bald man approaching a pretty woman who has recently been parking in that area. I don't know her name, but he called her Ms. Barton.

"He held out a folded piece of paper. It seemed unusual, but I can't describe why… but it made me curious. I watched as she took the paper, opened and read it. She looked up at him with a shocked expression and he said something to her.

"A white van with the panel door open pulled even with them and she got into the van followed by the man. There was no writing or identification on the van, but I took a picture of the back when it drove away. I think I have the license plate, if there was one. I also took a picture of the man. She showed the pictures and Pulanski asked her to text them to him.

"When the man spoke to her, I saw her crumple the paper and drop it on the floor behind her, next to what I assume is her car.

"The man slammed the van door and the van drove off. I confess, curiosity got the better of me and I retrieved the crumpled paper and read it. I think you should see this."

As she laid the opened paper flat on the desk, she said that she had taken the pictures at 5:22 p.m. Munoz read the note without touching it. He felt as though he had been hit hard in the solar plexus. He knew exactly what was going on.

He asked Ms. Malawi if anyone other than the man, Ms. Barton, and she had touched the paper. She said she knew of no one else other than she who touched it after Ms. Barton took it. He thanked Ms. Malawi profusely, complimented her on her thorough recitation and observations, and excused himself.

His phone rang and she nodded for him to answer as she saw herself out. The man on the phone advised Pulanski that one of his security men had been found unconscious on the executive parking level. He was assured that the man had not been harmed.

He telephoned the security office and ordered that surveillance footage from the executive levels of the garage and all entrances be downloaded and sent to his office immediately. He also ordered a list of all persons who parked on Level B of the garage where Ms. Malawi witnessed the incident.

He had recognized the name Barton immediately. On a hunch, he called Robert Munoz and advised him of the incident.

Munoz immediately ordered security footage of the hospital parking lot. The footage was sent to his computer and he quickly scrolled through it from 4:30 p.m. At 5 p.m., he saw a similar incident and recognized Dub Wade. He quickly phoned Detective Asimov.

Fortunately, Asimov answered his phone and Robert Munoz reported what he had just learned. Asimov called Pulanski, verified what Munoz had told him, and told Pulanski he would be there as quickly as traffic would allow, then called Evans.

"I think we have the thread on which to pull in the Clark/Barton matter." He relayed what he had learned from Munoz. Evans told him to get a car with full lights and a siren, and to swing by the DA's office and pick her up.

Asimov called Munoz and asked him to meet at ExxonMobil as well.

FIFTY-EIGHT

When Evans and Asimov arrived at the ExxonMobil campus, Pulanski had photographed the note and duplicated the security footage for his file. He had printed the photo from Malawi's phone. The note was still where Malawi had placed it on his desk. Next to it were a list of the employees who park near Barton and a copy of the pictures of the van and the man. The security footage was on his computer, ready for viewing. One of Pulanski's officers was calling every person whose parking place was near that of Liz Barton in hopes of gaining additional information.

Munoz arrived with security footage from the hospital just before Asimov and Evans.

The four of them scanned the footage and saw the abduction, but it was at a distance. They saw Barton enter the van followed by the big man and watched the van drive down the aisle, out the garage entrance, and turn right into oncoming traffic. They could discern what happened and identify Barton, but little else. They saw the big man and verified that he was the man in Malawi's photograph.

They scrolled backward and found the van as it entered the garage. It parked across from the entrance to the down ramp leading to the executive level. They saw the bald man walk to the control mechanism for the gate. He inserted two wires with prongs attached to the mechanism. They saw sparks fly and the gate rose.

"Electrical charge, probably a Taser," Pulanski said. "They shorted out the mechanism and it goes to open by default. Looks like they've done this before."

The van drove down to the executive parking where Liz's vehicle would be.

Asimov called the crime lab, described the van, and gave the exact time it turned on the street in front of the parking garage. He asked them to start examining traffic cameras for a possible match.

"Hey, Robert," Pulanski said, "are you aware of the problems Ms. Barton was having with a guy named Clark?"

"Yes," Munoz responded, "he was stalking her. She had dated him briefly and broke it off abruptly–for good reason, I was told. We had a couple of incidents with Clark at the hospital. Ms. Barton's boyfriend works at our hospital. A guy attacked him on the premises and was arrested. The guy's name is Hector Gomez.

"I know that name," Choksi replied. "Gomez works for Clark. We believe Clark sent him after Mr. Wade. This is an interesting corollary to the case at hand. We may have to talk to Gomez and Clark about all this–after we get the warrants issued. I'll get started on them right now."

By eight o'clock that night, Pulanski's staff had reached two persons who had noticed the van in the garage, but neither could give any more information than Malawi had provided.

PART 9

FIFTY-NINE

I came into a groggy consciousness. I was disoriented and felt a slight stinging sensation on the side of my neck. I was lying on narrow a cot. Awkwardly, I raised myself on one elbow and looked around. I was in a rectangular room approximately fifteen feet by ten feet. There were three cots, including mine, head in on the long back wall. On one side, there was a half door that appeared to open into a rudimentary bathroom. I saw the top of a sink and a toilet and the edge of an open shower stall. Both side walls and the back wall were constructed with cinder blocks. I guess the building had been a small manufacturing facility or warehouse and that the bathrooms had been added.

The facing wall was made of chain link fencing from floor to ceiling securely attached to round, galvanized steel posts that were solidly embedded in the floor and ceiling. There was a door of similar material in the fence wall. I saw a hall outside and a similar room across the hallway. The opposite room was empty, but I could hear voices occasionally–indistinct women's voices to my left and, once, a man's voice to my right.

I rose, walked to the bathroom, and peered in. It was five by ten feet and contained the basics, but it appeared to at least be clean. I stepped to the fence and saw that the room across the hall was identical, and it was empty. I looked left and right. I could see three similar compartments across the hall, so I assumed I was in the middle of two compartments on my side.

Across the hall to my right, the cell appeared to be a repository for rolled and bound carpets. That was strange.

At either end of the building was a large, steel rollup door. Each held a window in the center through which I could see daylight. The door to my right was farther away so I assumed there was an office or fourth room on either side at that end. The stream of sunlight through the window in the door to my left was longer on the floor, so logically it was either morning or evening.

I looked to see the time and discovered that my watch was gone. I patted my pockets–no keys, no wallet, no phone.

I considered my situation for a moment. I assumed that I had been kidnapped. There was no apparent reason for anyone to kidnap me, so I assumed that it was related to Liz and that she, too, had been kidnaped. I assumed similarly that it had something to do with what Evans had told us about Damon setting something in motion against us. I examined everything in the space that I could see, but I saw no avenue or implement of escape.

"Hello," I called out in a strong voice.

Immediately I heard a voice to my right say, "Quietly, amigo. Don't shout or they will come down here and use the Taser on you. That is very painful."

I was taken aback.

"Thanks for the information," I said quietly. "Where are we?"

"I don't know. I guess we are in Houston or near to Houston."

"Is there anyone with you?"

"There was a man who was here last week, but they took him away yesterday."

"Why are you here?"

"I am not sure. Someone comes every day to check my temperature and blood pressure. He did the same for the man who was here last week.

I think they intend to cut out my heart or some other body part and sell it. I'm worried. I've heard stories about this kind of thing."

That took me aback. I've read about human trafficking and kidnapping persons for body parts, but this was way too close to home for me. I know that it happens a lot and that Houston is a major area for trafficking. I have read that hundreds of persons are kidnapped or disappear every year and are presumed to be victims of human trafficking and the sale of body parts.

"Were you here when they brought me in?"

"Yes. They brought you yesterday evening. You were unconscious."

"Did they bring a woman in with me? A tall, auburn-haired woman?"

"Yes. She was unconscious as well."

"Do you know where they took her?"

"She is probably at the other end on the other side with the women."

"How many women are here?"

"I think just one plus her and another who has been here for some time who is named Leticia, I think. The cells seem to be identical, so nine beds on either side. There were two women at the end on the other side last week, but they're gone now. I don't think there is anyone else on our side right now."

"Have you seen them?

"Every day and every night. There are seldom other men. There are usually two guards. There are usually at least two or three girls here all the time. Whenever the guards get the urge, they just drag a girl down the hall and have her. Sometimes they strip her in her cell; sometimes they don't. But all the girls come back down the hall naked and crying, usually with red marks on their faces and bodies, sometimes with bruises.

"I'm pretty sure all of the women here are going to be sold or forced into a life of prostitution. These guys have no conscience. I've heard the girls screaming and crying and begging. The more they beg, the harder these guys make it for them."

I turned to the left and said, as loud as I dared, "Liz. Are you there?'

There was no response. I waited a moment and tried again.

A soft voice, that of a black woman, came back. "You want the red-haired girl that come in last night?"

"Yes. Is she all right."

"Don't know. She still be unconscious."

"Thank you. What's your name?"

"Leticia."

"Thank you, Leticia.

"Ain't no problem, Man."

"I'm, Dub. Will you let me know when she wakes up?"

"Yeah."

I said to my right, "What's your name?"

"James White. I work for the city. I was on a job alone in a remote area when I was grabbed. What's your name?"

"Dub."

"Like George W?"

"That's right." I paused. "What can I expect here?"

"Two meals a day, morning and evening. There should be a water bottle in your cell. Fill it in the bathroom. Don't expect clean sheets or more than one blanket on your bed. You're only the third guy I've seen and I've been here for over two weeks. They don't get many guys and don't bother the guys unless one gets loud or obnoxious. They all carry a Taser and a stun gun, and they like to use them.

"Most of them just tease the women and fuck them. One of them is a hitter, but the guy in charge tries to keep him in check. I heard him one time tell the hitter that no one cares if they fuck the girls, but the girls weren't worth as much if they had bruises and marks on them. I haven't seen the hitter now for a couple of days. The doc checks the girls, too, when he checks me.”

“Is it morning or evening?”

“It’s morning. I think today is Saturday, but I’m not sure.”

“Do you think there is any way to get out of here?” I asked.

“No. If there was just one guy, maybe you and I could figure a way to take him, but there are always two or three here and they all have Tasers. Maybe if there were a couple of big bull dykes down at the other end, they could take the guards, but these guys don’t snatch big bull dykes. Most of the women I’ve seen are small. And none of us are gaining weight on this diet.”

“Thanks, James. I need to think for a while.”

“Sure. I think I’ll take a nap. I do that a lot these days”

SIXTY

Asimov had an early breakfast and arrived at headquarters on Saturday morning, June twenty-fourth, early enough to be there for shift change in the lab. He knew the lab guys had worked through the night and he wanted to know what they had learned. He met the night supervisor as he was going off duty and the day supervisor was coming on. The night man brought them up to date.

"We enlarged the picture and got the plate number, but nothing from the plates. They were stolen, apparently several months ago. We ran the make, model, and color, but there hundreds of white Chevy step vans in Houston. Without a plate or some identifying marks, there is not much we can do. We followed the van to the entrance to the North Freeway but lost it in the traffic there. It was rush hour.

"We're still working on Clark's phone, but no luck yet. We got the number you mentioned off the phone and the computer is checking it against pings with the numbers called that day. We should have something soon.

"We lifted prints from the note. We found three sets, two of which we assume at this time are Malawi and Barton. We got a partial set that appears to be from a larger hand, probably the guy. We ran the partials through the FBI's NCIC–the National Crime Information Center–and got fifty-six possibles.

"But…" he paused and grinned, "we got a pretty good side facial from the photo of the big guy. We enhanced it and are running it through every facial recognition database. That's about it for now."

Asimov called Evans and brought her up to date.

Munoz and Pulanski spoke on Saturday and agreed that Evans should notify the families of Barton and Wade. Evans did so. ExxonMobil immediately made arrangements for Barton's family to return to Houston. Wade's parents resided in Houston. Munoz advised Jill and Vivian Hancock and Dr. Melbourne, who were very upset by the news.

SIXTY-ONE

I sat on the bed and tried to think logically. There had to be a way to escape. There had to be some weapon that could be created from what was at hand. I examined the bed. It was a typical metal frame cot. The head and foot folded out and made a single flat unit with a wire mesh webbing secured to the frame like a typical army cot. There were no bed slats, the mattress rested on the wire mesh bed of linked four-inch squares that hung from the rails of the frame. There was nothing else in the cell. As I stood and looked into the bathroom, I heard Leticia's voice.

"Mr. Dub. The lady be awake. She a little fuzzy right now."

"Thank you, Leticia."

"No problem."

I checked the bathroom. Other than the metal arm of the shower pipe, there was nothing to use as a weapon. Even the handles for the faucets were plastic, and the seat to the toilet had been removed.

"Dub?"

It was music to my ears. I heard Liz's voice again. "Dub. Are down there"

"I'm here, Liz. Are you all right?"

'I'm a little groggy, but that should go away. Physically, I'm fine." She paused. "Do you know where we are?"

"No. I don't. I'm guessing we aren't far from home right now. And I'm guessing this has something to do with what Evans told us. It is morning, but I don't know what time. My watch, wallet, and phone were taken while I was out."

"Mine, too.

"I think, for the time being, we should keep quiet and observe. I don't know whether they can see or hear us in here, but I imagine there is a camera and a recorder in operation somewhere."

"You are probably right. Give me some time to get to know my neighbors. I think that would be wise."

"I agree." I paused.

"Liz, don't be upset by whatever you are told or you see. Stay focused and objective."

"I'll try."

Neither of us said any more for a while.

SIXTY-TWO

Later in the morning, I was lying on my bed when I saw a lean, nondescript guy with a buzz-cut swagger down the hall. I followed his footsteps and it sounded as though he had stopped in front of the women on the other side. It was quiet for a moment, then he let out a low cat whistle.

I heard Leticia say. "Little early for that, ain't it?"

"Fuck you, Leticia!"

He walked back down the hall. As he passed me, he muttered to himself, "Damn. That is one fine piece of ass."

Then, he looked at me and grinned. No words were necessary. Now, I was worried.

Soon, another man came down the hall and stopped at my cell.

"I'm Jerry. I understand your name is Wade."

I nodded.

"The rules here are pretty simple. You'll get breakfast and supper. No snacks. No phone, no TV, no newspapers. If you want a book, I have a stack that I can bring for you to look through. No yelling, no cursing at the guards, and no threats to the guards or another resident. No fighting. Break the rules and you get Tasered as many times as I think is necessary. All the guards carry a stun gun and a Taser. Ignore the girls, whatever happens. Don't try to be a hero. Someone will come to check your vitals every day except Sunday. Any questions?"

"Where are we and what day is this?"

"You're still in Houston and today is Saturday. It's eleven in the morning. That's all you need to know for now."

"I'd like a book."

"I'm going out for a little while. I'll bring them to you when I get back." He went down the hall and I heard him tell Leticia to explain the rules to "the new girl."

About thirty minutes later, Buzz Cut sauntered back down the hallway. As he passed me, he leered and gave me a wink.

I followed his footsteps to the cell where Liz was locked up. I heard a repetitious clinking sound as he said, "Well, now; lookee here what I got."

I quickly moved to the fencing and looked left toward where Liz was held.

He was swinging a key on a chain against the lock. There was silence for a moment; then I saw and heard Leticia.

"What you think you doing?"

"Well, now, Leticia, I'm gonna get acquainted with Red, here."

He changed focus. "I like redheads. I'd like to have me a redhead. What's your name, Red?"

Silence. I could see Liz now, standing near the back wall.

"I asked you what your name is. You can tell me or I can make you scream and dance until you beg to tell me." He brandished his Taser.

"Ain't no need for that," I heard Leticia say. "Tell him your name, honey."

There was a pregnant pause; then Liz said, "My name is Elizabeth."

"Eee liz a beth." He repeated drawing each syllable out. "Ain't that a nice name. Like the queen. Are you a queen, Eee liz a beth?"

"No."

"Well, why don't you just come with me, Eee liz a beth, and I'll make you feel like a queen."

There was silence. I saw him take a step toward the door and insert the key. I heard the lock click and the door open.

"Whaddya say, Eee liz a beth? You wanna feel like a queen?"

Another silence.

"I think I'd rather stay right here, thank you."

"Aw, now Eee liz a beth, you're gonna hurt my feelings… and you don't wanna hurt my feelings do you?"

Another silence.

"I don't mean to hurt your feelings, but I would rather remain here."

"Aww, Eee liz a beth, now you've gone and hurt my feelings, and I just can't take no for an answer." He stepped inside and stood in front of Liz.

Silence, then I heard the pedestrian door at the right end of the building open and close.

He grabbed her arm and Liz screamed, "Let go of me."

Buzz Cut shouted, "Shut up, bitch; you're coming with me."

Leticia cautioned, "Don't fight him, honey."

I was furious, but I knew better than to say anything. I knew that I would only make the situation worse. But it was all I could do to contain myself. I knew Liz must be scared out of her wits. This wasn't like Damon in my house; this guy held all the cards here.

I heard even footsteps coming toward us. Out of the corner of my eye, I caught a glimpse of Jerry, moving unhurriedly, and thought, *Oh, shit; Jerry isn't going to do anything about this. He's going to let this guy rape Liz.*

Jerry reached my cell and stopped, watching as Liz screamed, "Please, don't."

"Fuck you, bitch. I'll fuck you right here on the floor in front of everyone if I want to. Who do you think you are?"

Buzz Cut pulled at the lapel of Liz's blouse and I heard buttons hit the floor. Then he grabbed a handful of her hair and forced her to her knees in front of him. Once again, Liz screamed, "Please, don't."

"Take off your blouse, bitch. Let's see those titties and then you can suck my cock."

I wanted my hands on the guy. I wanted to beat him to a pulp. I wanted to scream every profanity I had ever known—but I couldn't. I knew it would only make things worse for her. I could see the fear on her face and I could see her shaking as she started to cry.

"Who do you think <u>you</u> are?" Jerry asked calmly and evenly.

Buzz-cut jumped like a scalded cat and whirled toward Jerry.

"Oh, hey, boss. This bitch was being sassy and disobeying the rules. I was just gonna straighten her out."

"I was very clear to all you guys–no one touches this girl while she's here. Do you remember me saying that, Steven?"

"Well,… yeah, boss, but you didn't say she could break the rules."

"What's the number one rule here, Steven?"

"Do exactly what the boss tells you."

"There you have it. You can pick up your check Monday at the office. If you have anything down the hall, get it on your way out now."

You could have heard a pin drop as Steven turned and walked toward us. He gave me a hard look as he passed me.

Jerry watched until Steven was out of the door; then he walked to me. He leaned toward me and said, very quietly, "I did that to save my job, not for her. I'll be back with the books."

SIXTY-THREE

I was curious. Whoever ran this place and gave orders to Jerry obviously ran a tight ship. Jerry didn't seem like the kind of guy who was easily intimidated. I was impressed with his composure. In an environment like this, I would have expected him to yell and scream and be as obnoxious as Steven.

I heard Liz crying and I could do nothing to help her.

"Liz," I called, "it's all right now. You're all right now. It's over. It's over now."

"Oh, Dub," I heard her moan. "Oh, God, Dub."

I didn't know what to do.

I listened as Leticia talked soothingly to Liz until she stopped crying.

I felt so helpless.

I heard James next door say, "She got lucky. He'll move her out of here tonight."

Jerry returned with the books. I thanked him for the books and for Liz.

"I understand that what you did wasn't for her, but thank you anyway. No one deserves where that was going."

He paused, looking at me. He stepped close to the wire and spoke very quietly.

"You probably won't understand. I have an eighth-grade education. I read a lot and I'm not stupid. Years ago, I had no hope of getting a job that paid very much. These guys put me to work when I was twelve and I've been working for them ever since.

"I have a wife and two daughters. My daughters are bright. Both are in college. Neither my wife nor my daughters know what pays the bills. They think I'm in the import/export business. I've been doing this so long that I can't get out until I'm so old I die or they let me out. I know I'll probably rot in hell, but there isn't much else I can do that will pay for my family's needs."

"Why would you tell me that?"

"I don't know. You and the girl seem like nice people. Most of the girls who end up here never had much of a future to begin with. The others, all the others, people like you, were just in the wrong place at the wrong time. It's getting harder for me to look the other way."

He paused thoughtfully. "I've said way too much. Don't make too much of it. The only thing that matters to me is keeping my family on top of the water."

"How long will we be here?"

"Not long. Probably two or three days. There wasn't room for you this weekend where you're going."

"Is there any chance of moving Liz across from me?"

"I'm probably going to have to get her out of here. I can't trust that idiot and the others to leave her alone. If she stays here, I'm going to get my tit in the wringer."

I looked imploring, and he said, "Let me make a call, first."

Not long after that, Jerry came to my cell. "Boss says I have to move her out of here."

"Where will you move her?"

"Next building for tonight. The others can't get in there."

"Can I talk to her?"

"Boss says no."

He brought Liz back down the hallway. Her eyes were downcast, and she didn't look in my direction.

"Liz," I said quietly.

She looked up and the anxiety on her face was palpable.

"Dub?"

"Keep your wits about you," I said, as he pushed her on ahead of him. I watched her until the outside door swung shut behind them with an ominous thud. I have never in my life felt so helpless. I was scared for her and there was nothing I could do.

When he was gone, I called, "Hey, Leticia."

"Yeah, Mr. Dub."

"How long have you been here?"

"A year, maybe two years–not sure."

"How long are most girls here?"

"About a week."

"Does this work for you?"

"I ain't on the street or sleeping in no corners somewhere. And I ain't strung out on no drugs."

"Do you know where they took her?"

"Probably the building next door. She be safe there tonight."

So, Leticia is the one who maintains order and discipline among the women who pass through here. And she does what she can to protect them while they are here.

Supper came–grilled cheese sandwiches, a cup of pudding, some grapes, and water. I ate. James White had said nothing since that morning. I only heard subdued voices from the girl's cell. I never learned if there were women on both sides of the hall. I asked James, but he said he had seen no one enter the far cell on the left, our side. He said that there were three women across from my cell when he first came. He said four guards took them repeatedly that night for most of the night, but they were taken away the next day. He said the women screamed and cried and pleaded and, when the guards couldn't physically continue, they used their batons instead.

Shortly after supper, two new guards came down the hallway with a new girl. I guessed this was the night shift. A little later, they came back and removed the girl from Leticia's cell. The girl woodenly walked to the other end of the hallway, resignation visible on her face, eyes straight ahead. They returned about an hour later. Neither of the guys looked like a heavy hitter, so I could only imagine what the girl had done most of the time.

I didn't sleep all night. I worried about Liz alone in another building. She had to be incredibly scared. I worried about our fate. Did all this occur simply because of Damon Clark?

SIXTY-FOUR

Asimov called the lab again Sunday, June twenty-fifth, but there was nothing new. He asked if they knew how the entrance to the parking garage had been breached.

"Electrical shock. They hit it with a charge hot enough to fry the little brain inside. My guess is that it was a Taser. That would be an easy way to carry that much charge safely in something small.

"What's next?" asked Asimov.

"We will check with Delaware first thing in the morning for information on the corporation. They should have the name, address, and phone of the incorporator and the directors, maybe even an officer or two. Then, we run that information down in hopes of getting a name and address here in Houston. If we don't get someone here, we just start leaning on the names we get for information. No way to know at this point if we're close or not."

SIXTY-FIVE

At sunrise on Sunday morning, I was awakened by the sounds of the door opening at the end of the building. I looked and saw another new girl being marched down the center aisle by two new guards. She wore short shorts, a halter top, and sandals. She was tall, white, slender, and attractive in a tawdry way. I heard her coming as soon as she was in the door. She was mouthy and belligerent. I assume she had been taken off the streets late Saturday night and, from the sound of her, she was still a bit drunk or strung out on something.

When she reached the space in front of me, she stopped to look at me. When the guard pushed her forward, she swore and slapped him. He swore back at her, jammed his stun gun hard up between her legs, and pressed the button. She screamed and jumped at the shock, then launched into a long monologue about his pedigree and his legitimacy.

He told her to shut up as he reached for his Taser. She didn't and he Tased her in her abdomen. She screamed as though she were being tortured, piercing screams of agony until she arched and went rigid, falling onto her back where she bounced and bucked and convulsed like she was having a fit, screaming frantically the entire time. When she screamed, the hair stood up on my arms and the back of my neck. I had never in my life heard such pitiful, agonizing screams as the girl gave out.

She must have convulsed for at least a full minute or more. When she finally collapsed and stopped quivering, the two guards roughly jerked her to her feet, pulled the Taser prongs from her, ripped her clothes off, and viciously took turns with her right there in the hallway until she was too weak to fight or scream.

When they were finished with the girl, the guy that she had slapped kicked her between her legs and shouted, "How do you like that, bitch?"

They drug her down the hall and dropped her in front of Leticia. They returned, laughing about how hard she had convulsed and making coarse and crude comments about her.

Later that afternoon, they came for her. She tried to be brave, but the look in her eyes was pure fear. I watched them take her down the hall to the office. She walked gingerly and it was obvious she was still in pain.

I heard them laughing and her pleading until I again heard the same pitiful scream that she had expelled when she was Tasered and convulsed earlier. For what seemed like an hour, I listened to the laughter of the guards and her pleas to stop. Finally, one guard came down the hall carrying the limp, naked girl over his shoulder. Bruises and red marks covered over her body, and her nose was crusted with blood. Fortunately for her, she was unconscious. He deposited her with Leticia.

That night, when the guards changed, I heard raucous laughter from the office. I assumed the girl had been the topic of conversation. When the two relieved guards left, the two new guards went for the girl and the same scenario played out, but they returned quickly, carrying her under the arms between them. Her eyes were open, but they were dull and lifeless. I'm sure her usefulness to them had been stretched thin by the first two guards, and all semblance of attractiveness had been worn away.

I was appalled, but I kept my mouth shut.

SIXTY-SIX

Monday morning, June twenty-sixth, I was sitting in my cell when Jerry walked up. He told me we would be leaving that day. I described to him what had happened on Sunday. He just shook his head and said, "Yeah, I heard she had a mouth on her. Sometimes things happen. It's too bad she didn't get to Leticia before she hit the guard."

"What's going to happen to us?"

"Your girlfriend is either going to the Middle East or to some rich Muslim guy here in the states. I haven't gotten the story, but I know she's worth big bucks. And you, you're going to give your heart away."

He said it as though I had asked what was for breakfast. I was speechless.

"Don't worry. You won't feel a thing."

SIXTY-SEVEN

Asimov checked in again with the lab at mid-morning Monday, June twenty-sixth, and got some good news. He was told that there were no criminal matches on the prints or the pictures, but that the computer had found two passport photos that look like the bald guy.

"We checked and got two names. We ran those two passports and names through DMV records and got a match with the license of Yousef Ahmadi, so we're pretty sure he is our guy,

"We're trying to get information and background on Ahmadi now. We ran his home address from his license, but it turns out the address is some import/export business incorporated in Delaware called Marcos Import/Export Limited with a Houston address. We checked the address and there is such a business there–a good-sized building with two warehouses. Unfortunately, right now the computers at the Delaware secretary of State are down, so we can't get behind the corporate name yet, but the computer is sifting through various records looking for information on the business. All we can get from our Secretary of State is the name of the registered agent, who is a local attorney. We should be able to get in today."

PART 10

SIXTY-EIGHT

As I was slowly coming into consciousness, I heard a door open, then close, followed by muffled footsteps. I opened my eyes and saw that I was on a bed in what appeared to be a bedroom. To my left, I saw a bathroom with facilities and a shower. I felt weight pulling my left hand. I looked and saw that my wrist was handcuffed to a steel cable encased in plastic, like a bicycle lock chain. The cable was about ten feet long and was attached to an eye bolt secured into the wall next to my bed, between the bed and the bathroom. I looked to my right and saw a man standing near the bed, watching me. The man held a bottle of water in one hand and what appeared to be a plastic gun—which I knew from the recent incident with the girl to be a Taser—in the other.

"What's going on," I asked through dry lips.

"Ah, Mr. Wade. Good morning. I've been waiting for you to wake. I imagine you are very thirsty and that your mouth is dry. I have some water for you."

"What's going on and who are you," I repeated.

"I am going to hand you the bottle of water. Drink some water, then we will talk," he said as he gingerly extended the bottle near my right hand.

I started to slap his hand away but then realized that I wanted the water and that it would be wiser to avoid confrontation at this point. I took the water, opened the bottle, and drank greedily.

I looked at him and raised my eyebrows questioningly.

"You may call me Marco. You are in my home on my estate. Unfortunately, you are here because you are what is called collateral damage, as they say, associated with Ms. Barton. It will be better for all concerned if we can agree to cooperate and avoid confrontation while you are here. Will you agree to that?

"What day is this?"

"It is Tuesday morning, June twenty-seventh."

I narrowed my eyes and asked slowly and purposefully, "Where is Liz?"

He stared at me for a moment, then said, "Ah, yes. She is also here and should be waking soon." He paused.

"Will you agree to cooperate and avoid confrontation while you are here?"

"Until I know what's going on, I won't agree to anything. I want to see Liz and I want this handcuff removed. This is kidnapping."

"Unfortunately, your macho attitude won't work here." He unexpectedly stepped back, pointed the Taser gun at me, and pulled the trigger. I heard a crackle and immediately felt a tremendous electrical shock race through my body. Every muscle in my body spasmed as I involuntarily screamed and bucked uncontrollably. The pain eased and I could begin to think after a minute or two. A vision of the girl in the hallway as she screamed and convulsed flashed in my mind.

"You son of a bitch!" I intended to shout, but my words only came out weakly. "I'll get even with you!"

"That is a nice thought, but don't take comfort in it," he said as he reloaded the instrument and pointed it at my chest.

"I can do this all day until it kills you if I want. Or I can use it on Ms. Barton and you can listen to her screams. It's your call, Mr. Wade."

I was resignedly silent. I had never felt pain like that. My dentist inadvertently hit an exposed nerve once and I thought that was incredible pain. It wasn't even close to this. I decided it was better to cooperate and avoid confrontation until I could figure a way out of this nightmare. I nodded my head in acquiescence.

"Good," he said. "I'm going to leave you alone to contemplate for a while. I'll send someone up with lunch and dry trousers in a little while." He closed and locked the door behind him.

I realized that the shock had caused me to pee my pants.

Son of a bitch! When I get us out of this, I'm going to Taser him until he screams for his mother and pees his pants.

Soon, I heard a woman scream repeatedly. The screaming stopped for a few minutes, then I heard a long, agonized scream–the same scream made by the girl in the hallway. The scream went on for a heart-wrenching minute or two. It was followed by a woman's voice whimpering in pain or fear or both. It sounded as though it came from just below me. I knew who it was. It had to be Liz.

Liz. He used that damned thing on Liz. I'm going to kill him!

SIXTY-NINE

Somewhere far away, the muffled sound of a man's scream registered in Liz's mind. Slowly, she came to, roused by the sound, but there were no other sounds that she could discern. Her shoulders hurt and she became painfully and frighteningly aware that something was holding her hands above her head and that she was sitting on a chair. As consciousness returned, she opened her eyes, looked up, and saw that her hands were secured together by a leather wristlet above her head and that she was suspended by a rope threaded through a pulley secured in the ceiling. She looked around the room and saw that it was a large bedroom. The wall opposite her was covered with mirrors.

She looked at herself and recoiled. She was completely naked, hanging like a side of beef on a hook. She was at first simply surprised, then abject fear enveloped her and she involuntarily screamed. She screamed and screamed and screamed and her body bucked until she was hoarse and worn out. Her head dropped as her shoulders slumped against the strain of the leather around her wrists.

A memory of Phillip came to her mind. He had once told her that, when confronted with what seemed to be an impossible problem, to calm herself and keep her wits about her, to observe the problem and the surroundings, assess the situation, and formulate available courses of action. And he told her never to give the psychological advantage to the other side.

"Control the situation to the extent you can," he had told her.

This certainly qualifies as an impossible situation. Keep your wits about you, Elizabeth.

She looked around the room. With a few exceptions–the pulleys, a deadbolt lock on the door, and a fully mirrored wall–it seemed to be a normal, well-appointed bedroom. She could see an adjoining bathroom with a tub, walk-in shower, toilet, and a bidet. That was a surprise. She looked at the mirrored wall across from her and saw herself. She was completely naked. Her hair had been brushed and mussed, either on purpose to give it an appealingly healthy look or by all her struggles. And she wore fresh lipstick. Then she saw that she had been shaved smooth below her waist. She recoiled again. This frightened her, but she reminded herself of Phillip's advice.

She sat like that, observing and contemplating, for several minutes until she heard the deadbolt click. She turned toward the door as a man entered the room. He wordlessly closed the door, but did not lock the door, then stared at her. He was short and lean, with a large nose, thick black hair, and a swarthy complexion. He was not ugly, but neither was he even remotely close to good-looking. His eyes were dark, cold, and penetrating, like the eyes of a predator. He wore creased khaki trousers and a golf shirt. In one hand, he carried what appeared to be an expensive digital camera, in the other an object that looked like a pistol with a square barrel and two shiny prongs at the end.

With all the temerity she could muster, Liz asked in a controlled voice, "Who are you, why am I here, and who shaved me?"

He smiled wryly and said softly, in a slightly accented voice, "Do not speak until I give you permission."

He circled her, observing her with a calculating stare.

"Who are you, why am I here, and who shaved me?"

Without a word, he pointed the pistol and shot her in her left leg. She heard a crackle and felt as though she had been kicked by a horse as electrical current surged and pulsed, coursing painfully throughout her body. She screamed in agony, bucking and thrashing like a hooked fish on a line until she was again exhausted. Her wrists were bleeding from burns and abrasions caused by her thrashing.

As she hung inert, the man repeated, "Do not speak until I give you permission. If you can hear me, nod your head."

With difficulty, Liz nodded her head.

"If you agree, nod your head. If not, we shall have to do this dance again."

Liz again nodded, slowly.

"I am going to take some pictures of you. I may give you some instructions, which you will obey," he said. "If you agree, nod your head. If not…, we will do this dance again," he repeated.

She raised her half-open eyes to look at him and listlessly nodded.

"I need you to be alert. I am going to give you some orange juice, then some water, then a caffeinated drink. Do not resist me. Say yes if you understand?"

She again nodded and croaked dryly, "Yes."

He went to a large dresser against one wall, opened a door behind which was a small refrigerator that contained small bottles of orange juice and water. It also contained a small can of a highly caffeinated soft drink that Liz recognized. He took one of each drink from the fridge, then pressed a button on the wall that reduced the tension on the rope enough that she could hold a water bottle to her lips. He helped her slowly drink the water, then the juice, and then the soft drink.

He disposed of the empty containers, then sat across the room in a comfortable chair and observed her. "You will soon become more alert and feel no more effects of the Taser. Then, I will explain some things to you, and we will move forward."

Liz sat quietly, trying to flex her knees and ankles, and shoulders as well as she could. She was scared witless, but tried hard not to let her fear show. She tried to concentrate on Phillip's advice.

Eventually, she felt better and more alert, but she was dauntingly, incredibly aware of her nakedness.

After a few moments, he spoke. "I am going to take some pictures of you. You will cooperate and do as I instruct you. Do you agree?"

"Yes," she said perfunctorily.

He walked behind her to the button on the wall, pointed the camera at her, and instructed her to look at him. As she turned, he pushed the wall button. She was quickly pulled up and off the seat into a standing position, her arms stretched higher into a painful position, her toes barely touching the floor. She went wide-eyed with fear and he took her picture, capturing the fear on her face as she cried out, "No!"

He pushed the button a second time, lifting her feet from the floor and moving the chair aside. As the pain increased, her eyes widened again, and she sucked in her breath hard as he again took her picture.

"Very good," he advised as he released the tension to the point she could stand, heels raised, on the balls of her feet.

He circled her, taking more pictures. When he was finished, he told her, "Very good. Relax and I'll get you down."

He released the tension on the rope, removed it from the pulley, and untied it from her wrists. He coiled the rope and placed it on a shelf in the closet. He took a robe from the closet, gazed at her naked body for a long moment, then helped her into the robe. He led her to a comfortable armchair and motioned for her to sit.

She did as she gathered the robe tightly around herself and started to speak, hesitated, then asked, "May I speak?"

He shook his head. "In a moment. I will speak first."

He went to the fridge and took a bottle of water, asking if she wanted anything.

"Water, please."

He sat and they drank.

"Listen carefully to what I say. Many of your questions will be answered. Let me finish before you speak. I will tell you when I am finished.

He repeated Liz's first questions. "Who are you, why am I here and who shaved me?"

"My name is Marco. I am a businessman. I make much money in my business. I buy and sell women. Occasionally, I sell someone to another businessman who sells that person for body parts." He spoke matter of factly, as if he were describing any normal job.

Cold fear filled Liz. She trembled and a knot formed in the pit of her stomach. Her stomach roiled and she thought she was going to be sick, but she kept the bile rising in her throat in check and said nothing, trying to remain passive.

"You are here because you now belong to me. I paid your friend Clark fifty thousand dollars for bringing you to my attention–sort of a finder's fee, if you will.

"I shaved you because the man to whom I will sell you prefers to see you that way. I will send him the pictures we took earlier."

"You were to be sent to the Middle East, to an extremely wealthy man who maintains a discrete harem. He will pay me five hundred thousand dollars for you, if you meet his approval. He was here yesterday with several other guests. He advised me that he has purchased an estate in Palm Springs to which you will be sent, instead. I believe that is an ill-advised course of action, but it is not my business.

"Do not believe that you can tempt me to your advantage. I can have all the young women I want. I would not offend this man by so much as touching you.

"You will remain here for two or three weeks for indoctrination and training. When you arrive at his palace, he will expect certain behavior from you, and I will ensure that you have been properly trained. Most of your training will be cultural and will be presented on video.

"You will live in this room. Depending on your behavior and how much I believe I can trust you, you may be allowed outside this room, possibly even onto the grounds of my estate. You will find it impossible to leave and/or communicate with anyone outside this estate. In keeping with that line of thought, your treatment will depend on your behavior. Your fate, as it were, is sealed. The sooner you accept that fact and reconcile your future in your mind, the easier it will be for you.

"The Taser is your punishment for resistance; hopefully, it will not be needed again. You will not be harmed or molested while you are here unless you invite that kind of treatment.

"Tomorrow, a small, but adequate wardrobe will arrive for you. For now, there are underwear, hospital scrubs, and a nightgown in the dresser drawer, and toiletries in the bathroom. There is a form on the dresser of your sizes and preferences for you to complete. Fill it out later and slide it under your door with the pencil. Do not forget to return the pencil with the form.

"Just so you know, there are a housekeeper, a cook, a gardener/handyman, and my bodyguard in residence here. If you are seen where you do not belong, they will tell me."

"Now, you may ask your questions, but be brief."

"I was told you had Dub Wade and his life was threatened to get me here. Is he alive and, if so, where is he?"

Marco was pensive for a moment. "I'm sure you want to know, not that it will matter much. You will never be able to tell anyone who can reach me, even if they believe you.

"At this time, he is here. If you cooperate, he will be sold for body parts, which will be harvested humanely and without pain to him—he will die quietly on an operating table. If you don't cooperate, I may just have him killed and dump his body in the Gulf of Mexico."

His words were more than Liz could handle.

"Oh, my God," she moaned and wept uncontrollably. Her stomach again roiled, and bile rose in her throat as she struggled hard not to be sick. Marco waited silently while she cried herself out.

"Please don't hurt him," she pleaded. "Please don't kill him. I'll do what you say."

Marco simply nodded.

She composed herself and asked, "I suppose, from what you said, that no one will ever know what happened to me or where I am? Or Dub, either?"

"That is correct."

"Why? Why do you do this? Why are you doing this to me?"

"As I told you, it's a business. I make a million or more dollars each year from exceptionally beautiful, intelligent young women like you, and it's all tax-free money. I have another legitimate business that is above suspicion. That business brings in enough money to sufficiently obscure my income from this business, so why not do it?"

He went into the bathroom and returned with gauze, tape, and ointment. He treated the burns on her wrists.

"What day is this?" she asked.

"Tuesday. I kept you sedated last night. It is now noon."

He handed her a small phone. "You can text using this phone. You cannot make phone calls or text outside, but you can text me or the kitchen. I am 1001, the kitchen is 4004. The television works." he said nodding his head toward the television. I will visit you later"

"Why are you being so civil to me?" Liz asked.

He turned and paused for a moment. "As I told you, I am a businessman. You are simply a commodity. I find that business and life go better if one is civil and practical. You and I are going to be together here for two or three weeks. I would prefer that we get along while you are here. If we cannot get along, then there is always the Taser."

"I will bring you lunch soon." He left, closing and locking the door.

Liz felt hopelessly forlorn and vulnerable.

SEVENTY

At noon, I heard a voice from the hall tell me to sit at the table next to the bed. A key was inserted in the lock and the door opened. The large, bald man from the garage stood in the doorway with an automatic pistol in his hand. On a cart beside him were fresh clothes and a tray with food on it. When he saw that I had followed his instructions, he holstered the pistol and brought the tray and clothing into the room. He cautiously set the tray on the table in front of me and wordlessly handed me the clothes, then left, locking the door behind him. The tray contained a cup of water and a sandwich on a paper plate, plastic utensils, and a napkin.

He had given me underwear and a clean set of scrubs, much like what I had been wearing. I ate, then sat quietly, thinking.

I'm collateral damage. The object of all this is Liz. So, assess the situation.

I observed that I was tethered by a coated flexible steel strand cable about ten or twelve feet in length to an eye bolt screwed into the wall, most likely into a stud behind the drywall. I cannot reach the entry door, but I can reach the toilet, and the shower. I have a new toothbrush, toothpaste, deodorant, soap, and shampoo, but no razor or shaving cream. I'm beginning to show a shadow of a beard.

I have a bed, an easy chair, a small table and one chair, and a bedside table with a lamp. My room appears to be a small bedroom for a servant. I have a small refrigerator containing several bottles of water. There is no apparent way out of the room except for the main door. There is a window, but it appears I am on the third floor and I would hang by my wrist twenty feet above the ground if I tried to climb out the window unless I can remove the tether. I can see very large houses on large lots in the far distance with wooded areas in between. I can see a swimming pool below and a large garage to the right of the house.

I do not know how many others are in the house in addition to the bald guy and Marco. Since this room appears to be a servant's room, I assume there is at least one servant in the house, maybe more. I have heard what sounds like the whir of an elevator and the sound of an elevator door opening and closing, so I assume that this home contains an elevator. So, there are four ways out–door, window, elevator, and stairs. But no apparent means of escape.

From the scream I heard earlier, I assume Liz is being held in a room below me, probably just below me from the sound of the scream. It is probably safe to assume that she is shackled similarly. If she is below this room, it is reasonable that she is in a larger room, a guest room.

It is possible that someone saw my abduction or that of Liz, but that's a longshot. It is probably better to assume that no one knows yet that we have been kidnapped. Whatever these guys have in mind, I am sure that I'm secondary to their plan. They want Liz, but why? Does this have something to do with Clark? Whatever it is, it isn't good. Since we are being held and haven't been harmed, someone must be waiting for another person to make a decision or give directions. But, will that happen in hours or days?

Given the size of this place and the homes that I can see around this place, there is big money involved. Does Clark or someone he knows have that kind of money? Liz said he does pretty well with the delis, but he can't be doing this well.

So, *what weapons are available?*

The only weapons I have seen are the Taser and the pistol. It's possible that I could get the Taser away from the little guy, Marco, but

I'm not sure I can take the gun from the big guy, especially not tethered like this. I might be able to get the shower pipe off, if necessary. At least it would be a hard object with which to strike.

Soon, I heard the voice tell me to sit at the table. Baldy again opened the door, pistol in hand, and checked my position. He entered and cautiously retrieved the tray and the plastic utensils. He set them on the cart and returned with two magazines and two paperbacks. He walked to the closet and reached above the doors, sliding a panel to the side to reveal an inset television. He laid a remote on the bed, and left, again without a word and again locking the door.

I assumed I was going to be a guest for more than just a few hours.

SEVENTY-ONE

Liz dressed in clean clothing but was afraid to take a shower. She had been naked long enough in this room for the time being. She didn't trust the man who called himself Marco.

There was a knock at Liz's door, then she heard Marco telling her to step away from the door and sit at the table. She did, and he opened the door, Taser in hand, and a tray on a cart next to him. When he saw her seated, he pocketed the Taser and carried the tray with her lunch into her room, setting it on her table. It held a nice lunch, but only paper plates and cups and plastic utensils.

He told her that her pictures had turned out wonderfully and that he was pleased that the exercise would not have to be repeated. He left her to her lunch, telling her he would return later with some instructional videos for her. He locked the door as he left.

An hour later, he returned with a book and several computer discs. He removed her tray and laid the items on her table. Holding the book up, he said, "This is an English translation of the Koran, and" he picked up a pamphlet, "this is a study guide that will direct you to the portions that you should read and understand before your trip."

He retrieved the stack of discs. "These are instructional videos that you should watch over the next two days. I suggest you watch them several times and become well versed in the instructions that these will give to you. And I must impress upon you the seriousness of all this. You must know how to dress, speak, and behave in your new culture. If you offend your new master, the law allows him to flog you, beat you, have you stoned, or cut off your head. Your life depends on what you learn before you leave here. Do not take it lightly."

He took a small DVD player from a drawer and showed her how to operate it. "The DVDs will play in this device. You have much to learn."

He left, locking the door behind him.

Liz was frightened. She was angry. She was intimidated. And the true reality of her situation became clear to her. She ran to the bathroom and threw up. Then, she wept.

Marco returned with dinner, but she was too upset to eat and was noncommittal when he attempted to engage her. He left without comment and did not return.

SEVENTY-TWO

aldy returned that evening with dinner. We went through the same drill as before. I sat quietly at the table and watched him carefully. He carried his pistol in a shoulder holster, not at his waist. He had thick wrists and was big and strong. He didn't lumber like a lot of big guys, so I assumed he was pretty quick and agile

I assumed a non-threatening posture and asked politely, "Is Liz okay?"

He said nothing and I assumed that he intended to ignore me. But, he stepped back and looked at me. "If you are good, she will be all right."

Well, okay; he can talk.

I tried again. "Do you live here?"

He paused. "Yes. I work for Mr. Marco for five years. I live here."

"Do you like baseball?"

He chuckled. "Sometimes I watch baseball."

"Can I get the Astros on that television?"

He nodded and told me the channel number. I thanked him.

He seemed to want to talk. I imagine he had little chance to converse in this environment.

"Will I be able to go outside and walk?'

"Behave. Maybe you will."

"Do you have family here?

He shook his head.

"What do you do here?"

"I work. I do errands. I drive Mr. Marco. Whatever he wants, I do."

"What day is today"

"Today Tuesday."

"Do the Astros play tonight?"

He shrugged that he didn't know.

"Go now. No more talk."

"Thanks. Good night."

He left, locking the door behind him.

I watched the ball game and went to sleep.

A thought woke me at 3 a.m. I had tried unscrewing the bolt from the wall, but it was in too tight to turn by hand. I needed a lever and it came to me while I slept. I quietly went into the bathroom and examined the pipe neck from the wall to the showerhead.

A bit of good luck. There was a ten-inch forty-five-degree extension between the wall and the showerhead. It appeared to be standard issue. I tried to unscrew it, but couldn't with my bare hands. There was a rubber bathmat on the shower floor. I wrapped it around the neck of the pipe and twisted. It gave me a better purchase, but I still couldn't budge the pipe. I tried and tried.

Come on, Dub. Get it off for Liz.

I strained until I thought my wrist would snap and the cords in my neck stood out like whipcords. And I felt a slight give. I strained again and the pipe turned ever so slightly again. Another strain and it turned enough to make a revolution. Then, it unscrewed completely and lay in my hand.

Now, if only I had estimated right. I took the pipe to the eye screw in the wall. Perfect fit! It slid right through the eye of the screw with little room to spare. I used the pipe to spin the screw out of the hole. I spun it the other way until it was back in, tight. Then, I tightened it even more and tried to move it side to side in the hole. It moved a little. I screwed it out a quarter turn and moved it side to side again. I repeated this, over and over until I could screw it back into the wall with finger pressure, yet it looked tight, but I could quickly unscrew it again with just finger pressure.

The only problem was that it left the cable twisted one way or the either as I turned it. I would have to make sure that it didn't show when anyone came into the room.

I returned the pipe to the shower and tightened it just finger tight. I ran the shower and there was just a slight leak around the threads.

Okay. This is good. Two parts of the problem solved.

If either of my handlers checked the pipe fitting, it would just look like it needed a new washer.

I looked at my left hand foolishly.

You're still handcuffed to a piece of cable. And you can't cut the cable and you can't open the handcuffs. So, how far have you really gotten?

I knew this problem would take a real solution.

Go back to sleep. Maybe the answer will come to you in your sleep as it had just done.

When I went to bed earlier, I had coiled the cable on the floor next to the bed to avoid tripping myself when I got out of bed. I bent to coil it again, and I had the answer, as crude as it was. Assuming I had enough time. I would simply coil the cable around my waist, leaving enough play to use my hand and arm, but not tight enough to impede the use of the limb. I looked in the closet and found a robe with a sash. I could use the sash to tie the wound cable into place around my waist, if necessary.

I went back to sleep in hopes of another great idea coming to mind.

SEVENTY-THREE

Liz had lain awake most of the night, thinking about her predicament. She had thought about what Dub had told her and had taught her about self-defense. She had relived her response to Damon's intrusion at Dub's home. Dub had told her that the best defense was a good offense. She had decided that she would rather die in America than be sent to service some Muslim's ego.

She thought about the abduction, remembered each act, each moment. When she had turned to face the bald man, she had noticed a woman in the row next to them who took out her phone and appeared to take a picture. She didn't think the bald man noticed the woman. And she didn't think he noticed her drop the note.

If only the woman had seen it and retrieved the note.

Marco had told her Dub was here. He, too, had to be thinking of a way to get them out of this situation.

If I can just buy us some time and keep Marco off balance, she thought, *maybe we will have a chance.*

She was mentally exhausted. She finally went to sleep well after sunrise.

From somewhere far away, she heard Marco telling her to sit at the table. She groaned. She heard the door open and said listlessly, "I'm in bed. I don't feel well."

He entered with the tray and set it on the table. "What is wrong?"

"I didn't sleep all night. I have a terrible headache and my stomach is upset. I just want to go back to sleep," which was true. "Please just leave the tray and let me sleep. Please."

"Very well. Text the kitchen if you want food. Text me when you feel rested." He left, locking the door behind him.

Liz feigned illness the rest of the day and was left alone except for receiving meals.

On Thursday, June twenty-ninth, she again feigned illness. A doctor was summoned and he came late that morning to check her. He advised that she was just mentally and physically worn out. He examined the wounds on her wrists, re-dressed them, gave her a mild sedative, and left another tablet for her to take that evening.

SEVENTY-FOUR

Thursday morning, June 29, I showered, shaved, and had just finished dressing when I heard the elevator and then Baldy called through the door for me to sit at the table. I did and he entered, saw me, and reached for the breakfast tray.

"Good morning," I said. "Thanks for bringing breakfast." I began eating.

"You are welcome."

"What is your name?"

"Yousef."

"You don't talk much, do you?"

"My job not to talk. I do what I am told."

I nodded. "I understand. I will see you at lunchtime."

"Yes,' he said as he left and locked the door.

I finished eating and set to work. I had gotten a few other ideas in my sleep and was eager to implement them.

I went to the sink. It was a standard pedestal sink, with faucet knobs and a stopper with an attached stopper pull. I looked under the sink and found the rod that was controlled by the stopper pull. Like most sinks, it was a ten-inch, threaded bolt that went through a piece of strap metal below the pull and attached to the drain with a two-inch plastic wing nut. I removed the nut and the bolt, replacing the nut on the end of the bolt. I now had a stabbing instrument with a handle that I could control. One more weapon.

Now, I needed a small nail or something similar. I searched every drawer in the room, along the baseboard, and in and around the window. I didn't see any plausible place I had missed. And then, voila!

I looked up and I found a cheap metal coat hanger in the closet. I bent it and twisted it back and forth until I had broken off a straight piece, three inches long I used that as an awl and my shower pipe as a hammer to remove the door hinge pins one at a time. I rubbed soap on each of them before putting them back in place so they would come out easily the next time.

I thought about the door. It was locked with a key which meant a small deadbolt slipped into a hole when the key was turned. I examined the lock and it looked pretty standard. Since the door swung inward, it was unlikely that I could kick it hard enough to splinter the jam with just a couple of kicks. More than that would probably be heard all through the house. But I was pretty sure that I could remove the top and bottom hinge pins and, if I could pull the top of the door out from the hinge side far enough to get a good grip, I could probably pull the door inward and dislodge the bolt or splinter the wood around the metal seat for the bolt.

But how in hell was I going to get something wedged in the tiny space between the edge of the door and the jam that would give me enough purchase to pull the door to me? I looked everywhere for a sturdy thin metal object to force in the small space but could find nothing.

I sat and tried to think logically. If only I could screw a doorknob on the hinged side of the door. I looked at my small coterie of tools and wondered if I could screw the bolt from the sink drain into the hinge side of the door and get a grip tight enough to pull the door to me and pull the lock out of the receiver. That would take some doing and I wasn't sure I could maintain a grip on that slender bolt.

I pondered, looked down, saw the end of the cable, and had an idea.

I went to the closet. I had looked there for a nail with no luck, but I remembered seeing a couple of sturdy, thick wooden coat hangers. It had surprised me that something like that was left in the room. I removed one and examined it. A hard, lightweight steel hook at the top was screwed into the wide wood of the shoulder portion of the hanger. I unscrewed the hook and found approximately one inch of threaded metal screw with another half-inch of straight metal before the curve began.

Now, I had the beginnings of a plan, but it was going to be a little noisy at times. I would have to wait for the right time, but I didn't know how long we could wait. Each morning and evening, I heard the elevator come to the third floor, but no one came to my room. I assume that one or two servants, probably a cook and a housekeeper, had rooms on this floor as well. I could probably make a little noise during the day but would have to be careful at night.

Hell, I could probably yell for help, but I'm sure that would only result in a visit from the Taser. The day passed uneventfully.

SEVENTY-FIVE

Friday, June thirtieth, started quietly. Yousef brought me breakfast and lunch, and I chatted with him a little. After lunch, I heard the engine of a large lawnmower fire up. I looked out the window and saw that a team of gardeners was setting to work. This was as good a time as any, so I set to work, hoping the lawnmower would dampen or disguise any sound I made.

I unscrewed the eye bolt from the wall and wound the tether around my waist. I took the coat hanger screw, the shower pipe, the drain pipe bolt, and the small piece of coat hanger to the door. I hoped the lawnmower would not finish too soon. This might get a little noisy. And, it was going to be a slow, tedious process.

I took the piece of the coat hanger and, using the shower pipe as a hammer, tapped it into the door directly across from the knob and lock and about two inches in from the edge of the hinge side of the door. Tap, tap, pause, and listen for anyone coming; tap, tap and pause again. I tapped it in as far as I could which was only about one-quarter of an inch. I guessed that it took about half an hour. This appeared to be an expensive, well-built house and the doors were solid wood. This was going to be a very slow process, but I was glad the doors weren't thin and hollow. If they had been, my plan wouldn't have worked.

In a little while, the lawnmower shut down. I assumed they were finished with it for the day. I took the coat hanger screw and pushed the pointed tip into the small hole I had just made. I pushed as hard as I could and turned the screw just a little with my fingers. It was slow and tedious, but I eventually got a little purchase in the wood and the screw just started. I got the screw in about one-eighth of an inch. I removed the screw, inserted the piece of coat hanger, tapped it, and listened. I heard nothing and tapped it in another quarter of an inch and started over with the screw. I repeated the process until I heard the elevator start. I had been so intent on what I was doing that the sound startled me.

Oh, shit. How did it get to be so late?

I grabbed my tools and scampered to the bed, quickly screwed the eye bolt into the wall, hoping it would hold, and hurried into the bathroom, pivoting as I went to take the wound turns out of the tether. I hid everything beneath the shower mat just as I heard Yousef knock and tell me to sit.

"Just a second," I called out as I flushed the toilet. He came in as I was walking out of the bathroom.

I sat on the bed, pulling the tether close to me, looked out the window, and said, "The yard looks nice."

He cocked his head and looked at me inquisitively.

"I heard the lawnmower. Is Friday the day the yard service comes?"

"Gardener tends the yard on Friday," was all he said as he left my tray. He had left my door open, so my handiwork was on the backside and he didn't see anything.

He returned later for the tray, said good night and left, again without noticing the small hole in the backside of the door.

~ ~ ~

Liz woke on Friday morning, distraught and upset. When Marco entered her room with breakfast, she moaned, choked, and ran for the bathroom where she vomited in the toilet. Marco left the tray and told her to rest and to text the kitchen if she wanted anything.

She tried to sleep and was successful for a couple of hours. She asked for ice cream and Marco brought it. It helped her stomach and he brought her soup that evening. He said little to her all that day.

SEVENTY-SIX

Saturday, July first, Yousef brought my lunch which included a full cup of mousse. He told me the cook had made the mousse especially for guests and that it was very good, that I would like it. He was right. It was very, very good.

Shortly, thereafter, four cars arrived and men disembarked from them. All appeared to be Middle Eastern and the driver of each carried a suitcase into the house. The elevator went up and down to and from the second floor several times that day and into the evening. Once, it stopped on the third floor to bring Yousef who looked in on me, as if checking to see what I was doing, but he was in and out quickly.

"Do we have company?" I asked.

"It is meeting," he replied. "Nothing for you."

Right after that, I became unusually lethargic and drowsy. I realized that the pudding must have contained a sedative to keep me quiet while guests were in the house. I don't remember anything else.

Yousef woke me with dinner. He asked if I wanted to watch the Astros. I said yes and he turned the game on for me and left. I soon realized that I had slept through Saturday and this was Sunday. He had, indeed, sedated me.

I assume they had done so with Liz; then a cold, sobering thought occurred to me. Perhaps he had sedated me so that I wouldn't know that Liz had been taken from the house.

Yousef came for my tray and asked about the game.

I replied, then asked if Liz was still in the house. He paused for a long moment, then said, "She is here."

"Really, Yousef. You're sure?"

"Yes. She is here."

"Did you sedate me to keep me quiet yesterday and last night? I asked.

He nodded. "Better that way."

"Was she sedated also?"

He nodded.

"Did anyone molest her while she was unconscious?"

He paused and I thought a lie was coming until he asked, "What is molest?"

"Did anyone touch her or bother her?"

He shook his head. "No."

I didn't know whether to believe him or not, but he gave me no signs that he was lying.

SEVENTY-SEVEN

Yousef brought me breakfast on Monday, July third, and asked about the Astros game. I told him the score–six to one, Astros won.

He nodded and asked, "Do you like baseball?"

"Yes. I played as a kid and in college. Do you like sports?

He nodded. "Soccer."

"Did you play when you were a boy?"

"A little. Mostly in the streets with other boys."

"Do you like watching soccer?"

He nodded, and said, "I watch sometimes. Not often."

He turned to go and I said, "See you at noon."

He shook his head and pointed to the tray. I noticed there was a wrapped sandwich and an apple as well as breakfast. "Gone today. Your lunch is on the tray also."

"Okay. Thanks."

He nodded and left, locking the door behind him. I noticed that he had not locked it behind him when he entered. Nor did he notice the screw hole in the door.

SEVENTY-EIGHT

On Monday, July third, at seven-thirty a.m., the crime lab accessed the computer base of the Delaware Secretary of State. They printed the incorporation application and noted all names. The incorporator was a lawyer in Dover, Kent County, Delaware. The president of the company was listed as Masoud Kassam with a Houston address. There were also three directors listed with addresses in Houston.

Despite it being a holiday, Paul Radke, head of the Crime Lab, called Asimov and brought him up to date.

"We ran all four names, plus Yousef Ahmadi through the IRS database. We presume these guys are resident aliens, so we ran them through the IRS and ICE databases. They are resident aliens and they have addresses. Coincidentally, both Yousef and Kassam have the same home address according to IRS. We ran the address through Harris County Real Property Records and that address is a pricey home in The Woodlands owned by Marcos Import/Export, Ltd. The home is valued at two point five million dollars. You recall the address of Marcos Imports was the address on Yousef's driver's license and is the address on Kassam's driver's license, according to DMV. We're running down the other three guys, but these two look the most connected and promising."

"I agree."

"I called the company at eight o'clock and they are open today. I asked for Mr. Yousef and was told that he is out of the office for the day with Mr. Kassam and was unavailable. I asked what his job is. I was told he is the Driver for Mr. Kassam and is Mr. Kassam's factotum."

"His what?" asked Asimov.

Radke laughed. "Yeah. That one got me. I had to look it up. It's someone who does a variety of jobs, usually a handyman or the like. So, he is Kassam's driver and flunky. We ran his name through DPS and he has a concealed carry permit, so he is probably Kassam's bodyguard, too. He listed his address as the company address for his weapons permit.

The picture on his gun license is the same as the passport and driver's license–and the guy pictured in the parking garage. Looks like you have enough for a Warrant."

"Yep. I'll call Evans right now. Keep me posted if you get anything else."

"Will do."

Asimov called Evans' office but got her voice mail. He texted Evans: NEED YOU ASAP.

SEVENTY-NINE

Liz was up and dressed Monday morning. She had given her situation a lot of thought and had made a decision by the time a knock came at her door. Marco's voice told her to sit at the table. The door opened and he was there, Taser in hand, with a tray of food on the cart next to him. She was at the table, so he pocketed the Taser and entered with the tray, which he placed on the table. He did not lock the door behind him.

"I must go out today, so your lunch is also on the tray. You can put it in your refrigerator until you are ready for it."

"Did you sedate me over the weekend?" she asked pointedly.

Without hesitation, he replied, "Yes. The doctor advised that you needed rest and suggested a long-lasting sedative. I trust you are well-rested this morning."

She didn't reply, but she did feel well-rested.

Liz had decided that her best plan of action was to go along to get along, but to keep him off balance until she was better able to formulate a plan. She greeted Marco politely and thanked him for breakfast. She began to eat quietly, leaving him to start a conversation.

"Have you viewed any of the instructional DVDs?" he asked.

"No. I'm upset and am not ready to do that yet," she replied evenly.

"You must begin your education. You have lost several days. It is in our best interest."

"You are telling me that I have to voluntarily leave my family, my home, and my religion just to please a wealthy man from the Middle East who has no feelings for me. I find that very presumptuous."

"You must accept your destiny."

She continued to eat and replied, "Your words to me were that life would 'go better if one is civil and practical,' and that you 'would prefer that we get along while I am here.' You are being civil, but not practical. There is no incentive to induce me to leave my family, my country, and my religion to become a concubine in the Arab world. You tell me I'm worth five hundred thousand dollars to you and you have offered me no incentive to help you in this venture."

He was taken aback. No one had ever talked to him like this.

"I do not have to offer an incentive. I own you."

"No. You paid fifty thousand dollars to a man who gave you my name. He didn't own me and you don't own me. Right now, you aren't a businessman. You're a simple thug and kidnapper. If you are going to make this work, you need to work with me.

"If you want to make this work, it will cost you half of what you are to be paid for me, and I must be allowed to say goodbye to Mr. Wade and my family."

He pulled the Taser from his pocket and brandished it. "You must be taught a lesson."

"That won't change my mind. If you send me there, I'll tell the man to whom you send me that you raped me. He may have me killed, but he will demand his money from you or a replacement for me. Either way, you will have lost your credibility and I will have brought about your downfall."

"You threaten me with a claim of rape," he shouted in a shrill voice. "I have six men to whom I can give you. They can have you one after another until you cannot stand on your own or remember your own name. You have no idea what true rape can be."

"You may be right, but I would still tell and bring about your downfall."

"You insolent bitch," he shouted and angrily extended the Taser toward her, fiercely pressing the trigger button.

Liz screamed in agony as the unbearable pain coursed through her body. She fell sideways from her chair, convulsing and moaning on the floor.

He screamed at her. "I'll let them have you until they are tired of you. They will fuck you every way imaginable. Then, I will sell you as a common whore. I may even give you to the most objectionable man I know, just to teach you a lesson."

It took two minutes for her to begin to calm. When she could speak, she looked at him malevolently and whispered, "'Kill me. Or rape me yourself, if you're man enough."

He went livid at her words and Liz saw in his eyes and on his face that she had struck a nerve.

"It will only come back to haunt you, Marco. You had better think twice about what you're doing."

He was apoplectic. "I will give you until I return this evening to think about what you are doing. Then, I will be back to deal with you." He stormed out the door, slamming and locking it behind him.

EIGHTY

Below me, I heard shouting. I heard Marco shout "you insolent bitch," and then heard Liz scream. I assumed he had Tasered her again. I heard the door slam and assumed he had left and she was alone. Her scream had come from directly below me about six feet from the sidewall of my room. From my view out the window, I was certain that the wall was approximately just below my west wall.

I knelt and leaned against the west wall, cupped my hands to my mouth, and called Liz's name loudly against the wall. I hoped the sound would travel down the sheetrock, but not far enough to be heard by others. There was no response. I put my ear to the wall, tapped with my knuckles, and called her name again. Nothing.

I tried again and heard tapping from below me. I tapped twice, then once, and heard two taps, then one in response.

"Can you hear me?"

"Yes."

"Are you all right?"

"I made him angry. He Tasered me and stormed out. He is selling me to some rich sheik, I think. I'm scared."

"Stay calm and think straight," I advised her. "Is there a bathroom at the right end of this wall in your room?"

"Yes."

"Is there a window on the right side of the bathroom?"

"Yes."

"Go to the window and see if it will open."

There was silence for a moment, then her voice. "It will open. Do you want me to leave it open?"

"No. Not yet." I paused. "Are you shackled or handcuffed?"

"No."

"Can you move about freely?"

"Yes."

"I am in a small room right above you. I'm shackled to this wall."

"Oh, no! What can we do?"

"Keep calm. Does the big guy ever come to your room?'

"No."

"Is there anything in your room you can use as a weapon?'

"I don't think so."

"Do you have your purse?"

"No.

I explained to her how to remove the slender bolt from her drain plug and put the wingnut back on it. "Do that. You have at least one weapon. If you have to, drive that into his temple, his eye or his throat. Don't be squeamish about it. And keep at him, just like you did with Damon."

Silence again, then, "Okay."

"Let me think for a minute. Look for anything else you can use as a weapon. When you want to talk, tap three times. If you think he is coming, tap twice quickly."

"Okay. He said he was going out today and he brought my lunch with him this morning. Do you think that means we will be alone until late afternoon, at least?"

"I think so. They brought me lunch, also. I saw the Mercedes leave a few minutes ago and Marco was in the car. When he comes to your room, does he lock the door behind him when he is in with you?

Silence, then she replied, "No, I don't remember him doing that."

"Okay. At least, we have four or five hours or so to work on a plan. You look for weapons."

"Okay."

I thought. I didn't remember Marco or the big guy locking my door after them when either of them was in the room with me, either.

If I could get out of the window, I might be able to get into her room. At least there would be two of us. If Marco or the big guy didn't come to my room and find me missing, we would have the element of surprise. If either did find my room empty, then I would have the big guy and probably both of them to contend with in her room.

The problem with the window was that I had nothing to allow me to climb down. I could secure the steel cord to the bed, but then it wouldn't be long enough to allow me to get into her room. And I would be tethered to the bed and couldn't get free. But I might be able to tear a sheet into strips and get some added length that way. I scrapped any idea of going out of the window.

I knew I could knock the hinge pins out of my door and maybe get it open that way. I could get to her room, but it was locked. I would have to wait for Marco to come to her room, surprise him, overpower him, and get the key to her room–a long shot, at best. But I should loosen the pins and maybe remove one or two in preparation.

Other options?

I had the pipe from the shower to use as a weapon. I had the cable with a lock and sharp screw on the end that I could swing as a weapon. I had examined the bed. It had a metal frame, but the headboard and footboard were all one piece and the platform was like that of an Army cot–nothing there that I could take apart and use as a weapon. I looked at the table. The legs were square and were secured to the tabletop by bolts that screwed to the table frame. Maybe I could get a leg off and use that as a club.

I knew Marco and Yousef came up to my floor by elevator; I heard the sound each time they came and left. I guessed they did so when they went to the second floor as well, especially if they were carrying a tray of food. And neither had come back for my tray until they brought the next meal.

I heard three taps and put my ear to the wall, tapping twice back to her.

"I've looked but I can't find anything that wouldn't be obvious to him when he enters the room."

I had figured as much. A missing table leg would stand out like a sore thumb. "Okay. Sit tight and stay calm. Let me think for a while"

"Okay." Then, "Dub, I'm scared."

"I know. But right now, we're okay. One step at a time. You think and I'll think."

"I miss you."

That was a welcome surprise in the midst of all this. "I miss you, too, Sweetheart. Stay calm."

"I'll try."

PART 11

EIGHTY-ONE

Evans texted Asimov just before nine a.m. Monday morning, July third: I'M UP NEXT; IT WILL TAKE ABOUT THIRTY MINUTES. She called him at nine-thirty. "What do you have?"

He told her succinctly and she told him to call Arvin Choksi, give it all to him, and tell him she said to start working on warrants.

He called Choksi and they met in the District's Attorney's conference room with Paul Radke. Asimov and Radke walked Choksi through the evidence, exhibits, and suppositions from the very beginning. They spent an hour going through everything.

Asimov mentioned the instances of Clark's stalking Barton and Choksi replied that he knew that a guy named Gomez works for Clark. He said he believed that Clark sent Gomez after Mr. Wade.

"This is an interesting corollary to the case at hand. We may have to talk to Gomez and Clark about all this—after we get the warrants issued. I'll get started on them right now."

As they were preparing to leave, Radke's phone buzzed. He answered, listened for a moment and exclaimed, "Super. Way to go!"

He held his finger up to Asimov and Choksi to wait. He listened for another long moment, looking intently at Choksi and Asimov, as he did. He ended the call and said, "You guys aren't going to believe this. This case is getting weird and we're getting lucky."

He turned to Asimov. "You brought me a phone from that guy Clark a few days ago and we've been trying to trace the phone and the numbers on it. My guys just hit the mother lode.

"The number Clark called is a burner with renewable minutes. We could never get an answer when we called the number. We finally tracked it down. It was bought across the street from the address of Marco Import/Export with a company credit card. We're working on the numbers that were called from the phone.

Evans and Asimov went to her office to work on warrants.

EIGHTY-TWO

I tapped the wall for Liz. She tapped back. I called, "I am going to make some noise up here and it may take two or three hours. When I am finished, I will explain everything to you. Just sit tight until then."

"Okay. Can I ask what you are going to do?"

"I'm working on a way to get out of this room and to you. But there are still a lot of loose ends. I'll be working on those while I'm working on a way to get out of the room. Trust me.

"I do."

"Does Marco always have the Taser with him when he comes to your room?"

"Yes."

"Okay. Sit tight for a while."

I retrieved the coat hanger screw, the shower pipe, the drainpipe bolt, and the small piece of coat hanger. I used the shower pipe to unscrew the eye bolt in my wall and returned to the door. I hoped like crazy that Liz was right and they were gone for the afternoon. This might get a little noisy.

Once again, I began the repetitive process. I tapped the piece of coat hanger into the door, but this time I followed with the sink bolt and drove it into the small hole started from the coat hanger as far as I could, about one-quarter of an inch. I removed the sink bolt, took the coat hanger screw, and screwed it into the hole as far as I could. Thanks to my prior efforts, the hole was about three-eighths of an inch deep now. I removed the screw.

Now I had a hole about one-quarter of an inch in diameter, three-eighths of an inch deep and narrowing as it went down. I took the pipe drain rod and drove it into the hole using the shower pipe. I got it in to about half an inch. I guessed that had taken ten minutes. I needed to get the hanger screw in the full length before the curve. Ten minutes for half an inch; at least sixty minutes, probably more, to get the hanger screwed all the way in. The deeper I went, the harder it became.

I guessed that ninety minutes or so later, the hanger screw was in all the way. I removed the hanger screw, took the drain bolt, hammered it into the hole made by the hanger screw, and wallowed it around and around, enlarging the hole. I reached down, pushed the pointed, threaded end of the eye bolt secured at the end of my tether into the hole, tapped it with the shower pipe, then inserted the shower pipe into the eye. Using all the strength I could muster, I leaned into the screw and used the shower pipe as a lever just as I had before to screw the eye bolt into the door. I got it into the hole about half an inch, pulled it out, cleaned the threads and blew the dust out of the hole, and went at it again–pound the drain bolt, screw in the eye screw, clean hole, repeat. I guessed it took another two or more hours to get the eye screw into the door to the hilt. I pulled and the resistance made me hopeful.

EIGHTY-THREE

Monday morning, Masoud Kassam, a/k/a Marco was driven by Yousef to the Hotel Damascus, an exclusive hotel in the banking center of the city, ostensibly for a director's meeting, but actually to meet with five of his "special services" clients. He had reserved a large meeting room replete with dining tables, a horseshoe-shaped meeting table, and video equipment. He anticipated at least two new orders for women today and several to follow. In his locked briefcase, he carried several photographs of "possible candidates" and a set of the photos he had taken of Elizabeth Barton as she hung by her wrists, naked. He thought her photos would be an impressive example of what he could provide.

He opened the meeting with lunch, tea, coffee, and soft drinks, and alcohol for those who wanted wine or liquor, which most did.

After lunch, he slowly moved through a PowerPoint presentation of several young women who were already subservient to his organization, as well as a number who were targeted for future "indoctrination" and who could easily be made available upon request and payment. They spent a spirited afternoon of evaluation, comparison, comments, and pointed observation. Some placed orders for some of the women who had been presented.

When that portion of the afternoon was completed, Marco presented photographs of five especially beautiful and expensive young women who could be provided promptly for the right price. He received three orders and two possibles.

Then, he showed the photographs of Elizabeth Barton after advising that she was already spoken for but that she was an example of the truly exceptional young women to whom he had access. One very wealthy sheik offered to pay a considerable amount for her, more than she was to bring Marco, until another guest whispered in the ear of the sheik the name of the man for whom Barton was reserved. His offer was quickly withdrawn with apologies.

EIGHTY-FOUR

I got a drink of water and collected my thoughts for a minute. It was going slowly and I knew we needed more time.

Okay, Wade. Now, what do we do with all this preparation?

I tapped for Liz and called her name. She immediately replied.

"How are you doing?" I asked.

"Trying to stay calm and optimistic. Tell me something good, please."

"I have an idea, but there are a lot of variables that I need to think through. I just wanted to let you know I'm still working on it. Give me a little more time to work it out."

"Think fast, handsome."

"I will. Just remember what I've taught you and what we've worked on. Stay alert, be aware, and don't let the other guy surprise you. Don't react blindly."

"Understood. You've been a good teacher. I'll try to keep my wits about me."

"Good girl. Talk to you in a little while."

It had to be around three p.m. I closed my eyes, visualized, and planned. The big variables came when Marco returned. So far, Yousef had not accompanied him to Liz's room. Unless he was going to move us tonight, I didn't expect Yousef to be on her floor. She had said that Marco told her she would be here two or three weeks for learning, so I didn't expect a move tonight.

I knew that Marco had been taking Liz's meals to her, but after the conflict this morning, I thought he would go to her room to set her straight before he thought about feeding her. So, if he stayed in form, he would probably go to Liz as soon as he got back, take the Taser, leave the door unlocked behind him and confront her.

My big worry was Yousef. If he came to my room when Marco went to her room, I would have to deal with him. I wasn't sure I could deal with him. I thought I needed more than what Mr. McCain taught me. And, I'm sure Yousef has a gun. I worked it through in my mind like a flow chart. If A, then B. If C, then D. If B, then E. If D, then F.

I removed the table leg, gathered my sink rod and my shower pipe. I screwed the eye screw into the entry door securely and checked my paltry arsenal. I removed all the hinge pins in the door. And remembered one important thing I had forgotten.

EIGHTY-FIVE

Evans and Choksi had Warrants ready at one p.m., Monday. As they worked, they talked through the bones of the case they were making. They were sure they had Ahmadi by the short hairs and could convict him of kidnapping. They felt confident they could make a case of kidnapping against Kassam as an accessory to kidnapping.

Choksi apprised her of the coincidence of the Clark and Gomez case. "From the pictures on Clark's phone and what we've just learned from the lab, I think we may be at the doorstep of human trafficking and pandering."

As he said that, his paralegal came in with papers in her hand. "I did what you asked and got a surprise. Masoud Kassam was charged with pandering ten years ago. That was long before any of us were here. I read the file, which was pretty short, but there was an interesting note by the attorney who handled the charge. An employee of Marco Exports complained that Kassam solicited her to go to the Middle East and be a consort for some prince over there. She said she thought he was joking at first, but when she realized he was serious, she came to us, filed a charge of discrimination with the EEOC, and quit her job. A note in the file says she settled for a lot of money and a permanent protective order against Kassam." She handed Choksi a typewritten summary and asked, "Does that help you?"

Choksi looked at Evans and they both grinned from ear to ear. He looked at his paralegal, "Sharon, take the afternoon off and have dinner on me. It helps a lot. Great job!"

Evans had called ahead to her favorite district judge and arranged to bring her warrant applications as soon as she could. They gathered applications for arrest warrants for Yousef Ahmadi and Masoud Kassam, as well as search warrants for Kassam's residence and property, all automobiles registered in his name, and all buildings, offices, files, safes and other assets belonging to Marcos Imports/Exports, Ltd.

At one-forty-five p.m., she and Choksi appeared before the Hon. Evelyn Parcell and succinctly walked the judge through the warrants and supporting evidence. The judge read every document thoroughly and listened carefully to the recount of the pandering charge. She liked Evans because Evans was good and thorough. She found no fault with any of the applications, signing them as she wished Evans and Choksi good luck with the case.

EIGHTY-SIX

Masoud Kassam looked around the table with a smiling face. It had been a profitable luncheon and meeting. He had, indeed, received the two expected orders and a third with promises of more to come. As he reached to collect the pictures of Liz Barton, a swarthy, overweight man with porcine eyes motioned with his hand for the pictures.

"May I see those one more time?"

He took the stack and studied every picture slowly with a greedy countenance.

"Stunning. Absolutely stunning. I only wish I had known about her first. Find me one like this and I will gladly pay your price."

"She is spectacular, isn't she?" Kassam retrieved the pictures and looked at the top one. "I shall, of course, do my best to please you," Kassam said to the man, then his eyes took each man in the group. "I shall do my best to please each of you, as I have tried always to do."

The men bowed to one another and said their ritual goodbyes.

Yousef had guarded the door during the meeting, for obvious reasons. As the men began to leave, he entered the room and took Kassam's two briefcases from him after Kassam double-checked that they were locked tight. Each was heavy metal with a sturdy, combination lock. Youssef carried them to the parking garage where he loaded them and collected the car, then drove to the hotel entrance for Kassam.

As he entered traffic, he asked, "It was a good meeting, sir?"

Kassam sighed happily. "Yes, Yousef. It was a very good meeting. Our miss Barton stole the show. Now, I must improve her attitude and her behavior."

Yousef occupied himself with driving in the burgeoning traffic as Kassam leaned back, closed his eyes, and mentally counted his money.

EIGHTY-SEVEN

At two-thirty p.m., Detectives Rivera and Smock, followed by two patrol cars, pulled into parking spaces at the front door of Marcos Import/Export, Ltd. They entered, placed an officer at each exit, and walked to the receptionist, where they introduced themselves and asked to see the General Counsel of the company.

"We don't have a general counsel here," said the nervous woman.

"Then, please summon your chief officer," said Rivera.

"Mr. Kassam isn't here."

"Well, who is in charge right now?"

"That would be Mr. Khalil. He is a senior vice president."

"Get him. Do not call anyone else."

Khalil appeared and was served with the Search Warrants for the premises, offices, files, safes, desks, et cetera. He blustered briefly but had nothing of substance to say.

"How many employees are here right now, including the warehouse?"

"About twenty-five."

"Do you have a cafeteria or a large conference room?"

"No cafeteria. We have a large conference room, but it will be crowded with that many employees."

"Then have all your management employees go to the conference room, and all your nonexempt employees come to the lobby right now. No one may leave until we have met with him or her. Until we give permission, no one may call outside. If we see anyone with a phone in his or her hand, it will be confiscated and that person will be arrested. Do you have an intercom system?"

"Yes."

"Use it. Everything, just like I said."

"Check all of the warehouse buildings," Rivera instructed two officers.

They returned with James White and Leticia.

"This lady and gentleman were locked in cells in one warehouse. There are six cells with three cots each out there. Mr. White here says that they imprison mostly women out there. He says that Mr. wade and Ms Barton were removed from this location days ago, maybe as much as a week ago. He doesn't know where they were taken."

"Well, damn," exclaimed Rivera. "We may be too late to save them."

He called Asimov and relayed the information.

EIGHTY-EIGHT

At what I guessed to be around three-thirty pm, I tapped the wall and called Liz's name. She responded immediately. I knew she must be a bundle of nerves by now. I didn't want to tell her what to expect because I didn't know what to expect and I didn't want her to be confused if something went differently than I had said. I knew she was intelligent and resilient, but I also knew she was very frightened.

"How are you doing?"

"Hanging in there. Hoping for the best."

"Good girl. I can't tell you what to expect because there are a lot of variables that I can't control—the biggest one being Yousef."

"Who is Yousef"

"Sorry. He's the big, bald guy."

She paused, then said slowly, dejectedly, "Oh."

"Since he has never come to your room, I'm planning on that same behavior this afternoon. I'm hoping he doesn't come to my room when Marco comes to yours."

"What if he does… come to your room, I mean?"

"Be patient. If you hear me yell to run, kick the shit out of Marco and run. If you can't get down the stairs, jump out the window."

She was silent for a long moment. "You're serious?" she asked.

"Yes, but that is a very down the line, last resort.

"What about you?

"Don't worry about me. You get out of here any way you can. Avoid using the elevator and avoid Yousef."

"I can't leave you."

"You won't be leaving me. I may not be right behind you, but I will be on my way. I don't want to have to worry about you. Unless I'm dead, I will be calling your name and you will hear my voice. If you don't hear my voice, get out of the house and run screaming down the road. Trust me."

"I do."

"If Marco comes in and does not lock the door, try to stall him and keep him off balance. If he locks the door, keep him off balance until I can break in. Stay away from his Taser, but don't be afraid of him. He's a bully, just like Damon. Without his Taser, he's just a wimp with a mean toy and no backbone. I assume you have a table chair or desk chair. Pick that up by the back and used the legs to fend him off, if necessary."

"Umm...," she paused wordlessly, then said, "Okay."

"If you smell smoke or hear anyone other than me yell FIRE, don't worry. If you actually see fire or hear me yell FIRE, get out as fast as you can by door or window."

"Fire?"

I let that one pass.

As my first contingent plan, if we couldn't get free, I intended to start a fire in one of the far third floor rooms and hope the smoke and flames were seen and reported. Worst case scenario, I planned to set the entire upper floor on fire and hope the firemen arrived in time to save us. But, I was an optimist.

"The more you can do to keep him off balance and away from you, the better."

"If you see me behind him, do not acknowledge me or tip him off in any way."

"Can you get out of your room? Are you coming down here?" she asked me.

"If things go right, the answer to both questions is yes.

"If there is an opportunity to get his Taser or his phone, get them. And don't be afraid to use the Taser on him. Stand three to four feet from him and pull the trigger. Don't press it against him; that defeats the purpose. If you want to reload, new loads should be in his pocket but don't get close enough to him that he can grab you. Just hang onto the Taser itself."

"If he goes down, hit him over the head with a lamp or something. And hit him hard."

Again, there was silence for a moment. Then, "Okay."

"Enough of that for the time being, just relax for a few minutes."

"Okay."

She was quiet and I didn't know what to say. Telling a person over and over not to worry just plants the seed that she should be worried. I wanted something to take her mind off of our predicament.

She must have been reading my mind.

"Dub?"

"Yes?"

"Do you think about us when we're not together?"

"Yes. Constantly. I have to be careful when I'm in the operating room to keep you out of my mind."

"I'm sorry. I'm… sorry that I got you into this mess."

"Oh, I don't think you did. I think I'm the guy who asked if he could buy you a drink."

"You know what I mean."

"Of course, I do. We had four dates and finally slept together. Can't be much more circumspect than that."

She giggled. "I thought we would never get to be alone together."

"I think it was destined."

"Jill said the same thing.

"Dub?"

"Yes?"

"I don't want to lose what we have."

"I don't either. We just need to stay alert and be on our toes for a few more hours."

"I'll do my best. How will we know when something is going to happen?"

"Listen and watch out the window. A big, black Mercedes left earlier to take him wherever he was going. When it comes back, the show starts."

"Okay."

She said she had to go to the bathroom and I thought that might be a good idea.

When she came back, she tapped and called my name.

"I'm here."

"Put your hand against the wall. I want to be as close to you as I can."

I put my hand against the wall and softly patted it. I heard her do the same thing.

We heard the car coming up the drive at the same time.

"Gotta go," I said. "Keep your wits about you."

EIGHTY-NINE

Asimov and Evans were in Asimov's car. They were followed by six officers in three squad cars. They used sirens to get through the heavy traffic from the business location until they turned off the North Freeway. It took them longer than they had expected to reach the exit. They wound through the suburban streets, using a quick siren burst when necessary, as they passed through a business area and into more residential. The farther north and west they went, the larger the homes became.

"Do you think Barton will be at Masoud's home?" Evans asked.

"Don't know. If this is playing out the way it appears, unless they had a plane ready when they grabbed her or drove her out of state, I think he may have her for the moment. I hope he has them both."

"Right. We seem to have forgotten Mr. Wade."

"This must be incredibly frightening for her."

"I imagine so. But I talked to both of them after Clark broke in and she shot him. They both seem pretty solid. I guess we'll see."

Just then, Rivera's call came in to Asimov. He listened. "Talk to everyone there. See if anyone has any idea where they could have been taken."

He relayed the information to Evans. "It looks like we're the cavalry. Let's hope that they are at Masoud's place."

NINETY

I heard the sound of the Mercedes coming up the driveway. *Game time!* I had already screwed the eye bolt into the door next to the middle hinge as deeply as I could get it. I jumped to my feet, grasped the table leg and quickly wrapped the cable around it a few turns until I was standing about six feet from the door, slightly toward the doorknob side.

This has to work, Wade. It's our only hope.

I took a deep breath, held the leg horizontally with a reverse grip at shoulder level, and heaved backward pulling the hinged side of the door toward me and hard against the knob side of the door. The door pulled away from the empty hinges and swung precariously on the deadbolt for a moment. I pulled again. The bolt receiver tore loose from the door frame, and the door flew toward me.

As I jumped to one side, it dropped to the floor with a thud, but all together with much less noise than I had expected. I knew Liz had to have heard the noise and was wondering what was going on. I hoped Marco had not entered the house yet. I assumed Yousef would drop him at the door, then park the car in the garage.

As quickly as I could, I extracted the eye screw from the door, coiled the cable, and tied it around my waist with enough play to be able to use it as a weapon and to use that hand.

I shoved my smaller weapons into my pocket, shouldered my table leg, and picked up the last weapon that I had earlier forgotten to prepare–I had pulled the cord out of the lamp, the two copper wires hanging loose at the end. I could use it as a makeshift lethal Taser, if necessary, or to start a fire. I stuffed it into another pocket and looked carefully out the window, then to the garage.

I could see Yousef walk to the back of the car where the trunk lid was open. He removed two solid, heavy metal briefcases. He set them on the driveway, looked up at the house, and walked back into the garage.

I hoped he had not seen me or Jill looking out a window. If he did, his face gave no indication that he had.

I stepped into the hall and looked around. The elevator was directly across from me. The stairwell was on the left of it. There were two rooms on my side of the hallway to my left, and two to my right. There were four more rooms on the other side of the hall, two on either side of the elevator and stairs.

I raced to one end of the hallway, opened a door and burst in, hoping no one was in the room. Empty—thank God. I grabbed a bedspread and wadded it next to a wall socket near draperies. I reached into my pocket and pulled out the lamp cord. I laid the bare ends of the wires together on the bedspread and plugged the cord into the wall. Sparks jumped and crackled like crazy. I waited impatiently until the material began to smolder.

I stepped into the hallway, looked back, and saw a small flame growing in the bunched material. I heard the elevator door open on the first floor. I looked carefully to the stairs and heard the car began to ascend.

Please stop at two. It did.

I moved quietly to the stairs and descended slowly and cautiously as I heard the elevator door open on the floor below and footsteps cross the carpet. I heard a key being inserted and turned in a lock as I neared the bottom step.

Now, I could see the door to Liz's room. Marco swung the door open as I stepped soundlessly off the last stair onto the carpeted landing. I wordlessly watched as Marco confidently entered the room. I could see over his shoulder that Liz was sitting on the window sill, in the opened window, with one hand on the back of the desk chair next to her.

"What are you doing?" shouted Marco. He left the keys in the door lock, took two quick steps toward Liz, and dug into his pocket for the Taser.

When Marco shouted, I heard the rapid footsteps of Yousef on the tile floor of the entry below as he called, "Sir? Sir, are you all right?"

"What are you doing?" Marco shouted again.

"Why I'm just sitting here in the fresh air waiting for you, you pusillanimous perverted little piece of shit," Liz said sweetly with just the slightest touch of a southern drawl.

Well, I told her to keep him off balance. She was certainly doing that.

As I started for Marco, I heard the heavy footsteps of Yousef thundering up the stairs. He must have heard Marco's shout.

Marco had a Taser, was twenty feet away from Liz, and she had a chair as a defensive weapon. Yousef had a gun and would be within a few feet of me immediately. I had no choice but to turn from Liz to face Yousef.

As I did, I heard Liz shout and what sounded like Liz's chair strike something. I heard a grunt from Marco.

Yousef reached the landing on the second floor, gun in hand, and saw me as I moved toward him. I have never seen such a surprised look on a person's face. He stopped and hesitated. In that split second of hesitation, I swung the table leg, smashing it into the wrist of the hand that held the gun as he brought the gun up and fired twice.

We both yelped in pain. One of his shots grazed my shoulder with a quick, burning pain. He dropped the gun and fell backward against the stair rail as I swung again, clipping his shoulder.

I wanted to go for the gun, but he rebounded so quickly that all I could do was kick the gun away from him and swing for the fences with my table leg. I had to hand it to him. The guy was tough and quick. I caught him on the right shoulder and again he fell back against the railing. I hoped it would give way, but it didn't.

Behind me, I heard a guttural sound from Marco, a scream from Liz, and the sound of what I took to be the Taser prongs striking the chair seat, followed quickly by a wooden thud, and then a shout of pain from Marco.

Yousef was back in the game, but moving cautiously this time. His right hand hung limply, so I assumed that my blow had broken or disabled his wrist. He stepped backward, moving slowly down and away from me. I wasn't about to move down the stairs after him, so I stood on the high ground and watched him as blood soaked the sleeve of my shirt. He stopped and cautiously watched me.

"Get out, Yousef, while you can," I told him. He didn't respond, just stared at me.

Behind me, I heard Liz shout, then a grunt from Marco and another thud and another outburst from Marco. *She must be holding her own for the moment.* I chanced a quick glance over my shoulder at Liz and saw her in a jousting position with the chair in front of Marco as he dug into his pocket, I assume for another load for the Taser.

The second I averted my eyes, Yousef charged, low and away from my weapon. Mr. McCain always said to use offense as a defense. When the other guy moves toward you, don't back up, but move into him. I stepped into Yousef as if he were a fat, hanging change-up pitch. He threw an arm up to ward off the blow, but his effort was useless as I caught him square in the side of the head, and heard a wet sound. He went down like a sack of sand. He was lifeless. He wasn't just dazed; he was down for a ten count. Just to be on the safe side, I whacked his good wrist with all the gusto I had and heard a bone break. He was going to need someone to feed him for a few weeks.

I turned and ran into the bedroom. Liz and Marco were still jousting. He had reloaded. He was swearing at her as he thrust the Taser in his right hand toward her. He must not have had a handgun or he would have drawn it by now. She countered and parried with the chair. I wanted to watch, but she needed out of this dance.

He lunged toward her. She lost her balance, screamed in frustration, and fell backward against the wall. When she did, Marco grabbed one leg of the chair with his free hand and moved to Taser her with his other hand. As he did, I sprang toward him, swinging my table leg down hard on the top of his right shoulder. I heard a soft crack. His arm went limp and he dropped the Taser.

I thought it was game, set, match, but Liz rose, threw the chair aside, and reached for the Taser. Marco grabbed her wrist with his good hand and Liz, the good student that she had been, immediately turned her hand and wrist against the grip of his thumb as I had taught her, and she was free of his grasp.

She retrieved the Taser. Before Marco realized what she was doing, she brought the Taser up, pressed the trigger, and shot him in the belly from about six feet away. There was a loud crackle and both prongs made good contact, piercing his shirt and sticking. I have never heard a man scream as he did.

"That was for the first time you did this to me," she shouted at the screaming, thrashing figure lying on the floor in front of her.

The Taser was in her right hand. Marco was on his back, convulsing as if he had epilepsy. She swung her left fist and hit Marco in the right temple with the side of her fist, just as I had shown her.

"How do you like that, you little bully?"

Then, just like on a speed bag, she came back with the fist and hit him in the other temple.

"Do you still want to threaten me with rape by six guys?" she shouted, swinging again and making good contact.

What's that all about?

I was amazed as she timed each blow with his convulsions, and never missed once. She swung her right hand and hit him with the barrel of the Taser both going and coming.

I looked back and checked Yousef.

"Shit," I yelled as I saw him awkwardly try to rise. The guy was certainly resilient. He got to his feet, lost his unstable balance, and went to his knees. He groaned, lurched up, lost balance again, and tumbled backward down the stairs to the tiled entry. I heard a sound like a hammer hitting a coconut.

I turned to see Liz, a little wild-eyed, looking straight at me, and breathing hard.

"Do you think this thing is charged up again?" she asked me intently.

"Doesn't work that way," I replied as I stuck my hand into Marco's pants pocket and pulled out two reloads. When I did, I noticed that he had wet his pants, and I laughed.

I took the Taser from her, re-loaded it, and handed it back to her.

"It should work okay now."

"Well, we'll find out," she said matter of factly as she bent and aimed the Taser at Marco's wet crotch.

"No! Please!" He screamed.

She pressed the trigger. It was charged. The device again crackled, and Marco again screamed and bounced like a puppet on a string.

"That was for the second time you did that to me, you worthless little shit," she calmly told him.

She stood patiently, watching him as he convulsed, moaned and quivered, and the wet stain on his pants grew. After a moment, she looked up at me again and smiled. Part of her oozed malevolence, part of her gazed at me with doe eyes. She had another major adrenalin rush going.

She raised one finger and said softly as she shook her head affirmatively, "Just one more time. Then we can leave."

She handed me the Taser and asked politely if I had another load.

I hesitated, but what the hell, he had it coming. I pushed the load into the barrel and handed the Taser back to her.

"It's charged again."

Marco was lying on the floor, twitching and crying, and pleading with her not to do it again. She knelt, shoving the Taser into his chest, but I caught her in time just as he screamed, "No!"

"Hold it away from him. It won't work if you press it against him."

She smiled at me, nodded, backed up five feet, pointed at his stomach as he screamed again, "No, please. No!"

She blew him a little goodbye kiss, and pressed the trigger. The crackle was followed by another long stream of agonized screams.

"And that was for you Tasing the man I love," she said sweetly.

She looked up at me, concern in her twinkling eyes. "I'm sorry. That was presumptuous of me. You may not be ready for that."

I just grinned as she smiled lovingly and a bit wild-eyed at me.

For the second time in just a few weeks, she calmly asked me, "Do you think we should call the Sheriff now?"

We both roared with laughter, just as we heard a pounding on the front door and a voice shouted, "Police. Open the door." We laughed even harder.

Then, she saw the blood on the left arm of my shirt. "Dub, he shot you!"

"I'll be okay."

I took the Taser from her, put my good arm around her shoulders and we left the room. At the door, I nodded toward the keys in the lock. She locked the door and took the keys. At the landing, I picked up Yousef's gun by the barrel with thumb and forefinger, and we walked together down the stairs to where Yousef lay inert.

As I laid the gun and the Taser on a small table, Liz opened the entry door. At the first crack of daylight through the door, it was pushed wide open and we heard a harsh voice state, "Police. We have warrants for..."

Detective Asimov stood there, warrants in hand, speechless. He looked incredulously at me. No one moved.

"Detective Asimov," I said as I extended my good hand to him, "come in. We were just about to call you. Glad to see you."

He wordlessly looked at my shoulder, then took my hand and grinned from ear to ear.

I nodded toward Liz and said, "I don't think you've had the pleasure of meeting Elizabeth Barton."

Liz extended her hand to him and said sweetly, "Detective, it is truly a pleasure to meet you."

The three of us burst into laughter and seven faces behind Asimov grinned happily.

Asimov pointed to Yousef, then to the cable coiled around my waist. "I really want to hear this story."

NINETY-ONE

The fire department and medics arrived. Yousef was revived, and he and I were treated for our wounds. The Search and the Arrest Warrants were served on Marco. He and Yousef were arrested, and the house was thoroughly searched as soon as the fire had been extinguished. We stayed for two hours giving succinct synopses statements to DA Evans and were then allowed to leave.

Liz held up like a trooper. She recounted all of her treatment by Marco while she was there. And I learned about the threat of rape by six guys. If I could have gotten my hands on Marco, I would have beaten him to a pulp with my table leg. But she handled everything surprisingly well.

We assured Evans several times that we were all right physically, but I suggested it might be good to have someone talk with Liz that night. I tried to appear calm, but inwardly I worried about her. And I was pumped full of adrenalin, as well. Asimov and Evans both said they would be in touch in a day or two.

An officer drove us to the hospital where we were examined for physical injury, and then a resident psychologist talked at length with Liz and me. When he was satisfied that we were dealing with the events for the time being, he gave each of us a sample of a mild prescription sedative and told us to return the next morning to discuss how the night went.

The officer who drove us to the hospital had waited. When we were ready, he drove us to my home.

I closed the door behind us and took her hand, which shook perceptively. She turned to me and I said gently to her, "You're safe. We're home. It's over."

She came into my arms and we held each other. She was shaking and her breath quivered against my neck. I think she wanted to cry, but she was still too wired. It felt wonderful to hold her, but the muscles of her back were as taut as a board, and she couldn't relax. It was obvious that she was, once again, feeling the adrenalin rush. She stepped back and looked at me with a sentient grin.

"I'm so full of adrenalin, my head is about to come off."

She took my hand in her shaking hand and led me down the hall to my bedroom as she said matter-of-factly, "I think we know what to do about this."

We dropped clothes all the way down the hall and I did my best to help alleviate her adrenalin rush. It didn't hurt that I, too, was still pretty pumped. After two frantic times, she rolled over and pulled me to her. We were soaking wet from perspiration.

"I think we should rest for a minute," she said.

A minute later, we were reaching for each other and she was again squirming against me, belying her suggestion of rest.

When she finally came down, she said softly, "Hold me. Just hold me."

I did and she nestled warm against me.

After a moment, I kissed her and said, "You do know what to do with an adrenalin rush, girl. Once again, that was incredible sex!"

I had repeated myself from the last time and I saw her smirk just as she had before.

"Yes. It was; wasn't it?" she said brightly,

We laughed heartily and I proclaimed, "Deja vu, all over again!"

She chuckled, then pulled me to her. "It was wonderful. You were wonderful. But, I think I've had all I want of adrenalin rushes for a long time to come."

She looked into my eyes. "Thank you for rescuing me, Dub. We're laughing now, but I've never been so scared in my life."

Her face reflected the fears and memories that were running through her mind.

"I thought my life as I know it… our life together as we've known it was over, and that I would never see you again." Her voice quivered and she said, "I wanted to curl up and die."

She whimpered and shook and came into my arms, where she had a good, long cry.

EPILOGUE

Liz and I both have been seeing a counselor weekly for two months, and we listen when the other needs to talk. She is a strong woman and has dealt with what happened well. We were very fortunate; things could have ended tragically for both of us. I was afraid the episode would adversely affect her feelings for me or her interest in us, but she hasn't shown those signs. I try to be gentle with her and attentive.

Two nights ago, she snuggled close to me and whispered, "You treat me as if I were made of delicate china. I'm not going to break, baby."

I pulled her close to me and said softly, "I was really scared that I was going to lose you and that I wouldn't be able to stop what was happening. I don't ever want anything bad to happen to you again, and I won't let it."

She kissed me. "I know you won't. You saved me, Dub; and I love you… for saving me, for saving us, and for who you are."

Interestingly, the counselor said that Marco was an incredible narcissist and egoist, who also displayed strong signs of an inferiority complex. Therefore, he wanted those he attempted to control to like him; and he believed they would because he believed he showed concern for them. Interesting observation, but, if correct, that behavior mitigated our short-lived nightmare.

Thankfully, it was Marco's ego that not only mitigated our experience but led to his downfall. I was told by Evans that he believed he was Liz's benefactor, which led to his rather benign treatment of her compared to most women in the same predicament.

We both returned to our jobs and life as we had known it before Damon Clark and Marco. Jill soon returned to work and Vivian returned home. In the beginning, we seldom talked about what happened. I didn't want to bring up bad memories for her, but our counselor suggested it would be good therapy for both of us.

"It happened," she had said, "and the two of you can't pretend that it didn't happen. You should talk about it together."

We did and have gotten to the point that we can even joke and laugh about some of the things that happened.

I often ask, "Pusillanimous?"

And we both burst out laughing. And other things made us laugh. Some were not so funny. Some were damned frightening. She was ashamed that I knew she had hung naked and on display, and that Steven had shamed and frightened her as he did. We had to work that out, too. And we did.

I learned from Detective Asimov and DA Evans–and dozens of news reports and newspaper accounts–that Marco's only hope of any defense at all swirled down the drain the moment the briefcase was opened and they saw pictures of Liz hanging from the ceiling. Apparently, Marco went to a meeting the afternoon of our rescue with several men who participate in slavery, worldwide prostitution, and the sale of body parts. Names, addresses, and contact information were in the briefcase. The deeper they dug into his files and his organization, the more they learned.

The chain of events that began with Damon Clark's telephone call to Marco–actually with Liz's rejection of Clark–led to evidence of such crimes on a worldwide proportion that new information is still coming to the surface. Marco was only a small-time player who fancied himself a purveyor of premium merchandise, for lack of a better term.

Liz and I could have suffered greatly, and probably would have, if our captivity had drug on much longer. I found it unnerving to know how close I had come to being body parts. We learned that a dozen or more young women were located and returned by governments of countries in which they were being held, but that was only a small number of the women affected by that heinous coterie of jackals and others like them. We learned that James White and Leticia were found and freed. That made me happy.

We still have a difficult time thinking about all the unknown women who suffered and are suffering because of Marco and men like him. And I still have nightmares about that young girl who was raped right in front of me, and of the anguished screams of Liz.

Think what you will of me, I relish the memory of Marco's seemingly endless screams as Liz Tasered him.

Marco, Damon Clark, and Yousef were all convicted of a variety of crimes. Damon took a plea of insanity, so he is locked down pretty tight for quite a while. They all took pleas in exchange for information. There has been one attempt on Marco's life in prison. They are all serving long sentences. The fortunate aspect of all this is that Marco does not have diplomatic immunity. Unfortunately for him, he is sufficiently close to those in high places so that he has become the whipping boy, and very few of those involved at the top will ever be punished. Moreover, the investigation of him and his organization, while revealing, didn't significantly diminish the problem of human trafficking either in the U.S. or worldwide.

A few months after her counseling and soul-searching, and as our lives had become more normal, Liz brought up her last comment to Marco as she Tasered him. I had put her comment out of my mind until then.

We were sitting on the patio with a glass of wine after dinner. She turned to me and smiled her wonderful, gentle smile. For the most part, she was back to being the Liz that I had known after the day of Jill's accident four months ago.

"You've never mentioned my comment to Marco about you."

"Do you mean when you hit him with the last Taser shot?"

She nodded.

"I just assumed that it was the adrenalin and your anger at him that made you say what you said. I had come to your rescue, so to speak. So you stood up for me."

She was quiet for a moment, never taking her eyes from mine. "It was some of that… but what if there were more to it?"

I looked at her. Her eyes were intent and she wore an anxious smile. "What would you say if there were more to it than that?"

"More to it, like… you meant what you said about me?"

She sat quietly, watching me for a long moment. Then, she gave me a little smile, a little nod of her head, and said softly, "Uh-huh."

I was quiet for a long moment.

"Well," I said, drawing the word out and pausing for a second, "then we're of one mind."

I paused, gazing at her, at the uncertain expression on her face.

"I love you, too, Liz."

I took her hand, kissed her palm, and asked, "Shall we see what lies ahead for us?"

Her one-word answer was soft and adamant.